The Fighters

A TRILOGY

Also by Robert Johns

———◆———

O'Brien's Broken Play

PRAISE FOR
THE FIGHTERS: A TRILOGY

"*The Fighters: A Trilogy* is a fascinating collection of three stories linked through common underlying themes of love, loss, and the willingness to fight to overcome challenges. Author Robert Johns creates a fine line that each protagonist must walk between determination to follow their perceived destiny and the expectations of those they love, respect, and desire in their lives. Johns does an excellent job of character development, which allows readers to fully identify and empathize with each of the main protagonists. This is an enjoyable and thoughtful book that I appreciated immensely. I highly recommend it."

—READERS' FAVORITE REVIEW, 5 stars

"*The Fighters: A Trilogy* by Robert Johns weaves three disparate stories together to create a cohesive book about the many confrontations of the self we face throughout our lives. Antiwar protests, smear campaigns, and family conflicts drive these absorbing protagonists to their edges, where they are forced to make tough decisions and fight for what they believe in. Johns's ability to deeply dive into complexities such as political clashes and family rivalries is truly something to behold. Pick up *The Fighters* for the stories and stay for the inevitable connection you will feel for these characters."

—KOLINA CICERO, author of *Rosie and the Hobby Farm* and the *Words on Words* literary newsletter

"Johns writes each story with an approach that meticulously follows each protagonist as they move from idea to rumination to planning—with all trying to find a new way to move through their world. . . . Johns . . . lavish[es] attention on interpersonal relationships that take on clear importance. The characters convincingly self-reflect, and they work to be upfront and in-tune with their emotions, which will have readers rooting for them."

—*KIRKUS REVIEWS*

The Fighters

A TRILOGY

ROBERT JOHNS

RIVER GROVE
BOOKS

Published by River Grove Books
Austin, TX
www.rivergrovebooks.com

Distributed by River Grove Books

Design and composition by Greenleaf Book Group
Cover design by Greenleaf Book Group and Anna Jordan
Cover images © Maryia Bahutskaya / Adobe Stock,
veneratio / Adobe Stock,

Publisher's Cataloging-in-Publication data is available.

Print ISBN: 978-1-63299-897-2

eBook ISBN: 978-1-63299-898-9

First Edition

To George, Larry, and Mike

*I'll always remember you
as great friends and storytellers.*

Contents

Christmas
1968

1

Not long after she started work at an advertising agency in downtown Chicago, Janice Wagner realized how much she enjoyed Susan. Janice liked her outrageousness and sense of humor, and especially her readiness to stand up to the male culture. At lunch, Susan would regale her fellow copywriters about advertising and the account managers who ran the business side, leaning back with her hands raised to make her point. Regardless of what Susan ridiculed, Janice found her to be incredibly bright and funny.

"Advertising is an enterprise to persuade people to buy things they don't need, while poor children go without food and clothing," Susan told them, her voice rising above the din of the crowded sandwich shop, where the six of them sat together around a speckled beige table. "And account managers are so focused on making money that they've lost their souls. They worry about what three-piece suit to wear for their client meetings—herringbone or pinstripe."

Janice joined the others in laughing at Susan's performance. Even though Janice worked on the business side supporting the account managers, she saw the humor in how Susan depicted them.

Susan had opinions about everything, and Janice was a devoted member of her audience. But one day after work as they left their office building, Susan confided in Janice that the copywriting supervisor had taken her aside, counseling her not to bite the hand that fed her.

"What do you think?" Susan asked. Janice leaned toward her to better hear her above the traffic noise.

"I think your supervisor is right. You might want to only share your thoughts with people who think like you."

"Yeah, you're right. I didn't even think about that," Susan said. She quickly hugged Janice, adding, "You know this business world so much better than me!" and raced off, presumably to the L subway station a few stops from her apartment on the north side. Janice walked to Union Station, following the hordes of people taking trains to their suburban homes.

Janice was surprised after that by how frequently Susan sought her out to hear her observations about the agency and its hierarchical relationships. Janice seemed to provide a grounding that Susan depended on. And Janice gladly gave it, in return for the eye-opening impact Susan's opinions had on her.

Over time, Janice realized that she shared an independence bordering on defiance with Susan, although expressed much differently.

"You know, even though you're quiet, you can be pretty cocky. I mean, in a good way," Susan said one day during a coffee break. "How did you get to be so confident?"

"I guess I started to feel more comfortable with who I was back in high school, because of sports. I was a pretty good basketball player," Janice said, smiling. "I loved to steal the ball from the boys and drive around them for a basket."

"Ha! Yes . . . there's nothing quite like beating those boys. I used to do it in debate club."

"That must be where you got your cockiness, but you're definitely not quiet. I'm guessing you never had that problem."

Susan smiled brightly. "You guessed correctly."

Janice wanted her husband, Jim, to meet Susan. She knew they might have differences, but she wanted to see what he thought of her new friend. One Friday after work, Jim met them for a drink in a bar on Chicago's near north side.

"So, the two of you rent a house in the suburbs?" Susan asked.

"Yes," Jim said. "I guess we like the peace and quiet and have met some good neighbors."

"Are you going to have babies?"

Jim turned, smiled at Janice, and said, "We hope to, once we buy a house." Janice was silent, as she always was when Jim talked about having children. She wasn't ready to consider it, but she hadn't told him that. She looked at the tables next to theirs, where men and women her age were laughing loudly and ordering more pitchers of beer.

"It sounds like that won't take long, with both of you having good jobs," Susan said.

"Yeah, we're doing well," Jim said. "I like Monsanto. There's opportunity to advance while improving agriculture."

Susan didn't reply, looking at Janice and then at Jim. The music in the bar seemed to grow louder.

"How about you, Susan? What are your plans?" Jim asked.

"Oh, I'm having a great time living near Lincoln Park with my roommate, Jill—she's a hoot. No marriage and babies for me."

"What are your interests outside of work?" He lifted his beer and took a drink, but not before Janice caught his smug expression.

Susan smiled, seeming to find humor in Jim's question. "To start with, work isn't an interest. I've got to get out of the corporate world. I've also got two guys I'm going out with now." She hesitated and smiled. "Although that might end if they find out about each other."

Jim was silent, his lips pressed together. Janice turned to him. "Copywriting isn't Susan's goal. She's not against corporations in general—it's just that advertising isn't a fit for her."

"Who said I'm not against corporations? But advertising is the worst. It isn't fit for anyone! Right, Janice?"

Janice hesitated. She worked hard at her job and didn't know what else she would want to do. Her throat tightened. She didn't want to appear to disagree with Susan in front of Jim.

Janice had thought she knew what she wanted when she enrolled at State College of Iowa in the fall of 1962 with her friend Michelle from Blairsville. Janice's family—especially her aunt Rose—thought it was sweet how they were both planning to become grade-school teachers. After two years, they decided to change their majors and try out a bigger school. They were accepted by Iowa State and quickly learned about the social opportunities for girls, who were outnumbered by boys three-to-one. Janice kept up her good grades, and so did Michelle, but their career plans became secondary, and the focus on dating grew in importance, with the unspoken goal of finding a husband.

Janice reached for her beer and thought about how to answer Susan's question. She knew that if she agreed with Susan that advertising was awful, Jim might react negatively to her antibusiness view. She valued Jim's steadiness, often seeming more rational compared to her emotional swings.

When Janice was at Iowa State, she and Michelle attended fraternity house parties where girls could drink beer for free. Janice was open to the charms of good-looking boys and once allowed herself to be led to a couch in a dimly lit corner, where a handsome fraternity brother made her laugh and kissed her. She let him cup her breast, but she pushed his arm away when he moved his hand under her sweater. He overpowered her, forcing his fingers under her bra, and she exploded. "Get your hands off of me, asshole!" She pushed him away with a hard shove and stood up, face hot with rage. "Are you stupid?" People in the room turned and watched as she walked out with a glare that dared people to stop her. They stepped back, and she slammed the door against the side of the building as she left. After Janice met Jim, she no longer had to deal with these situations.

"Advertising definitely doesn't fit you," Janice finally said to Susan. "You might kill someone if you stay there much longer!" The three of them laughed—even Jim—and Janice was satisfied that she had avoided answering Susan's question.

"Yeah, it's a bad fit," Susan said.

"I bet that you'll eventually want to have children," Jim said to Susan. He turned to Janice. "What about your friend Michelle? She has at least one kid, right? Didn't she say something once about no babies for her?"

"Yes—she has two kids . . . after getting pregnant and dropping out of college. She complains about being a stuck-at-home house-wife," Janice said. "She feels trapped."

"Yeah, that's out of the question for me," Susan said. "What I'm most interested in right now is helping end the war in Vietnam."

Jim stopped smiling and drew back from leaning on his elbows. "I think it'll end soon with a U.S. victory," he said.

Susan's eyebrows rose. "What's a U.S. victory? It's a civil war. We have no business being there," she said, raising her hands.

Jim straightened his posture. "If we weren't there, the communists could win, and other countries could follow."

"That's crazy," Susan said. She took a long drink of her beer and looked at Janice. The number of people in the bar had grown, and the music and crowd interactions produced a constant loud noise. Two women at the table next to theirs had moved onto the laps of two men, making room for newcomers, laughing so hard they almost fell off.

Janice didn't know what to say. Susan and Jim had squared off, each seeming ready to continue their argument. She had never heard Jim defend the Vietnam War so strongly, and she hadn't been aware of Susan's interest in helping end the war.

Janice had met Susan in their orientation sessions at the advertis-ing agency, where they started work the same day. The agency had two parts to its organization: the business side, where Janice was assigned as an administrative assistant, and the creative side, where Susan was hired as an entry-level copywriter. Like Janice, Susan had recently graduated from college, an English major from the University of Wisconsin. She was tall and thin, with long legs exposed by a miniskirt like those made famous by Twiggy—a contrast to the traditional skirt and blouse that Janice had chosen to wear. The two of them spent their first day having thirty-minute introductory meetings with agency leaders in gray, fabric-covered cubicles and glass and metal-framed offices.

Susan erupted when they finally had free time for lunch at a nearby sandwich shop. "God, those account managers are stiff. Are you sure you'll be able to handle working for them?" Janice nodded, thinking how the business suits worn by the account managers reminded her of her husband's. Susan continued, "But there are some intriguing artists—the long-haired guy was in his own world." On her way home, Janice kept thinking of Susan. She had encountered a whirlwind force, never having met anyone like her. Janice was drawn to her energy, and although she didn't know why, she felt Susan was also drawn to her.

Jim and Susan continued to stare at each other as the noise in the bar increased.

"We don't need to solve the world's problems right now," Janice said, hoping to turn the conversation back to something less charged.

Ignoring Janice's attempt, Susan finished her beer and narrowed her eyes in her stare-down with Jim. "This war is really about making defense contractors rich!"

Jim rolled his eyes. "Our military and business partnership is keeping communism in check. I don't know how you can criticize it."

This certainty was typical of Jim. Janice had first met him during her senior year in high school. She played on the Blairsville basketball team, which had made the state tournament as one of the Sweet

Sixteen girls' teams. One of her Wagner cousins brought his friend Jim, a Des Moines high school senior, to watch the first game. Afterward, Janice's uncle John suggested the two boys come with them to have pizza with Janice and her family. Jim was about six feet tall and lanky and wore penny loafers, blue jeans, and a letter jacket. Janice was intrigued to learn that he played baseball, and he seemed equally intrigued that she was an all-state basketball player.

Janice didn't think about Jim again until he called two and a half years later, after she had transferred to Iowa State. He asked if she would like to meet him for a Coke in the student union. She found herself attracted to his good looks, polite demeanor, and openness in discussing his plans. He was majoring in business and saw himself advancing in a corporation, possibly in Chicago. He wanted a family, a nice house in a friendly community. When Jim asked about her plans, she felt her ideas were underwhelming compared to his. She told him she was exploring the social sciences, especially anthropology.

The noise at the bar grew so loud that it was unsettling, while Susan's narrowed eyes bore into Jim. "Communism!" she said. "My God."

Janice's stomach tightened.

"We just bought the latest Rolling Stones album," Janice said to Susan. "Jim's not too crazy about it, but I love it. How about you?"

Susan turned to Janice with an impassive look and then nodded slightly.

"Jim, it's growing on you—right?" Janice said.

Jim didn't even nod, just looked at her with squinted eyes.

Janice's breath shortened in the awkward silence. She was not at a point where she wanted to choose between her husband and her new friend, and she searched for a way to facilitate an end to their battle.

Jim finally broke the tension by looking at his watch. "If we leave soon, we can catch the next train." Susan smiled, looking triumphant over Jim's withdrawal. They finished their beers and walked to the train station to say goodbye. Susan hugged Janice before they parted, while Jim turned and started walking.

Janice and Jim were quiet on the train ride home, reading as they did every evening commute. But Janice's heart still beat from the confrontation between Jim and Susan. She prepared a simple supper of pasta and shrimp with a salad while Jim watched the news. When she told him supper was ready, he sat down and began serving himself.

"I'm surprised you're so close with Susan," he said, offering her the salad bowl.

Janice's face warmed. "Susan means a lot to me."

"The two of you are so different," he said, finally setting the bowl down—Janice hadn't taken it from him.

"What do you mean?"

"She's antibusiness, antiwar, and anti-family," he answered matter-of-factly as he began cutting the pasta and shrimp into small pieces on his plate. Her own plate remained empty. "And she can't even keep a steady relationship."

Janice stared at him, her forehead furrowed and jaw clenched. "Why are you criticizing a person who means so much to me? I've done everything you wanted in this move to Chicago. Can't I have my own friends?"

"Why are you so angry?" he asked. "You don't have anything in common with her."

"How do you know? You don't even know me!"

He put down his fork and looked at her closely. "I thought I did. I thought we agreed on our goal to buy a house and start a family. Susan doesn't have much in common with that."

"I don't know what I want! But I'm so pissed at you for fighting with her that I'm not even hungry."

Janice pushed her chair back, got up, and went to the living room. She put on a Rolling Stones album and lay on the couch with headphones on and eyes closed.

Jim spent the evening in their second bedroom, which he had arranged as a study, while Janice kept her headphones on even when she had stopped listening to music and leafed through a magazine. Jim tried to talk to her again when they went to bed, but she turned her back to him without a word.

By the following morning, she felt calmer. She fried eggs and bacon for their breakfast. Before they started eating, she looked steadily at Jim. "I'm sorry I got so angry last night," she said. "But I don't want you to criticize Susan—she's very important to me."

"Okay," he said. "But I don't need to see her again. And please don't take up smoking—I could smell it on her at the restaurant."

Janice nodded. They seemed to be back to normal.

2

Janice looked for a chance to apologize to Susan. She didn't want the awkward meeting with Jim to hurt their relationship. When she spotted Susan by the water fountain, she hurried over.

"I'm sorry that meeting Jim didn't go so well," Janice said, placing a hand on Susan's forearm to impress upon her how truly awful she felt about the whole thing. "I didn't know he felt so strongly about the Vietnam War."

"It's not a biggie, Janice." Susan patted her hand. "The whole country's debating Vietnam right now. Let's try that new salad place for lunch today. I'll round up our lunch crowd."

"Sure," Janice said. She had an open invitation to eat lunch with account management staff, but she usually ate with Susan and a group of young copywriters and artists. They all had similar views of their employer.

"So, Janice, as a cultural anthropologist, how would you analyze the account manager subculture versus the creative staff subculture?" one of the artists asked with a smile after they had gotten their salads. It was the long-haired guy who had caught Susan's attention on orientation day. Danny—she was starting to remember all their names.

Janice smiled, recalling the language used in her anthropology classes. "Well, the values and norms on each side are certainly quite different."

Danny cocked his head playfully. "Do you find that norms for the account managers all have to do with making more money, no matter the sacrifice? Even if it's their dignity and humanity?"

Janice laughed. "I guess some might have norms that go that far. But few of them value what the creative staff values—art, laughter, color, and poetry."

At this, Susan nodded with feigned seriousness, chiming in to say, "Yes, we are all dreamy little rainbow people over on our side! Not a care in the world other than creating beauty."

Janice loved participating in this banter and could relate to the creative group's rebelliousness. She didn't find herself being quite as negative, though, about the account manager side as the artists and copywriters were.

"What do you do for those account managers anyway?" a copywriter named Martha asked.

"Let's see. A lot of stuff. But mostly, I keep customer contact info up-to-date, tabulate customer ad purchases, prepare presentation slides, help them with their customers."

"Do you like it?"

"I don't mind the work—I'm pretty organized—and I like being appreciated by them. Most of them do show it, even though they're uppity at times."

Susan observed her with a smile, saying, "I still don't know how you do it."

"Maybe it's because I grew up doing farm chores," Janice said. "I learned how to work."

"If you're talking about cleaning manure from cow pens, I can see the analogy," Susan said.

The waitress stopped by their table and offered refills on coffee, interrupting their laughter. Martha and another copywriter went up to the counter and picked out cookies from the display case for dessert. When they were settled back in their booth, Martha turned to them.

"I'm glad Janice likes some of the managers, but it isn't Shangri-la over there," Martha said. "I heard that one of the married managers is having an affair with his secretary. She left the office early the other day, crying."

"That's the jackass who said to me on my first day, 'Aren't you looking sexy!'" Susan said. "Not even a good line. That secretary should know better."

A female artist, who was about thirty and usually quiet, surprised the group by blurting out, "How disgusting!" They stopped their conversation and looked at her.

"This is straight out of *The Feminine Mystique*. Have you read it?" she said. "These asshole men think a woman's main job at work is to support them. Never mind the actual role they were hired for. This jerk probably wants his secretary to be his work wife."

As the usually quiet artist continued to give an impassioned speech, Janice listened to her intently and made a mental note to buy *The Feminine Mystique*, which she did the following day.

———•◦•———

Janice liked Susan's look. Her miniskirts kept getting shorter, and she grew her straight brown hair to the middle of her back. She sometimes wore platform shoes, which made her tower over the women and many of the men. Her long cigarettes, balanced between her slender fingers, made her look cool. After her copywriting supervisor had cautioned Susan to be careful in ridiculing advertising, Susan turned her focus and sharp tongue to the Vietnam War, particularly in mocking President Johnson.

"Do you know he's killed almost ten thousand American soldiers so far?" Susan said at lunch the day after the president had explained in a speech his rationale for increasing the number of U.S. troops in Vietnam. She took a deep drag off the cigarette she was smoking. "I think we should all go out on Michigan Avenue and yell as they do in Berkeley: 'Hey, hey, LBJ, how many kids did you kill today?'"

Janice began reading the *Chicago Tribune* to learn more about the country's political divisions. She felt like she was experiencing a new stage of her education, much different from what she had learned in college. Her eyes were being opened, and it felt exhilarating. Nothing was black and white, and the huge gray areas were fascinating to think about. It wasn't about memorizing facts, but forming her own opinions.

She saw herself agreeing with Susan, not satisfied with the country's direction, and ready to demonstrate her difference from the older generations. When Janice arrived at work with a new hairstyle, parted on the right and covering her left eye when it hung down, Susan exclaimed, "All right! Keep that hair growing!" She did, even though Jim said he didn't care for it.

Unlike Janice's daily stimulation from Susan and others at work, her life with Jim developed into a set of routines they followed in the days and weeks of living together. One evening, Jim grilled chicken breasts while Janice prepared a salad and vegetables.

"I had a great meeting today with an ag cooperative," Jim said after they sat down to eat. "They could be a customer for many Monsanto products—seeds, fertilizer, pesticides."

"That's good," Janice said. She was used to hearing about Monsanto customers and products.

"One of their members talked to me afterward—he wanted to hear more about our latest pesticide. I told my boss about it, and he said that I should start attending sales meetings in other states. Isn't that exciting?"

"Very. I had a pretty good day myself—my account manager liked the slides I prepared for his client meeting."

Jim looked out the window at some birds at the bird feeder. "My boss said these would usually be overnight trips, sometimes involving a weekend conference. You'd be okay with that, right?"

"Yes." It might be good to have the house to herself on occasion, she thought. "Of course."

"There's so much opportunity. I can already see how the stock I'm getting as part of my pension plan is growing in value."

Janice waited for him to ask to hear more about her success with her manager, but he was silent.

"My account manager said he planned to recommend a raise for me at the end of six months," she said.

Jim came alive and beamed at her. "That's great news! If we both keep getting raises, we can buy a house and start our family sooner."

Janice was silent after listening to his words. She had gone on the pill, and it was a huge weight off her chest, not worrying about becoming pregnant. She hadn't told Jim yet—he would no doubt be upset.

———•••———

Through Jim's initiative, they made friends with a couple in their neighborhood who were a couple years older than them. The woman, Tamara, had graduated with an art history degree. She and her husband, Bill, an engineer, had decided to start a family immediately after their marriage, and she was staying home as a housewife during her pregnancy. Janice thought Jim was envious of their decision, but she was not.

Janice wondered what Tamara did all day in her suburban home, so different from the bustling downtown of Chicago that she herself had grown to love. She occasionally persuaded Jim to join her in taking the train downtown on the weekend to see concerts by rock bands. She was thrilled that they could attend a Rolling Stones concert.

"So much energy," Janice said on the train ride home after a concert, voicing her thoughts on the show they'd just seen. She could still feel the tingle of the music flowing through her. "I felt like I could relate to it. All those young people, artists . . . Would you ever consider renting a place downtown instead of a house in the suburbs?"

"No, are you kidding me?"

"How come?"

"It's too crowded—too much traffic. And it's unsafe. I'm okay working there, but I want to come home to a town with people like us."

Janice turned to stare out the window, but only her face reflected back at her, and Jim's hazy profile behind her, staring ahead. What had intrigued her about him?

After their Coke date in their junior year, Jim asked if she would like to go to his fraternity party the following weekend, a "woodsie" with a keg of beer in a farmer's grove of trees. She had agreed to go, although she was wary from her past fraternity experiences. They rode with Jim's friend and his date. Once they arrived, Jim spread a blanket for them to sit on, and Janice sipped beer from a mug Jim gave her. It was engraved with the Greek letters of his fraternity. She had stared at it, questioning if she belonged there. Most of the girls were from sororities, with heavy makeup and an air of superiority, like the girl Jim's friend brought. Janice imagined they were judging her, a girl from the dorms brought by Jim to their exclusive gathering.

But Janice spent most of her time talking to Jim, and as the beer loosened her inhibitions, she found it easy to make him laugh, and she was drawn to his smile and attentive eyes. When he asked her if she'd like to walk the three miles back to town, she was thrilled to accompany him under the moon and stars in the cloudless sky. They strolled down a tractor path through a field until they reached the road, with her holding his arm tightly against her as they savored the cool air and quiet country night. She was ready for his kiss at the dorm entrance and went to bed smiling at the image of him bending down to meet her lips.

Janice tried to think of good memories like this when Jim talked about having a home and family in the suburbs. Could she love him now like she did then and give him what he wanted?

One Saturday evening, Tamara and Bill invited Janice and Jim to their house for grilled steaks. Janice helped Tamara prepare snacks in the kitchen, and Bill offered Jim a beer and put the steaks on the grill over the hot coals. While waiting to turn the steaks, Bill picked up a football and motioned for Jim to go out for a pass. Jim leaped in the air and caught the high pass, yelling, "Touchdown." Bill and Jim laughed and drank their beers.

Janice helped Tamara prepare a veggie plate and dip and watched the laughing men through the kitchen window. She wondered if Tamara had fallen in love with Bill like Janice had with Jim and whether she and Bill still had that love.

It wasn't long after the night of the fraternity woodsie that Janice and Jim began seeing each other every day. At social gatherings, they often sat by themselves in a corner. Their friends joked that they no longer mattered. They began driving to the edge of the city park in Jim's old Chevy and had long kisses in the dark, their hands caressing their bodies to the sound of crickets in the warm night. Janice sensed they both were inexperienced, and she wanted to explore sex with him, her first steady boyfriend. But Jim often stopped before Janice was ready to, seeming to want to control himself from becoming too aroused. He would talk about where their relationship was going, and Janice didn't discourage his ideas, although she didn't feel as he did about the need for the church to bless their relationship. Jim gave Janice his fraternity pin that spring, signaling their next step was to become engaged.

As Janice carried Tamara's cheese and crackers into the screened-in porch, she heard a bit of Jim and Bill's conversation, making her stop.

"I should take you to the new strip joint in Greenfield west of here," Bill said. "It leaves nothing to the imagination."

"We used to find small-town bars around Ames where there were no zoning laws on dancing," Jim said. "Some of those women were wild."

"That's Greenfield."

Janice felt awkward and cleared her throat to signal to them she was coming through the screen door. She had never heard Jim talk about going to strip bars and was disgusted by the thought.

"Great, the snacks are here," Bill said. "Served by two beautiful women." Tamara followed Janice with chips, veggies, and dip. Janice and Tamara sat on the light blue padded patio chairs while Jim continued to stand next to Bill at the grill. After Bill turned the steaks, he offered to make drinks, and everyone chose a gin and tonic except for Tamara, who wasn't drinking alcohol when she was pregnant.

"You've grown!" Jim exclaimed to Tamara. "Have you picked names for the baby yet?" Tamara smiled at Bill, saying that they were negotiating.

When Janice went to the kitchen with Tamara to bring out the salad and dinner rolls, she had an opportunity to ask Tamara a question on her mind. "Do you ever feel lonely, not having a job and being at home all day while Bill works?"

"No," Tamara said. "My job is to support Bill and be a mother to our children—we'd like to have three or four."

Janice nodded, but she couldn't relate to Tamara's goals. She would go crazy if she had to stay home alone all day.

Their talk over dinner focused on the two men's work and the best suburbs for buying a house. Janice tried to change the subject, asking if anyone would be interested in attending a rock concert in downtown Chicago. But Jim interrupted her, starting a lengthy discussion with Bill on the prospects for the Chicago Bears that fall.

Janice stood to help Tamara take dishes to the kitchen. When they loaded the dishwasher, Tamara showed her a file of recipes, saying she would gladly loan any of them to her. She also showed her the catalog she had used to order maternity clothes and recommended a set of slacks with elastic waists for when Janice became pregnant.

Janice noticed the new flowered drapes in their living room that matched a new couch and side chairs. "You're way ahead of me in decorating the house," she said. But as the words came from her mouth, she felt a restless sort of dismay wash over her that she couldn't quite put a finger on.

"When Bill comes home from work, I want this house to be a sanctuary for him," Tamara said.

Boredom. That was what it was. Their conversation was boring. But before Janice could contemplate it further, Bill and Jim joined them, and Tamara put her arm around Bill's waist, looking up at him with adoring eyes. Janice wondered if Tamara would be so adoring if she knew her husband went to strip joints on occasion, instead of coming directly home to her sanctuary. What did he tell her? That he was working late?

Janice tried to be friendly and show interest in Tamara's activities, but when they left, she knew that Tamara's life was not for her. While Jim worked outside on the lawn the following day, Janice began reading *The Feminine Mystique*. She could see that Tamara's role as a housewife and mother was the American ideal for women, as described by Betty Friedan. Janice marveled at how Friedan skewered these dreams, saying that women with these goals often lost who they were as individuals.

Janice lay back on the couch and looked at the ceiling. She felt drawn to Tamara on one hand—primarily through Jim's wishes—and to Susan on the other. But if she had to be stranded on an island with one of them, for the rest of her life, she knew who she would choose.

3

During one of Jim's business trips that fall, Janice had a chance to experience Susan's world. She'd suggested to Susan that she could stay downtown after work for dinner, and Susan was ecstatic. "I'd love for you to meet Jill and my other friends."

Janice entered Susan's apartment, and her eyes were drawn to a huge peace sign facing her on the wall above the couch. Instead of doors, long strings of beads hung in doorways to separate the rooms. A stereo system with prominent speakers sat against another living room wall on top of wooden fruit cartons, with a long line of albums stacked on the floor. A pretty tapestry in deep greens hung over the well-worn brown corduroy sofa. Janice liked the mustard-colored throw pillows.

"How do you like this?" Susan asked. "This is the home that Jill and I've created to counter the military-industrial complex. It helps me leave the advertising world when I walk in here every night."

Janice smiled, thinking of Tamara's perfectly decorated home. Susan's apartment had a casual edginess mixed with a political statement. And it was warm and colorful.

Janice and Susan had dinner with Jill and two of Susan's friends at a café near Susan's apartment. They stepped out on the sidewalk afterward, and Susan lit a cigarette, exhaling a big plume of smoke into the crisp night air. "I wish you would stay overnight," she said. "I'd like to take you out on the town."

"I better get home tonight before Jim calls."

"I assumed you probably hadn't told him about having dinner with me. He would be shocked if he knew! The scandal!"

Janice laughed, imagining the look on Jim's face. They walked to Susan's subway stop, hugged each other goodbye, and separated. As Janice's train sped by suburban towns, she remembered the days of making plans with Jim for their future.

After being inseparable in the spring of their junior year, they had worked summer jobs at home, with Janice helping on the farm and Jim interning at a bank in Des Moines. They tried to see each other every weekend, but the three-hour round trip was difficult. They met the other's family, and everything seemed to go well, although Grandpa Cole was uncharacteristically quiet after he shook Jim's hand and listened to him describe his plans.

Janice and Jim were overjoyed to return to campus in the fall. They immediately got engaged. Janice favored living together, just like she favored going all the way in sex. She talked excitedly about the former, making up for her reticence in promoting the latter.

"Why not live together?" she had asked. "We're almost married."

"We have a lifetime to live together. Let's do what the church would want us to do. We can live in married student housing next semester."

"But, honey, don't you want to be close?"

"Yeah, but, like I said, the church would want us to wait until we're married. It's what's right, right?"

She looked down, rocking slightly on her feet. Where did this preoccupation with the church come from?

He stepped toward her and hugged her, his hands on her hips, pulling her toward him. "We'll have plenty of time to enjoy ourselves very soon," he said. "Be patient."

She embraced him silently and after a moment pulled away. She couldn't help but feel a little irritated at the implication that she was being impatient, like some petulant child. But perhaps she was? It was something her dad had scolded her for, when she rushed the farm chores.

Since a fancy wedding had never been one of her dreams, Janice offered her mother the chance to plan it, which she accepted enthusiastically. Janice's Cole and Wagner families and a smaller group of Jim's family joined Janice and Jim at the wedding to celebrate their marriage in January of 1966. Janice's aunt Rose could not stop hugging Janice, saying, "I had my doubts about this tomboy, but she's picked herself a good one! Let's toast Mrs. James Scott!"

Janice was happy that everyone had a good time, but she would have been fine if she and Jim had just gone to a justice of the peace. Sometimes she wondered what she had done, following Jim lockstep on the path he was creating for them. But she didn't have an alternative and accepted his plans as the right thing to do.

At her train stop, Janice got off and walked to her car in the parking lot. The temperature had dropped rapidly—fall was giving way to winter—and the rush of the wind made Janice's nose cold. When she got home, she sat on the couch instead of changing clothes, still deep in thought.

Jim had become so serious in the spring after their marriage, interviewing for jobs. It didn't take him long to find one—a Monsanto sales trainee position in Chicago. He also enlisted in the National Guard, since his student draft deferment was no longer in effect. He made arrangements with Monsanto to start work in the summer after completing his basic training.

They moved to Chicago after graduating and rented a small house in the suburbs. Janice looked for employment while Jim was in training and found a job in an advertising agency, where she started work in July. When Jim finished his training and started at Monsanto, they commuted together by train to their Chicago Loop jobs.

Janice's thoughts were interrupted by the phone ringing.

"Hi," Jim said. "How's home sweet home?"

"Great. How was your day?"

"I made some new contacts—very promising. We'll have more talks tomorrow to see if we can close a deal."

"Good," she said. She could have told him she also made some good contacts—meeting Susan's friends at dinner north of the Loop. But she didn't.

When they hung up, she thought more of Susan's words—that Jim would be shocked about Janice having dinner downtown with her—and realized it wasn't funny. Why couldn't she do what she wanted without worrying about Jim's judgment? She had repeatedly followed his directions and given in to him. She was irritated at herself for not being more assertive.

A few weeks after her dinner with Susan, Janice had an opportunity for an overnight visit. Jim would be in Cincinnati for a conference on Friday and Saturday.

On Thursday evening, Jim was packing for the trip when she came into the bedroom to see if he needed help with his shirts. "I might stay with Susan Friday night," she told him. He said he hoped not, but she ignored him, quietly moving on to fold the pants. When the suitcase was full and Jim was zipping it shut, she left the room.

⁕

Susan and her friends took Janice to a bar and restaurant to eat, with live music played by a blues band. When they returned to the apartment, everyone was in a good mood.

"I have something for us," Susan said to Janice. She went to her bedroom and returned with a joint that she lit and passed to one of her friends.

Janice watched Susan's friends hold the smoke, often coughing when they blew it out. Susan turned on a fan to blow the smoke out the window, lessening the pungent odor of burning marijuana.

When it was Janice's turn, she felt no effects from the smoke other than making her cough. But then Susan approached her, bending down and looking at her face. Susan's eyes, nose, and lips seemed to slowly move, her mouth growing huge as she smiled at Janice. They started laughing, unable to stop.

A roommate played an album by The Byrds, and they all sang along to "Mr. Tambourine Man." Janice swayed to the beat, never having felt such an intense pleasure listening to music. Susan then brought out some cookies, and Janice quickly ate two of them, feeling the chocolate chips melt on her tongue. The following day, they were subdued, with Janice getting up first from where she had slept on the couch. She took the train home around noon. She felt surprisingly well rested, and was glad she had spent the night at Susan's over Jim's objections.

Jim arrived home Saturday evening, and he glared at Janice. "I tried to call you last night several times. Were you at Susan's?"

Janice was prepared for his anger. "Yes."

Jim grimaced. "Jesus. So, what did you do—get drunk, take drugs, go dancing with her men?"

"I enjoyed meeting Susan's friends and going to a restaurant in their neighborhood." Janice had rehearsed this line, expecting Jim to grill her.

"You're turning into somebody I don't understand. I don't see how you are attracted to her—her qualities are so far below yours."

Janice turned to him, her eyes squinted. "I told you not to criticize my friend. And I haven't subjected you to her, per your request." She walked into the living room and turned on the news.

They made it through Sunday with a distant silence. Janice was glad when Monday came and they returned to their routine of commuting and working.

One Sunday evening in November, Janice prepared a pot roast with potatoes and carrots for supper. The delicious odors of the cooking food permeated the house as a north wind blew the trees and the outdoor temperature dropped.

After sitting down to eat, Jim surprised Janice with a declaration. "I think it's time to buy a house. We've saved enough money for a down payment, and interest rates are reasonable."

Janice was ready to nod in agreement, but he didn't stop there. "I also think it's time for us to start a family."

Janice was silent for several seconds. "I'm not ready. I'm on the pill."

"You've been taking the pill and haven't told me?"

"Yes—I'm telling you now." Her eyes narrowed and her face dropped, preparing to take his verbal blows as if they were physical slaps.

"I can't believe it. When will you be ready to go off of it?"

"I don't know."

"There's no point buying a new house larger than this one if we're not ready to have kids."

She didn't respond and went to clean up the kitchen, her stomach churning as she scrubbed the plates. They didn't discuss it again until the following week, when they learned that Tamara had given birth to a baby boy and that Bill's offer on a new house had been accepted.

"What about our dreams of a family and a home?" Jim said. "Your indecision is getting in the way of our goals."

"I never promised you anything," she said.

Jim backed off. Janice knew he hoped that time would bring them together, but she did not want to follow Tamara and Bill's path.

In the fall of 1966, Janice and Jim traveled to Iowa for Thanksgiving, staying two nights in Blairsville for the Thanksgiving meal at her parents' farm. They both were good actors and covered up any tension between them in front of Janice's family. Janice thought her mother and Grandpa Cole were too smart, though, to not notice something. Grandpa Cole, now eighty-two, could not speak very well because of a stroke, but he kept looking at Janice with inquiring eyes.

After their Thanksgiving meal, Janice joined her cousins in the den, where the wood paneling always made Janice feel safe and cozy.

"Did you hear about Rick Peterson?" her cousin Laura asked.

"No, what about him?" Janice said.

"He was killed in Vietnam."

"No—Rick Peterson? From the same graduating class as me?" It was easy to believe, yet impossible.

Laura's blond curls bounced as she nodded. "Yeah, he was transferred there last year and was killed in a battle against the North Vietnamese."

"That's terrible!" Janice said, her throat catching on the words. She stood, wiping her eyes, and hurriedly left the den to step out onto the porch. She closed the door behind her, and the chilly afternoon greeted her, seeping quickly into her clothes. She looked out over the barren field.

Rick had grown up on a farm on the other side of Blairsville from Janice's farm. He was a gentle soul and good friend, physically slight and artistic. She knew he had been drafted after dropping out of college and was stationed in Germany, but she wasn't aware that his army division had been reassigned to Vietnam. She couldn't imagine him carrying a rifle through the jungles of Vietnam wearing a soldier's uniform and helmet. She regretted that she had lost track of him.

Janice thought of Susan's strong feelings against the U.S. involvement in Vietnam. Why was the U.S. in this war? Why had Rick died? What was the cause he was fighting for?

In college, Janice and Jim had talked about the Vietnam War, feeling fortunate that he hadn't been drafted because of his student deferment.

"There were five hundred North Vietnamese soldiers killed yesterday," Jim said while reading the paper at breakfast. "If we can keep up that rate, the war will soon be over."

"I guess," Janice said. "I don't even know why we're over there—such a tiny country. We're bound to win. I just don't want you to be drafted."

Rick's death made the war real to Janice. She no longer was detached, assuming this war had little impact on her life and that it would be over soon with a U.S. victory. She wanted to learn more about it.

4

Later that Thanksgiving Day evening, Janice took *Newsweek* magazines upstairs to her childhood bedroom, where she and Jim slept during their visit. She propped her pillow up, turned on the bedside lamp, and pored through articles about the Vietnam War while gusts of cold wind blew across the farm fields. Six thousand American soldiers had been killed during the past year alone. She was amazed that boys like Rick had been sent to a war that was killing thousands of them each year.

She read about the speech by President Johnson that Susan had mocked, his somber reasons for why more troops were needed to counter the threat of communism. Janice reacted like Susan did. These reasons made no sense; North Vietnam was no threat to the U.S.

After Jim came to bed, he reached across her to turn off her light and gently pulled her toward him. She resisted, quickly turning the lamp back on.

"I'm sorry," she said. "I want to finish reading. This war killed my friend, Jim. This is important to me."

"Aren't you overreacting a bit?" he asked, a change from the initial sympathy he had shown after hearing about the loss of her friend Rick.

"What?" Janice put the magazine down. "My friend is dead, and you're saying I'm overreacting?"

Jim turned onto his back instead of facing her. "It's a war. People die."

"Oh, God. Shut the fuck up." She couldn't believe Jim was mocking her when she was trying to understand why Rick had died. She moved away from him. He slid to the edge of his side of the mattress and turned his back toward her. She was silent, listening to the wind and trying to control her anger. She finally got up, put on her bathrobe, and went downstairs to the living room, where coals were still hot in the fireplace. She sat in the dark, watching the embers glow, wondering how she had gotten to the point of bringing such an insensitive person into her childhood home.

When Janice and Jim said goodbye the following day, Janice again noticed her grandpa's inquiring look. She put her arms around him and didn't let go for several seconds, coming close to tears. She wrote him a long letter afterward, confessing that her marriage was challenging but telling him not to worry. She would get through it—she had learned from him to play the cards she had been dealt.

In a month, they returned to Iowa, but this time to visit with Jim's family. The two days they spent with Jim's parents over Christmas were uneventful. Jim and his father enjoyed discussing business, agreeing that the Johnson administration was hurting the economy with too much focus on social programs. Jim's mother—a housewife and mother during her entire marriage—had little in common with Janice. Janice guessed that she was eager to have grandchildren. Fortunately, Janice could break away to visit her Wagner cousins in Des Moines, which made the two days go faster.

Little changed as Janice and Jim began the new year—with extended periods of silence when they were together. They acted like things were normal during holiday parties and get-togethers with neighbors and

Jim's work friends. But when they were alone, Janice was constantly on edge. Jim's frustration was expressed with bursts of anger, either over her silence or over what he said was her obsession with the war. He wanted to have sex, saying that intimacy would bring them back together, but his anger failed to inspire her in that department, and they moved to opposite sides of their bed at night without touching.

Janice subscribed to *Newsweek* and also to the *New Yorker*, which Susan recommended. Jim brought it in with the mail one day.

"You're subscribing to the *New Yorker*?" he said, tossing the magazine on the coffee table as if it were a contaminated piece of evidence.

"Yeah," Janice said, lifting the magazine and placing it on her lap. She braced herself for yet another attack from him on her left-wing beliefs, but he just shook his head, seemingly in resignation.

Jim surprised Janice with dinner for their first anniversary at a fancy restaurant downtown. She tried to make the evening work.

"How's your job going?" she asked.

"Good. I'm in line for a promotion, maybe next quarter."

"That's great!" Janice said, knowing she hadn't supported him like this for months. He looked at her with curiosity.

On their ride home, Janice continued to ask him questions about his job, trying to be a good listener. He responded, seeming to appreciate their conversation. But they were interrupted by a car cutting sharply in front of theirs.

"Asshole!" Jim shouted. He accelerated and tailgated the car for at least a mile, saying "stupid shit" multiple times.

Janice tensed up, her back rigid against the seat and her hand gripping the armrest all the way home. She went to bed quietly sobbing, releasing the tension she'd felt the whole evening, especially in the car. Jim made an attempt to apologize, but she didn't respond. She allowed him to hold her while she cried, and she could feel his tears on her face when he kissed her.

"You're crying," she said.

Jim sniffed and cleared his throat. "I love you, Janice. I just want us to be together."

She hugged him and rubbed his back, trying to comfort him, but still crying herself, knowing their relationship was in trouble and not knowing what to do about it.

———•••———

Janice's job gave her a welcome distraction from her misery at home. She was efficient and responsive in supporting account managers, so much so that her supervisor talked about promoting her as an assistant account manager. He invited her to client meetings, and she gained confidence in helping define what customers really wanted. But none of this brought her closer to desiring a career in advertising. Instead, it confirmed that business success was not what she wanted.

Her job was not a total escape, either. Images of her recent arguments with Jim often stayed with her. One day, Susan stopped by Janice's desk with a questioning look.

"Are you okay?" Susan asked. "Everything all right at home?"

Janice was surprised, thinking she had disguised her feelings about her marriage pretty well up until this point. She looked at Susan and told her that she wasn't doing well. Susan suggested that they chat after work.

They walked to a nearby coffee shop in the rain and ordered tea. Before Janice started talking, her eyes filled with tears, and Susan gave her a tissue.

"I'm thinking of leaving Jim."

Susan handed Janice another tissue as more tears came.

"I don't know how I ended up with him. We're so different."

"You were college sweethearts—he's good-looking and nice—but now you're in different worlds."

Janice sipped her tea, ready to hear what Susan had to say.

"Your differences aren't just about Vietnam. Your values are different."

Janice raised her eyebrows.

"Do you know that Monsanto's making money off the war with Agent Orange? It's a toxic defoliant."

Janice had seen news reports of Agent Orange being sprayed on farm fields and jungle cover for Vietnamese soldiers. She didn't realize Monsanto was the manufacturer—Jim would probably defend it as an impossible-to-forego business opportunity.

Janice shook her head and dabbed her eyes with the tissues. Susan refilled their cups with more tea and reached across the table to put her hand on Janice's. "I need to start planning next steps," Janice said. "I can't keep living with him."

She sipped her tea, and it seemed to help release the tension from her shoulders. She felt spurred to action, even though she wasn't ready to make an immediate move. Seeming to sense Janice's new resolve, Susan asked if she wanted to attend an antiwar demonstration planned by the National Mobilization Committee in New York City.

"I hadn't mentioned it before because I knew Jim would be opposed. I didn't want to make any trouble for you, but now it seems like there might be nothing to lose."

Janice was quiet, knowing how Jim would react if she said yes. But Susan was right. "Saying no to going won't save my marriage," Janice said quietly. The thought of protesting in New York City excited her. "Sure. Why not," she said.

Susan smiled and squeezed Janice's hand.

That night, Janice told Jim of her plans to go to the New York protest.

"What's the protest?" Jim asked, his mouth turning down and his eyes narrowing.

"It's a march against the Vietnam War." She steeled herself, anticipating his ridicule.

"That's just unbelievable. I don't know what made us get married. We're totally different people."

Janice silently nodded.

———•••———

On April 15, 1967, Janice and Susan joined hundreds of thousands of people in the MOBE march from Central Park to the United Nations. They chanted antiwar slogans, amazed at the noise and power of the crowd. They watched several young men burn their draft cards and were enthralled by Martin Luther King Jr.'s speech against the war. Susan put her arm around Janice's shoulders after the applause died. "You look happy to be in New York," she said.

Janice nodded. She had absorbed the crowd's energy and felt that her participation was the right thing for her to do. When she returned from New York, she and Jim seemed ready for the end.

After a silent supper, Janice said, "We need to talk."

"What about?"

"I don't want to live together anymore," she said. "It's killing both of us."

Jim didn't seem surprised or angry. He stood up and looked out the window at their backyard.

"I want a divorce," she said. "You can keep most of our things."

"Okay," Jim said. He stood still with his eyes closed for several seconds.

"I'll move into the guest bedroom until I find a place to live," she said. She felt like her sentences were punches, imagining he was shrinking from the blows. But he stood and took it.

"Is that all?" he asked.

She nodded.

"I'm going to go find a movie." He put on his jacket and left.

Janice moved to the guest bedroom that night. She got lucky the next week at work, learning a secretary needed a roommate. Susan and two friends came out on a Saturday to help Janice move—a day Jim had purposely gone to work to avoid being there. That same weekend, Janice bought a used car, a seven-year-old Ford Falcon. She was ready to restart her life.

5

Although it would take some getting used to, Janice was now free to make her own choices. Her mind immediately turned to leaving her advertising job and thinking about her future. She recalled her Iowa State advisor telling her that a social science degree, like the one she was pursuing in anthropology, provided an excellent educational base for graduate school. That idea had intrigued her then, but any thoughts of pursuing a graduate degree were buried once she married.

She poured through a University of Iowa catalog at the local library after determining she wanted a change from Iowa State. When she read about a new interdisciplinary program in environmental studies offered by the Earth Sciences Department, she decided to apply. Maybe she could eventually work toward improving environmental practices in farming. She had some knowledge base there.

The university informed her that she had been accepted and could start her graduate studies in January 1968. She decided to work into December to save money for college expenses.

In the meantime, the months before she was set to move went by quickly. Janice often spent weekends with Susan, twice participating with her in Chicago rallies against the war. During the week, she spent evenings in her bedroom reading or watching TV on a small set she had purchased, while her roommate led an active social life, coming and going with her boyfriend. Although Janice didn't miss Jim, she was sometimes lonely and looked forward to interacting with her friends at work and starting a new life in Iowa City.

She didn't realize how much her work friends meant to her until they had a going-away party in December, during the week before her last day at the advertising firm. A core group led by Susan stayed up late, drinking beer with her at their favorite bar. When they said goodbye at the train station, Janice hugged them with tears, saving her longest hug for Susan. "I'll visit soon as you're settled and ready for me," her friend told her.

When Janice got home to her apartment, she stared at herself in the mirror and cried.

———•••———

Soon after her resignation, Janice packed and loaded her possessions into her Ford Falcon and drove west on Interstate 80 across the plains of Illinois. How flat the land was, she thought, stretching into the distance. Her college friends at Iowa State from the East Coast had joked about how flat Iowa farmland was, but Iowa was hilly compared to the corn and soybean fields in Illinois, where she could see a single tree on the horizon from miles away. The steady driving in the predictable landscape, with tires humming on the pavement, released Janice's tension. She was leaving behind the emotional ups and downs of a broken marriage.

As she approached the Mississippi River, the land changed, with smaller fields of farmland interspersed among hills and wooded areas. The final miles to Iowa City went by quickly. She loved climbing up the hill to the downtown, with the Iowa River and park on her right, full of trees. She eventually made her way to an economy motel on the Coralville strip and bought a newspaper, which she used that night to circle rental listings.

On the following day, Janice visited several apartments. She chose an upstairs apartment in an older white house owned by a retired university librarian who lived downstairs. In addition to a nice-sized bedroom, Janice had her own bathroom and a second bedroom that had been converted into a small kitchen and eating area. She also had her own entrance by climbing stairs on the side of the house to the small deck off her bedroom. It was the perfect place to dedicate herself to her studies.

After writing checks for her deposit and January's rent, she walked around the peaceful university campus, hearing birds chirping that she had never heard in the Chicago Loop. She observed students closely, most of them younger than her. She wondered if she would fit in. She ended her walk at the building that housed the Earth Sciences Department and searched for the department offices. When Janice asked if the department head was available, the receptionist escorted her to his office.

"Welcome!" the department head said, greeting Janice with a firm handshake and motioning her to sit down. "We're excited to have you in our environmental studies program."

"I'm excited, too," she said, "but I'm concerned that my physical sciences background might not be strong enough."

"Our program focuses more on interdisciplinary skills than the theory and math of a physical science major. I'm sure your anthropology degree will be a great foundation."

After thanking him and leaving, Janice pictured herself walking daily to classes with fellow students. She couldn't wait to return from her parents' farm after Christmas and begin the spring semester, putting a turbulent year behind her.

———◆◆◆———

Janice's Christmas visit with her family in 1967 was the first time they had seen her since over a year ago, when she and Jim had spent two days with them at Thanksgiving. Normally, Janice might also visit her family in the summer, but the past summer was when her marriage fell apart. She had kept her mother informed in phone calls about the ending of her marriage.

"Why don't you come home for a vacation. You deserve some rest after what you've been through," her mother said at the end of one call.

"I'm not organized yet in my apartment, I need to get my Falcon tuned up, and I've just begun talking to a lawyer," Janice said. "My plan is to stop in Iowa City on my way home in December and find an apartment for spring semester. Then I'll be ready to come home and relax."

"Okay," her mother said. "I'll have your favorite cookies baked when you get here."

When Janice arrived at the farm a week before Christmas, her mother exclaimed over the length of her hair. Encouraged by Susan, Janice had let it grow below her shoulders, still parting it on the right side. It was thick and wavy and often covered her left eye, causing her to push it back frequently.

"It's so thick and healthy," her mother said.

"I admit, I'm a little proud of it myself," Janice said, smiling broadly. "Thank you for noticing." She gave her mother a hug that felt as if it could last forever.

Her father, however, acted as if he didn't notice this change. His typical silence made it hard for her to tell how he felt about her leaving Jim and changing the direction of her life. She had worked hard as a child to make him proud, but unlike Grandpa Cole, he often seemed to keep her at arm's length, perhaps with one exception: when he was cheering for her in her basketball games.

Once, when Janice expressed her frustration with her father's silence, her mother told her that he was sometimes moody because of memories of fighting in World War II. In recalling those words now, Janice wondered if her father had guessed that she was against the

Vietnam War, most likely on opposite sides from him. She decided not to test that assumption.

Her brother, Tim, was not silent. Janice was amazed at how much he had grown, and she enjoyed talking with him about his basketball season. She loved watching him play on the sophomore team in a game during the holiday break. He led the scoring in their victory over a team from a nearby farm town. She was surprised to hear that Tim also had a perfect grade-point average.

Janice had been anxious about the Christmas Day gathering with relatives. She had not seen them all year but assumed they all knew about her divorce. Her anxiety disappeared after Grandpa Cole hugged her and her cousins teased her.

"Good that you're home," Grandpa said. He looked at her with understanding eyes, and she knew he would be willing to talk about her divorce, but only if she initiated it.

The only relative who made her uncomfortable was Aunt Rose. She nodded coolly to Janice in a brief greeting and ignored her for the rest of the gathering.

At the end of the week, Janice's mother packed a container of Christmas cookies for Janice to take to her apartment. On the second of January, a sunny day with a temperature of five below zero, Janice said farewell to her family. She drove to Iowa City, ready to begin her life in the new year as a graduate student. She had learned during her trip to Iowa City that her new apartment was near a food co-op. She unpacked her car, brought her things into the apartment, and walked to the co-op to buy food. A large sign dominated the bulletin board inside the front door: "Stop the War in Vietnam!"

6

Janice entered the meeting room at the student union and was struck by how young the students were and how extreme their hippie clothing was compared to hers. Women who looked to be under twenty held their long, straight hair in place with thin leather headbands and wore beads and medallions of peace signs around their necks. The men also wore long hair, some with sashes around their foreheads. Their jackets and boots were from army surplus stores.

Janice was feeling good about her new start—she had bought her books, had her first set of classes, and completed her initial assignments. Everything had gone smoothly. She had adapted to the routines of studying, getting to know the faculty's expectations, and comparing notes with fellow students. Her life as a student was under control, and that meant she could explore other interests, especially the antiwar movement on campus.

She learned from an op-ed piece in the campus newspaper, the *Daily Iowan*, that an Iowa congressman who supported the war planned to visit campus. The author of the op-ed piece, Ben Keller, a law school student, invited students to join a protest during the congressman's visit and asked them to meet in the student union the night before his visit. This was her opportunity to be part of something that had begun to mean a lot to her.

When Janice signed in, a young woman at the desk with blond hair down her back directed her to a woman named Cathy standing across the room. Cathy was a stout woman dressed in a long peasant dress, with hair pulled back in a single loose braid down her back. She had inquiring eyes and a sparkling smile, and Janice guessed her to be similar in age to herself. They exchanged information about their fields of study, discovering they were both in graduate school. Cathy was pursuing a degree in social work and was impressed to hear about Janice's interdisciplinary program on the environment. Janice smiled, overjoyed to meet a woman who seemed to be at a similar stage of life as she was, someone who had probably experienced the ups and downs of the real world as she had, in contrast to the undergraduate students who were getting restless waiting.

"What's being planned for the protest tomorrow?" Janice asked.

"That's what Ben wants to talk about tonight," Cathy said. "He wants ideas on how to call attention to the congressman's support of the war."

"Ben wrote the *Daily* piece?"

"Yeah. He'll be happy to see you have joined us," Cathy said. "The immaturity of some of these undergrads drives us crazy. Anyway, Ben decided to take this year off from law school to work on the antiwar protests. He's really active in the antiwar National Mobilization Committee, or MOBE, which he joined when he was an undergrad in Boston."

"I went to the MOBE protest in New York City last spring," Janice said. "I would've liked to have done more, but my husband was about to kill me by then—we were not in agreement about the war."

"You're married?"

"No. We got divorced last summer."

"You've been in the real world. Here comes Ben now."

They turned to the room entrance and saw Ben talking to the young woman with the long blond hair at the desk. She stood up and hugged him, laughing at whatever he had said to her. Turning to survey the room, he saw Cathy beckoning him to come over. Janice watched him slowly move toward them, greeting people on the way. The younger students stopped chattering and sat down at the cafeteria-style tables as he approached them. When Ben reached Cathy, she introduced Janice and told him she had marched in the MOBE protest in New York last year.

Janice pushed her hair out of her face and looked closely at him. His dark eyes sparkled, set off by a full black beard. He seemed to be hesitating as he looked at her. His barrel chest made him seem bigger than he was, capable of great strength and energy. Janice didn't let his hesitation bother her. She was intrigued by the impact of his presence.

"It's good that you've joined us," he said. "I want to hear about your experience at the MOBE march." He introduced Janice to Liz, the young blond-haired woman who had walked over to stand close to him, and then turned to face the crowd, saying he'd better start the meeting.

Ben welcomed everyone, and the room quieted down. He told them that when the administration heard he was planning a protest, they canceled the plans to have the congressman give a public speech. "They're concerned about hecklers and disruption, especially with what happened at the University of Wisconsin. He'll still be meeting with the Board of Regents, so I suggest we protest outside the admin building—the meeting will be in there."

There was silence when Ben stopped to ask for comments or questions—the group seemed ready to do whatever Ben told them. Janice decided to be bold and raised her hand. Her conversation with Cathy and her observations of the students gave her confidence.

"How about taking the protest inside the building?" Janice asked. "I assume the Regents meetings are open to the public."

Ben looked surprised, maybe seeing Janice's words as an interjection that might lessen his control of the meeting. But then he smiled. "I like that idea," he said. "Whether the police let us in or not, we might get more publicity than walking back and forth outside. What do the rest of you think?"

"Let's do it," Cathy said. Others nodded in agreement. Ben then went over the logistics of the protest, read the talking points he was prepared to use with the media, and adjourned the meeting, matching his eyes with Janice's as the students filed out.

Cathy walked out with Janice. "I think you got Ben's attention. Did you feel it?"

"I don't know. What did you see?"

"He seemed interested in you, especially after you surprised him with your idea," Cathy said. "I could feel his charming side emerging."

"I think the blond girl Liz felt it too. What's her story?"

"Ben seems to attract groupies—she's the latest. Fortunately, I don't have that kind of relationship with him. I suggest you be careful."

Janice smiled at Cathy, and Cathy laughed. When they parted, they hugged each other briefly, a spontaneous act that confirmed their new friendship. Janice walked home, knowing she needed to read a few chapters for an assignment that night, but her mind kept returning to Cathy and Ben and her own part in planning the next day's protest. It had been a wonderful evening. Cathy's warning about Ben made her curious, but she didn't let those thoughts linger.

About twenty-five students gathered to protest the congressman's visit outside the university administration building. The local press was there, including a TV camera operator who started filming the protesters when they arrived. They paraded with their signs, and shortly after the Regents meeting was scheduled to start, Ben led them up the steps to enter the building. When the campus police stopped them, Ben told them it was a public meeting, and they wanted to attend. Another police officer joined the first one, and they blocked the door.

Two young male students behind Ben started chanting: "One, two, three, four, we don't want your fucking war!"

The police moved toward them, telling them to walk back down. Janice was a couple steps behind Ben and watched as the two young students started pushing toward the door. Ben tried to keep people calm, but a police officer began shouting threats to arrest them. One of the chanting students—in full hippie garb with long hair dyed bright red—made it past the police, flinging the doors open and racing into the building toward the stairs that led up to the meeting. He pulled a chain for locking bicycles out of the large pocket in his army surplus pants and wrapped it around his waist and the bottom post of the railing. He then drew it tight and snapped a padlock through the links of the chain to secure himself against the post.

The police yelled at the student to unlock the padlock, but he refused. Ben stepped inside and was immediately pushed out by the police. He went down the steps to where reporters had gathered. They asked him what was happening, talking over themselves. Ben responded in a voice deep with emotion. The camera operator stationed himself in front of Ben, filming him as he spoke the short sentences he was prepared to use:

"We are against the war and oppose the congressman upstairs who supports it! We believe the university should also oppose this war, which has resulted in the deaths of thousands of Americans! They should stop consorting with politicians responsible for killing women and children!" As camera shutters clicked away, he added another point: "One of our protesters has chained himself to the stairs inside and will not leave until the university joins us in opposing the war!"

The reporters pushed their microphones near Ben's face and asked him questions he didn't answer. Janice, motivated by Ben's words, started shouting, "Stop the war! Stop the war!" The other students joined in. The camera operator kept filming Ben and the chanting protesters. When a police van pulled up, the reporters rushed to it. A police captain stepped out and raised a bullhorn to his face. "Disperse immediately," his voice boomed, "or you will be arrested."

Ben signaled it was time to leave and led the protesters away. Janice looked over her shoulder as they filed away and watched a police officer with a bolt cutter go inside. A moment later, the red-haired student was led to the back of the van in handcuffs. The door slammed loudly behind him after he entered. And that was it. The protest was over in less than thirty minutes.

Ben, Cathy, and Janice walked away together, and Ben suggested they stop at a coffee house. When Janice stepped inside, she noticed the bulletin board near the front door contained clippings of antiwar protests and announcements of political events.

After finding a small table and settling in, Ben told Janice and Cathy that the protest was a great success, and they nodded. He was confident it would be a headline story on the TV evening news and in the next day's newspaper.

"Your idea to move the protest inside really worked out well," Ben said to Janice.

Cathy nodded. "We took a risk," she said, "knowing some of our kids might get out of control, like the redhead did."

"But that was okay—I bet that's what the media will focus on," Janice said.

"I agree," Ben said.

"It's too bad that he'll probably spend the night in jail," Cathy said.

"But his willingness to go to that extreme is understandable," Janice said. "If the war doesn't end soon, he and his friends could get drafted."

Later in her apartment, Janice reflected on the protest. Unlike the large rallies she had attended, this was a small protest with a specific target. She replayed her role as a leader in the event.

She had made an impact.

The protest that spring received national attention, particularly the student chaining himself to the stairs. Janice was proud of her contributions in helping produce that publicity. She joined Ben and Cathy in monitoring activities at other universities—the weeklong student occupation of certain buildings at Columbia University was a highlight. They also followed protests outside of universities, by the Berrigan brothers, for example—Catholic priests who broke into a draft board office and burned the files using napalm. Ben, Cathy, and Janice worked together on ideas for protests that would support this national movement.

Cathy organized a letter-writing campaign to several Iowa elected officials and candidates running for office, urging them to take positions against the Vietnam War.

Janice helped Ben plan and publicize a protest at the campus buildings where corporate recruiters interviewed students for jobs. They targeted Dow Chemical, the maker of napalm used in the incendiary bombing of Vietnamese troops—which often also killed or injured villagers. The Dow protest drew almost one hundred students—their largest group yet—and attracted local and national media.

After the Regents' protest, a large campus police presence was always at the ready, prepared to head off anything like a student breaking into a building. In a couple smaller protests, Janice had gotten to know Sergeant Greene, who was the point person for the campus police. She sought him out at the beginning of the Dow protest.

"We're planning to march in a circle," she said. "Will that work for you?"

"Yeah, as long as you don't go across this sidewalk," Sergeant Greene said. "That's where I'll have most of our troops."

When the protest began with a larger crowd than predicted, about ten students crossed the sidewalk. Janice immediately ran to them to have them move back, before the police did it. Sergeant Greene thanked her and moved his troops out of the way so the students could step back.

Ben smiled as Janice crossed back over. "You're quite the facilitator," he said with a grin. "You can get either side to do whatever you want."

"Better watch out, or I'll have Sergeant Greene move you," she said, laughing.

After the protest, they walked together to meet Cathy for lunch. Ben kept laughing about how everyone obeyed Janice, and Janice joined him, almost reaching out to take his arm. "That was probably the most orderly protest in the country," Ben said. "Cathy, you should have seen Miss Facilitator—she was in charge."

"I'm sure she was," Cathy said. But she also gave Janice a concerned look that seemed to say, *Do you know what you're doing?* Just then, Liz arrived, and Ben stood to make room for her in their booth. Janice had been feeling closer to Ben, but Cathy's look and Liz's arrival put a brake on her feelings and imagination. She stopped thinking about where her relationship with Ben might be going.

She became more businesslike with Ben and Cathy, as the three of them began making plans to attend a national protest at the Democratic Convention in Chicago in late August. They reviewed a newsletter drafted by Ben informing University of Iowa students about these plans and asking for volunteers to join them, continuing the momentum they had built at the end of the school year.

It was an ambitious trip, and she was a key part of it. One night, she sat cross-legged in her bed, her notes scattered around her, and began jotting down details about the logistics that she knew Ben would want her to lead—coordinating transportation, finding low-cost hotels, and scheduling daily activities with protests planned by national organizations. She thought of watching Grandpa Cole schedule his plans for raising crops and livestock on a large calendar when she was in grade school. She also thought of Ben praising her for her organized plans and smiled, feeling warmth rise to her neck.

———•••———

Janice stayed in Iowa City that summer, taking two classes and working on planning the August trip to Chicago. As usual, she kept in touch with her family through phone calls to her mother.

"I hope you'll come home for Laura's wedding in August," her mother said to her on one call.

"I wouldn't miss my favorite cousin's wedding."

"Good, because we haven't seen you since Christmas."

"I've been busy."

"You've been studying hard?"

"Yeah, I'm getting good grades." Janice stopped with that answer. She didn't want to tell her mother—who would tell her father—about her involvement in protests. And she wasn't at all ready to tell them she would be traveling to Chicago for a national protest only days after her cousin's wedding.

7

On her drive home from Iowa City, Janice passed through the small town of Blairsville, about five miles from her parents' farm. She drove by the Methodist church where her cousin would get married and by the town's only school, where she had attended all grades and graduated from. She thought of the changes she had been through since her graduation day in 1962, a little over six years ago. She pictured herself then: medium-length hair curled with rollers, pleated skirts and sweaters, and flat shoes with bobby socks.

She drove up the farm's lane and parked her car in the gravel area near the farmhouse. Her mother opened the front door and quickly walked toward Janice as she exited her car. Her mother hugged her, molding Janice to her large body, and then, stepping back, looked at Janice's faded jeans, tie-dye T-shirt, and rubber flip-flops.

"That must be the Iowa City style of dress," her mother said. She smiled, looking down at her farm dress and apron. "I wouldn't fit in." Janice's father followed her mother and also hugged her, but he didn't comment or even seem to take notice of her looks.

The days before the wedding were fun—a chance to visit Grandpa Cole, who she learned would not be attending the wedding, having recently experienced a mini-stroke and requiring a wheelchair. She also saw most of her cousins, especially enjoying her Cole cousins on her mother's side: Laura, the bride, and her brother Steve.

When Janice greeted Laura and Steve at their parents' farm a couple of days before the wedding, Laura joked that Janice was a changed person, with her long hair and bell-bottoms.

"Are you living in a commune yet?" Steve asked.

Janice laughed. "No, I'm living in an apartment—the second floor of an old house—and spend most of my time studying. Alone. Quite the opposite of a commune."

Laura pointed to Janice's car—the rusty old Ford Falcon, its bumpers plastered with "Stop the War" and peace sign stickers. "How do you have time to study with all the protests you're attending?"

Janice appreciated the good-natured teasing, but also sensed her cousins' genuine interest in her beliefs.

When she ended her visit and walked to her car, Steve opened the car door for her.

"Laura and I agree with your feelings about the war," Steve said. He looked toward the house to make sure his parents weren't listening. "We need to be a bit careful living here, surrounded by such conservative folk."

⸻

On Laura's wedding day, Janice talked to several relatives and friends from Blairsville and the surrounding farms. They asked about her studies, staying away from topics related to divorce and politics. After the wedding ceremony, she moved to the church's fellowship hall for the reception, hugged the bride and groom, and followed others in line to get punch and cake. Her aunt Rose stood behind her, and she and Janice conversed with family members and friends around them. The hum of conversations in the packed hall produced a steady background of noise.

Aunt Rose was a tall, thin woman, and her gray hair, wire-rimmed glasses, and thick leather shoes gave her the look of a woman beyond her actual age. She turned and stared at Janice in a way that put Janice on guard—she'd experienced her aunt's strong feelings before.

"Nice bell-bottoms, but this is a wedding," Aunt Rose said. "Don't you have a dress?"

Janice wore one of her best outfits, a peach-colored silk top and black dress slacks that flared at the bottom. She didn't respond to her aunt, knowing there was probably more to come.

"And what about a haircut? I can barely see your face."

Janice lifted her arm and pushed her thick hair back from the side of her face to look directly at her aunt. "I'm fine."

"I used to think I knew who you were, living with your husband in Chicago," her aunt said. "But you left that for Iowa City and its hippies."

Janice looked at her aunt, thinking this was familiar and predictable but still feeling the sting. "I like Iowa City. I've made some good friends."

"Like the protesters we see on TV? It's a shame they don't love our country."

Janice's eyes narrowed. She hesitated, knowing she should stop rising to her aunt's bait. But she reacted anyway.

"I think they do love our country and hate to see the direction it's moving in," Janice said. She stepped forward to fill the gap in front of her in the line.

Aunt Rose followed her. "Do you mean the nomination of Richard Nixon? That's the best thing that has happened to us for years."

"I think it could be the worst thing," Janice said, her voice rising. She felt her face warming as she thought of Nixon's law-and-order campaign. She was about to continue when she saw that people in the line had stopped their conversations and turned to look at her and Aunt Rose.

Aunt Rose smiled, obviously basking in the attention she had attracted. She looked at Janice's father, who had been observing the exchange from a few yards away. "Carl, you've raised quite a daughter." Janice looked at her father's face to see if he was in agreement with her aunt, but he was expressionless. Aunt Rose moved away from Janice and started conversing about the weather with the people behind her.

Janice was not surprised at this exchange. Aunt Rose was an outspoken leader of the fundamentalists in the Methodist church and framed most topics in terms of whether or not God would approve of them. She was closely allied with conservative politicians, who had supported her when she led a rally against removing a stone carving of the Ten Commandments from the front lawn of the city hall.

Janice knew all this but still let her aunt get under her skin. Aunt Rose's provocations seemed driven by more than her conservative political beliefs. Maybe as the childless older sister, Aunt Rose was jealous of her brother's family and his children. Perhaps she took out her bitterness on Janice.

Still, Janice was now twenty-four. Why couldn't she control her anger when provoked, especially in public? She didn't have patience with people like her aunt who supported the war, but there was no reason to start yelling about it in the middle of a wedding reception.

She took comfort, though, in knowing that Ben and Cathy echoed her strong feelings. They would be appalled by her aunt's right-wing, fundamentalist views, which they believed were leading the country toward fascism. Janice thought of their upcoming trip to Chicago—she couldn't wait.

———•••———

After Janice got her cake and punch, she went outdoors to the small patio, feeling the hot August air surround her, more relaxing than uncomfortable. She was surprised to find her brother, Tim, sitting alone at a table under the shade of an oak tree in the church's yard, his tie loosened and sport coat draped over a chair. Tim—she still called him Timmy—was sixteen years old and already a head taller than she was. Like many siblings far apart in age, they had always been close, with Janice often babysitting him as he grew up.

She sat down and reached over to mess up his hair, which was drooping down his forehead. He pushed her hand away, and she laughed. He'd grown handsome over the last year, his jaw square and his forehead broad and smooth.

"How do you think your basketball team is going to do this year?" she asked.

"We can win the conference if our center keeps improving," he said.

Janice knew this was not small talk for Tim—that he was impressed with her basketball knowledge and accomplishments. He had attended all of Janice's high school games, watching her become a star basketball player on Blairsville's six-on-six girls' basketball team. One of their team's three guards, she took pride in her defense, making up for her lack of size with her skill at stealing the ball from the other team's forwards. In her senior year, she was named an all-state player, and her team made it to the Sweet Sixteen in the state tournament.

"If you improve like you did last year, you'll have a chance to be all-state," Janice said.

"I don't know about that."

"If I can do it, you can. If you need to be motivated, talk to Grandpa Cole."

"Grandpa's been after me ever since he heard about my test scores—he thinks I should be valedictorian of our class."

"You're a lot better student than I was. If Grandpa believes in you, you know you have a chance."

Tim looked at Janice and nodded, seeming to appreciate her encouragement. She smiled, thinking she was lucky to have a younger brother who looked up to her and glad that Grandpa was encouraging him like he had her. She felt responsible for helping guide him through his teenage years.

The reception ended, and Janice and Tim went inside. They joined everyone in throwing rice at the bride and groom as they walked to their car, ready to drive to Minneapolis for their honeymoon. The older cousins had decorated their car with balloons, streamers, and "Just Married" signs.

The bride and groom's departure in the decorated car brought back memories of Janice's wedding with Jim. She didn't remember any celebrations beyond a reception and Aunt Rose's toasts. She did remember wondering whether she was following too much in lockstep with Jim. But Janice pushed these memories out of her mind as she watched the bride and groom drive away. After farewells to her relatives, she and Tim returned to their farm with their mother and father.

Janice's mother put out a light meal of sandwiches and a salad for TV trays, and Janice joined her parents in watching a news-hour show her father had chosen. It included an update on the Democratic Convention scheduled in Chicago at the end of the month. Tim reclined on the couch, reading a basketball sports magazine. It was a humid evening; occasionally, they could see some heat lightning flashing in the distance through their open windows.

Janice had followed the 1968 events affecting the Democratic presidential nomination, especially once she had decided to go to Chicago to protest. President Johnson was initially expected to be the nominee, but Senator Eugene McCarthy surprisingly won 40 percent of the vote in the New Hampshire primary. Janice remembered how thrilled she, Ben, and Cathy were to hear that news. They were shocked, however, by the assassination of Robert Kennedy in June, with the country still recovering from the assassination of Martin Luther King Jr. in April, not long after Janice became active in the Iowa City antiwar efforts. She worried about the state of the country.

When the TV reports showed clips of battles during North Vietnam's Tet Offensive, Janice moaned, exhaling deeply when the TV showed wounded American soldiers carried away on stretchers and body bags of dead American soldiers lined up to be taken by helicopters.

"It's so sad when our soldiers are killed," her mother said.

"Our soldiers shouldn't even be there, Mom. There's no reason for this war."

Tim raised his head at the sound of a potential conflict. "Why shouldn't the soldiers be there?"

"It's a civil war that needs to be resolved by the Vietnamese people," Janice said. "We're making things worse by being there; plus thousands of our soldiers are being killed."

Their mother looked at the two of them with a frown and suggested they talk about something else, glancing sideways at Janice's father. She added that she thought the war would end soon.

Janice's father got up to get a cup of coffee and stood by the bar separating the kitchen from the living room. He looked the same as he always did—average height, slender with broad shoulders, and gray hair in a short crewcut.

"You're too optimistic, Mom," Janice said. "All General Westmoreland did was ask for more troops, and there's no evidence that Abrams is changing anything."

Her father remained standing apart. "U.S. generals usually know what they're doing," he said. Janice knew he was referring to his time in the Pacific during World War II.

"But the generals you fought under were defending the U.S. after the attack on Pearl Harbor," Janice said. "There's no reason for us to be in Vietnam."

"We're keeping Asian countries from becoming communist. They could fall like dominoes if North Vietnam wins." His posture stiffened as he looked down at her.

"That's what Johnson keeps saying, but more of our soldiers

are killed each year," Janice said, her jaw tightening. "Rick Peterson was killed too. Remember him? I want it to stop."

Her father looked out the window toward the cornfields. Janice followed his sight and saw a flash of heat lightning, causing the dark clouds to glow for a moment. He turned back to her with a frown.

"Is your aunt Rose right? Have you been involved in protests?"

"Yeah," Janice said. "We need to counter the Aunt Rose views."

"I want you to stop protesting and focus on your studies."

Janice considered ending the conversation, knowing she couldn't change her father's mind, but she resented his command.

"I'm not going to stop acting on what I believe. I've been meaning to tell you—I'm going with friends to Chicago to try to influence the Democratic Convention."

"Janice," her mother said, shaking her head. Her father stared at her with his blue eyes, his forehead furrowed.

"You're going to join the hippies to demonstrate against our country?"

"I'm going to help change the direction of our country."

"You're what?" her father yelled. "You protesters have no idea how the real world works." He suddenly raised his right arm and slammed the palm of his hand on the kitchen counter, rattling the dishes in the sink. He glared at her, the furrows in his forehead deepening and his chest heaving. He seemed to have given up talking and left the room, heading outside to the porch. Janice's mother went after him, appearing more sad than angry.

Janice watched them leave, staring at them with surprise. She glanced at Tim, who had a look of confusion and excitement on his face.

"Why is Dad so mad?" he asked.

She shook her head and stood up to go to her room. "You need to start thinking about how to avoid going to Vietnam after you graduate." She walked upstairs, not knowing what to do or how her father's fury would affect their relationship. She had never seen him so angry.

8

Janice walked down the lane from the farmhouse shortly after sunrise, her father's anger still weighing on her. She crossed the gravel road, heading toward the cornfield and the grove of oak and maple trees on the other side.

A calf bawled in the barn behind the house, signaling to its mother that it was time to nurse. Janice could tell the pigs were feeding by the clanging of the tin hog feeders. The stirring of the livestock meant that her father was up and had begun his morning chores. She hurried her step to enter the field across the road so that she would be hidden by the corn.

The cornstalks on both sides of the tractor path towered above Janice. She reached the grove, which owed its existence to a trickling stream that flowed through a small valley in the middle of the cornfield. She sat on a fallen log and didn't move, listening and watching. She soon heard red-winged blackbirds and watched them chirping and flitting among the reeds near the stream.

Janice had planned to get up early, sit alone in the grove, and think about her conflicts with her father and Aunt Rose. It didn't take her long to conclude that if her aunt, father, or whoever argued with her over the war, they would have to deal with her emotions. She was going to continue protesting, regardless of what people thought about it.

She focused again on the grove and its wildlife, surrounded by farm fields. She remembered being fascinated by deer as a child, their size and grace bringing her a sense of peace. Sometimes they came from the larger stand of trees where the stream emptied into the creek, looking for corn to eat.

One summer evening, when she was a teenager and Timmy was about five, her mother had interrupted her dishwashing to come into the living room and tell them that two deer were on the front lawn. Janice and Timmy gently opened the screen door to the porch. It was warm, and the air was still except for the crickets, whose soothing sound helped muffle any noises that might startle the deer. Timmy stepped off the porch and walked slowly toward the deer. Suddenly, a rabbit darted out from under the oak tree on the right side of the lawn. The deer jumped into the air and ran, and Timmy let out a scared cry. Janice's heart beat faster as the deer leaped toward the road and bounded into the cornfield, their white tails flashing in the dusky evening light.

Janice's fond memories of her family and farm life were being shaken by political disagreements. She loved her family and wanted their support, but she needed to do what she thought was right. She got up to walk back to the house, thinking about what she might say to her father and mother before returning to Iowa City that morning. She didn't want to be angry, but she wanted to be heard. As she walked amid the cornstalks, she heard a car come down the farm lane and turn onto the gravel road.

Janice entered the house and smelled the delicious aroma of breakfast cooking. Her mother was in the kitchen making blueberry pancakes, Janice's favorite.

"Where's Dad?"

"He went to town."

"For what? I wanted to talk to him."

"His weekend horseshoe games."

Janice looked at her mother. "Didn't he know I was planning to leave this morning?"

"He said he wanted to play horseshoes and left."

"He doesn't even want to talk to me—he just left to avoid me."

Her mother looked at Janice and sighed. "I've never seen you knock heads like you did last night. Come now—have some pancakes. I'll call Tim."

After eating, Janice brought her bag from her bedroom, preparing to leave. Tim stepped in front of her, holding a basketball.

"Let's play HORSE. I bet I can beat you."

"Okay, let's do it. You need to be taught some humility." Janice smiled, sensing that he wanted to connect with her, maybe because of the argument with their father.

They took the basketball to the court in the barn and went back and forth, each getting a letter after missing the other's shot until they were tied at the letter S. She missed a hook shot, and Tim took the ball out beyond the free-throw line. He swished the long shot, and she missed it. Tim smiled, trying to act as if beating her wasn't a big deal. But she knew it was.

They went inside, and her mother gave her some cookies and fruit to snack on during her drive. Janice packed the food and hugged her mother and brother, asking them to say goodbye to her father for her. Tim frowned when she mentioned their father. "I'm sorry," Janice told him. "I know that this is affecting you."

Tim just shrugged, and she hugged him again, climbed into her car, and began the drive to Iowa City.

———•••———

During the drive, Janice put the family conflict behind her and thought about the coming weeks. She realized how comfortable she felt with the direction her life was going in—especially when she considered her anxiety the previous fall when arriving in Iowa City. Everything seemed to have fallen in place—her choice of environmental studies as a career field, her apartment, new friends, and working to end the war. She turned on the radio and hummed along with songs as she rode by fields of corn and soybeans.

After arriving in Iowa City, Janice focused on what she needed to do that week. Even though the semester didn't start until after Labor Day, she wanted to buy books for her fall courses and schedule an appointment with an advisor to discuss thesis topics.

Grandpa Cole wrote his plans every January on a large calendar on his office wall in the old house across the lane from the new one her parents had built. He wrote the year's schedule for planting and harvesting crops and for raising livestock. When the weather changed the farming plans on the calendar, Janice asked him what he was going to do and was reassured by her grandpa's calm adjustments. Sometimes there were crop failures or diseased livestock, which worried Janice's mother. Her grandpa would say, "Barbara, we need to play the cards we're dealt."

The organization and discipline to get things done that Janice learned from Grandpa Cole were hardwired into her. She would successfully carry out her plans for the Chicago trip and her upcoming semester. She would do something significant one day in improving the environment. But managing her emotions was a different story.

She couldn't wait for the Democratic Convention in Chicago, her impatience for its arrival filling her up. It was less than ten days away, and she had trouble sticking to her daily routine. She was eager to see Ben and Cathy and discuss their plans. But more than anything, she found herself thinking of Ben.

On Monday, Janice was running late as she walked across campus to meet with her advisor when she saw Ben walking toward her.

"Hey," he said, "you're moving fast!" His eyes sparkled and he laughed his infectious laugh.

Janice felt flustered, wanting to stop and talk but knowing her advisor was waiting. "I'll see you tomorrow," she said.

"I can't wait," Ben said, his eyes boring into her.

She quickly waved and started her swift walk again. But she also remembered Cathy's warning about Ben. Did he feel about her the way she felt about him?

Janice's daydreams about Chicago protests and a potential relationship with Ben were disrupted by a phone call from her mother Monday evening.

"Jim called," her mother said.

"What? Why?"

"He wanted your Iowa City phone number. I imagine he'll call."

Janice was silent. That was just what she needed—a call from her ex-husband. She had no desire to talk to him.

"Also, your father wanted me to ask if you're still planning to go to Chicago," her mother said. "We hope you've decided against it."

Janice remembered the sound of her father's hand striking the counter in anger.

"I'm still going." She tried to be matter-of-fact, but her face warmed when she thought of her father's disapproval. "I need to get all my work done before then, and still need to pack." She ended the call, although she knew her mother wanted to talk longer.

Janice looked out her window at her landlord's flower garden. She thought Jim would also disapprove of her Chicago protest plans and inwardly groaned. Why did these two men still have a hold on her? Could she ever find a fresh start, a relationship in which she was free to be herself?

9

Janice learned from Cathy that Ben had scheduled a meeting on Wednesday evening for all the students planning to go to Chicago. He wanted to meet with Cathy and Janice at the coffee house on Tuesday to prepare for the meeting.

As Janice entered the coffee house, she thought about her chance meeting with Ben the day before, when she had acted like an excited schoolgirl in his charming presence. Her next steps with him were unclear. But her uncertainty about Ben did not diminish her sense of self. She hadn't felt so motivated for years and had arrived at the coffee house early. She took her notes out of her backpack and ordered coffee while she waited.

Ben and Cathy walked in together. Cathy wore a loose, floor-length peasant dress, and Ben seemed almost small beside her. But when Ben sat down, Janice was drawn to the energy coming from his flashing eyes and big smile.

"So, did you convince your Iowa relatives to oppose the war?" Ben asked.

"Not quite," Janice said, thinking of Aunt Rose. "I was told not to hang out with hippies."

Ben's laughter filled the room. "You're in the wrong place to avoid being around hippies."

Janice smiled. "I would rather be called political strategists," she said. Ben laughed again.

"All right, you two," Cathy said. "Can we get to discussing the student meeting now?"

Janice was prepared. She handed them copies of her notes on who was driving to Chicago, the hotel arrangements, and the tentative schedule of demonstrations, highlighting the closing march a week from Wednesday.

"This is great," Ben said. "Can you present these plans at our meeting tomorrow?" Janice nodded, her face warming to his praise.

"I thought of another angle," Cathy said. "I could lead a discussion on how to behave. These students need to be reminded that any violence will hurt the public support for ending the war."

"I agree," Ben said. "I'm glad you suggested it. Let's add that to our agenda, too." As Ben spoke, his eyes were more on Janice than they were on Cathy. Janice could feel their intensity.

Janice's connection to Ben was disrupted when she saw a flash of blond hair near the coffee house entrance. "Liz! Over here," Ben said. Liz sat down, and Ben explained to Cathy and Janice that he had asked Liz to stop by the student union to confirm the room arrangements for the meeting. "Everything's set," she said. "And I'm bringing name tags since we're expecting some new students. So exciting!"

Janice felt like rolling her eyes, but she worked to look professional.

"Okay, good," Ben said. "Anything else we need to cover?"

No one spoke. They parted, with Liz latching on to Ben's arm as they walked away. Janice went home, intending to begin looking at her textbooks for her fall classes, but she had difficulty stopping herself from thinking about Liz holding on to Ben's arm. She was irritated that she allowed herself to be excited whenever she was with him.

———◆———

More than fifty students showed up at their meeting, a much greater number than anticipated. Many students had returned to Iowa City early, before the start of the fall semester, to participate in the Chicago trip. Liz had come down with a cold, and Ben asked Janice to handle the sign-in and name tags. Janice inwardly questioned this for a moment, not liking him delegating to her, but it worked out well given the unexpected arrival of new students. She matched them with rides and confirmed they had places to stay as they signed in.

The students sat at the tables, with fluorescent ceiling lights illuminating the student union meeting room. When everyone was settled, Ben began the meeting with an enthusiastic welcome.

"I'm glad you're all here to learn about our plans in Chicago," he said. "We have a chance to join a national protest against the war and influence the Democratic Party's antiwar platform."

Janice watched Ben closely—as did others—captivated by his deep voice that grew stronger as his passion increased.

"Thousands of people will be there. We want to show the American people our broad opposition to the war through a large, orderly demonstration."

Janice noticed he had left the top two buttons unbuttoned on his light blue denim shirt. The color contrasted with his tan face and blue jeans.

Ben described the three locations for the protests: Lincoln Park on the near north side, the Conrad Hilton Hotel next to Grant Park, and the Amphitheatre, where the Democratic Convention would be held. He closed by saying they would depart early Sunday morning, with plans to participate in a demonstration organized by MOBE at two o'clock that afternoon. "You're free to choose where to protest after that, but be sure to attend the closing march on Wednesday," he told them. He then introduced Janice and Cathy.

Janice put aside her thoughts about Ben and spoke authoritatively as she reviewed the trip's logistics. She handed out copies of a map of downtown Chicago, saying as she did so, "It's easy to take the Chicago L subway trains to wherever you need to go. And the drop-off and pickup location is circled on the map." After answering a few questions, Janice turned to Cathy with the satisfaction of having done her job.

Cathy asked everyone to stand up and take three deep breaths. After they sat down, she spoke to them again. "You are part of a great peace movement. I urge everyone to avoid any violence. We don't want to give Mayor Daley the opportunity to use the Chicago police and National Guard." She closed by asking them to shut their eyes. "Think of the people you love," she gently reminded them. "Your demonstrations for peace are for those loved ones—to help create a better country and a better world."

Janice smiled at Cathy in admiration, and Ben adjourned the meeting, saying, "Thank you! Thank you all. We're going to make a difference!"

Everyone stood and filed out of the room, until just the three of them remained. Ben was beaming, saying, "That was great. That was really great. Why don't we celebrate? Drinks on me."

Janice agreed, but Cathy said she still had things to unpack in her new apartment. They walked out of the union. When Ben's back was turned, Cathy looked at Janice with raised eyebrows, as if to say, *Do you know what you're doing?*

Janice and Ben began walking in the warm August evening. Janice was glad she had chosen no more than a T-shirt to wear with her bell-bottom jeans. Ben suggested they walk up the hill to the Airliner bar. Janice nodded, looking at him as she pushed her long, thick hair away from her face. She realized this was the first time they were alone together other than their brief moment on campus, and she felt a little tremble run through her. Her first sip of wine relaxed her as they sat looking at each other across the table in their booth, waiting for a cheese plate Ben had ordered with the carafe of wine. A song by Buffalo Springfield played in the background.

Ben began the conversation, his dark eyes never leaving hers. "You've already lived quite a life," he said. "Marriage . . . and working in Chicago. You're twenty-four, like me, right?" She nodded. He asked about her job, and she told him stories about the advertising agency that made him laugh. She described her close friend Susan, who deserved credit for getting her to think about the Vietnam War. He poured each of them another glass of wine.

"When you were going over the maps with the students . . . I could tell you know your way around Chicago. I've only been there once—it'll be cool to see it again."

"But big cities aren't new to someone from the East Coast," she said. "Iowa must be pretty boring compared to Boston and New York."

"No, I was ready for a new part of the country," he said. "I love Iowa—particularly its beautiful women," he added with a smile.

"You mean like Liz?"

He laughed. "Liz is a nineteen-year-old girl. A kid."

Janice looked at him quietly, this time allowing her eyes to gaze deeply into his. He glanced down for a moment and then returned her look.

"Liz just likes to hang out with me. How about if we continue our conversation at my place?" He reached across the table to hold her hand.

Although Ben's touch was electric, Janice resisted turning her hand with her palm facing his, not ready to return his affection, but she kept her gaze on him. Her hand was warm inside his; she thought she could feel his pulse.

"Okay, I'd like to see how a hippie leader lives," she said. His face sparkled as he laughed. They finished their wine, and he waved to the waitress for the check.

They began walking. Ben told Janice he lived on the bottom floor of an old house about three blocks away. She asked him about his time growing up in New Jersey and attending college in Boston.

"My father was an eye doctor," he told her. "He commuted to New York City every day of the week, never missing a day—ended up building his own clinic. He had great vision, you see."

Janice laughed at the silly pun.

He smiled and took her hand. This time, she returned his grasp, interlocking her fingers with his. Feeling the wine, she moved closer to him as they walked.

When they entered his apartment, she faced him as he turned back from closing the door. He put his arms around her, and they kissed. She began unbuttoning his shirt, and he moved her toward the bedroom. They quickly shed their clothes and lay in bed, caressing and kissing each other. They joined together eagerly, and she matched his increasing motion, faster and faster, culminating with an explosion. They rested, quietly catching their breath. Ben turned the lamp off, and they slept, their bodies entwined.

They woke to sunlight streaming into the room. Ben apologized, saying he had to get up for a MOBE conference call on East Coast time. "I can make you some breakfast before the call, if you're hungry," he said.

"That would be great," Janice said. "Thank you." She smiled and stretched, feeling an intimacy she had never felt after making love with Jim, who would rush out of bed in the morning to attack his to-do list. They dressed, and she watched him scramble eggs with onions and green pepper, filling the apartment with the aroma of delicious food cooking. They discussed the MOBE call, which would cover final plans for the next week's protests.

Their ease of communication had worn off without the effects of wine, but Janice felt that Ben was caring. Their passionate beginning had promise. She liked listening to his voice and sat close to him as they ate breakfast. She decided to be bold and asked him when she would see him again. He laughed and suggested they could have a picnic at Lake Macbride that afternoon. She offered to bring food.

"I'll bring wine," he said. "Pick you up at two?"

She felt satisfied; any sense of awkwardness had disappeared. Before leaving, she hugged and kissed him, and she liked how he looked at her.

10

J anice couldn't stop thinking about her night with Ben when she got home. But it was Thursday, and she had things to do—the Chicago trip was drawing closer, and classes began the week after. She created a list of priorities, with the top item being to call Susan to see if she could stay with her in her Lincoln Park apartment. A robin chirped in a tree outside her window, as if urging her to start to check off her list.

Susan shrieked when she heard Janice's voice. They had stayed in touch after Janice left Chicago—Susan had resigned from the advertising agency and accepted an editor position at the Midwest office of Amnesty International. "I can't wait to tell you all about my new job and hear how school's going for you," Susan said. "My couch is all yours, for as long as you'll stay—the very couch that got you in trouble with your husband," she added.

"Yeah, he was not happy about that. And about a lot of other things."

"I guess I was the bad influence!"

"You sure were!" They burst into laughter.

Janice and Susan discussed the demonstration schedule. Susan planned to participate in protests in Lincoln Park on Saturday, where two college friends intended to camp. "I'll be at your place on Sunday evening," Janice said, "after the MOBE protest."

"I can't wait to see you," Susan said. "Really."

Janice next drove to the co-op to get food for the picnic with Ben. She bought sandwiches and fruit and then had a moment to relax in her apartment before Ben arrived. She lay on her bed and closed her eyes, trying to rest, but her thoughts kept returning to Ben's body pressing against hers the previous night.

Ben picked her up at two, and they drove to Lake Macbride, finding a picnic area near the water. It was a beautiful day, warm but with low humidity and a slight breeze. They parked and spread a blanket on the grass at the end of the picnic area near the woods, where they were all alone. Ben poured Janice a glass of wine, surprising her by using wine glasses instead of plastic cups. When they were done eating, they lay down on the blanket. Ben talked about his invitation to attend a MOBE meeting in Chicago led by Tom Hayden, the committee's national leader.

Janice rested her head on his chest as he stroked her hair. He stopped talking about MOBE and said, "Your hair is so beautiful." After kissing and holding each other for a while, Ben said he had an idea; she lifted her head and looked at him. He smiled, hesitating, and then said they could take the blanket into the woods. A slow smile came over Janice's face and she laughed.

They rolled up the blanket and entered the woods, looking for an open area. They found a spot under a large tree, the ground cushioned with a layer of fallen leaves. It was far enough into the woods, with no path nearby, that it was unlikely anyone would see them. They unrolled the blanket and undressed. As they embraced, Janice closed her eyes, feeling the warm breeze on her bare skin. They caressed each other, looking down at their bodies in the dappled sunlight coming through the trees. Making love, they took care not to raise their voices. Afterward, they lay quietly, letting the breeze cool their bodies. They dressed and walked out of the woods, with Ben's arm around Janice's shoulders and her arm around his waist.

Ben dropped her off at her apartment, telling her he had agreed to get together with law school friends that evening. They kissed and Janice went inside. She sat quietly in her easy chair for several minutes.

On Friday, she prepared for her fall semester graduate courses. By now, instructors had posted readings for the first week of classes. She walked to campus to find the postings outside of instructors' offices, copied the assignments, and ensured she had all the required textbooks. Then she went home and started on the readings. She thought Ben might call her, but she didn't hear from him. She caught herself—maybe she was expecting too much so early in their relationship.

At around four, Janice's phone rang, and she hurried to answer it, thinking it might be Ben. But it was her ex-husband.

"I wanted to see how you're doing," Jim said.

She sat upright in her kitchen table chair. "I'm fine."

"I am, too. I just got promoted."

"That's great." Janice was quiet, wondering where this was going. The relationship had ended for her over a year ago when their divorce was final. She'd wanted to avoid fighting over assets—as she knew Jim would—so she let him keep the furniture. She didn't even bring up his shares of Monsanto stock. Her generosity seemed to take any fight out of him. They found a lawyer to write the divorce agreement and switch her name back to Wagner. Jim was sarcastic at times, angry that she was destroying his dreams, but when they signed the final documents, Janice felt that his overriding emotion, like hers, was one of sadness. She remembered it now, an emotional finality that, for her, marked the end. She didn't want to talk to him.

"I hear you're coming to Chicago next week," he said.

"How did you hear that?"

"Your aunt Rose."

"What? You're in touch with my aunt?"

"She called me after the divorce to apologize. She couldn't understand why you left."

Janice was speechless. She would never have imagined it. Her aunt had apologized to her ex-husband for her leaving him.

"She and I always clicked on politics," he said. "She called me again when Nixon was nominated, and we celebrated over the phone."

"We haven't talked for over a year, but you've been in touch with my family without me knowing. Incredible."

"Your dad told your aunt that you were going to the protests next week, and she called me to see if I could talk some sense into you."

Janice took the phone away from her ear and stared across the room, not believing what she was hearing. After a long silence, she returned to the phone and said, "You're too smart to believe that you could do that."

"I'm also calling because I hoped I might be able to see you."

She winced. Did he have some hope of getting back together? "We agreed to end things."

"Yeah, but I've learned some things about myself that I want to talk to you about. I want to apologize."

"I'm going to be busy at the protests."

He was silent, making her feel guilty at first and then angry that he still could influence her emotions. He finally spoke. "Call me if you have some free time. We could meet for lunch."

She hung up and walked over to the window to look down at the well-kept flower beds on the lawn. Apologize? It was way too late for that. She kept staring at the flowers, wishing her life had their beautiful order. She tried to return to her reading assignments, but thoughts of her aunt and ex-husband periodically interrupted her. She was reminded of her father's disapproval of her. That night, she dreamed about being on the blanket in the woods with Ben, until she discovered three people silently watching them: Jim, Aunt Rose, and her father.

Janice woke up early on Saturday morning. She put the conversation with Jim behind her and decided to surprise Ben. She showered, put on shorts and a tight-fitting top, and started walking to his apartment. The bright August sun rose quickly, accompanied by still air heavy with humidity. She knew Ben slept late and planned to give him a wake-up treat, growing excited as she envisioned climbing into his bed. Stepping up on his porch, she tried the front door, happy to find it unlocked. She walked quietly into the house, starting to pull her shirt off as she turned to his bedroom. She heard a noise and stopped as she stood outside his bedroom door—she looked in and saw long blond hair cascading down a bare back. Liz straddled Ben, riding him with rapid breaths and soft sighs.

"Holy shit," Janice muttered.

Liz screamed and turned around. "Jesus Christ! What are you doing here?" She leaped out of bed and ran into the bathroom. Ben pulled the sheet over himself and raised up on his elbows.

"You asshole!" Janice said.

Ben got out of bed, wrapping the sheet around him. He looked toward the bathroom door that Liz had shut and moved toward Janice.

"Janice, let me explain."

Janice's face and head were warm and sweaty. "There's nothing to explain," she said. "I was just a change of pace for you."

"No, that's not true. Let me deal with Liz, and then I'll come over to talk."

"No!" Janice said. Breathing rapidly, she started to leave, and he reached for her. She whipped around and slapped him hard on the side of his head. It was more than a slap; the heel of her hand hurt from hitting his cheekbone. "You fucking asshole!" she yelled. She strode out of the house and slammed the door behind her.

11

Janice walked, almost ran, back to her apartment in the heat and humidity, tears mixed with sweat dripping down her face. She'd been so gullible, charmed by Ben's charisma. She couldn't get the picture of Liz on top of him out of her mind. She didn't care how many women he'd been with as long as she was the only one right now. But she wasn't, and she wasn't about to share him with a nineteen-year-old flower child. It was over. She thought about their trip to Chicago the next day. Fortunately, they were driving separately, and she was staying with Susan, so she'd be able to keep her distance. She entered her apartment, and her phone rang. It was Ben.

"I'm sorry, Janice. I was going to break things off with Liz. I want to be with you."

"Too bad—not interested," Janice said, gritting her teeth as she hung up. The phone rang again, but she didn't answer.

She walked into the bathroom and looked at herself in the mirror, a face of fury mixed with sadness and disgust. How had she not seen the real Ben, especially after being warned by Cathy? She shook her head. "Goddamn it!"

When she was ten, she joined a church basketball league and fell in love with the sport. Her parents attended her games and cheered for her, but Grandpa Cole encouraged her in a different way. He watched her intently but rarely changed his expression. When she scored a basket or stole a pass, he would just look at her with a slight smile. He would look the same if she lost the ball or committed a foul.

After her games, Grandpa often invited her to his office in the old house and asked her what she thought of her play. He listened quietly as she talked about needing to shoot or dribble the ball better, never criticizing or telling her what he thought she should do. He asked her what she had learned when they lost, moving her away from self-criticism to an awareness of her game. When they won, he did the same thing, moving her from elation to thinking about the lessons she had learned.

Janice looked in the mirror again. She put on her gym shorts, shirt, and shoes and ran down to the river and up to the student gym. She checked out a basketball and went to the courts, finding only one game underway and several open baskets. She picked one and spent an hour shooting, starting with long shots and running in to get rebounds and lay them in. She did this repeatedly, from all points on the semicircle facing the basket, her bouncing ball echoing in the large gym. Her tears over finding Ben with Liz flowed again, and she increased her shooting pace, tamping down her anger and pain by leaping to get rebounds and dribbling back to the top of the circle to shoot again. Her shirt and shorts were drenched with sweat, and she breathed heavily. She reached a point of exhaustion and slowed down; she had emptied herself. She jogged home, not caring if people noticed her sweaty hair and soaked clothes.

Back at her apartment, she did stretches on a towel to cool down and then took a long shower. After drying herself and dressing, she sat quietly on the landing at the top of the stairs to her apartment. A slight breeze countered the oppressive heat, and she turned her chair to face it. Thoughts of Ben kept coming to her, but each time, she pushed them away while watching branches on the giant oak tree in the backyard sway in the breeze. She imagined herself talking to her grandpa after a painful loss to an archrival, hating herself for not playing better. He would eventually steer her to talking about what she had learned. She thought about what she needed to do.

She had to tell Cathy what had happened before they all met the following day to drive to Chicago. She called her, and they made plans to meet at the coffee house that afternoon. Janice bought coffee and blueberry muffins for both of them. They sat down, and Cathy looked at Janice with curiosity.

"I've had two days of heaven with Ben and one day of hell," Janice said. "I caught him in bed with Liz."

"What a jerk," Cathy said. "It's not the first time."

"I feel so stupid." Janice looked down and slowly shook her head back and forth.

Cathy reached over and put her hand on Janice's. "You really fell for him. Sorry that he hurt you."

"I should've known better. I thought we were in sync, but he isn't ready."

"Ben's a great charmer."

Janice looked up with a slight smile. "He won't charm me again. I slapped the hell out of him."

"That's a first," Cathy said, laughing. She looked at Janice closely, hesitating before going on. "It's probably best it didn't work out. Ben uses people, including me. I've had to stop him when he's giving me orders."

"You're right—he uses us. I'm worried that it will be awkward in Chicago."

"I don't think so. Ben will be pursuing the limelight, on stage with Tom Hayden and MOBE," Cathy said. "It's complicated. He's a good antiwar leader—we follow him."

"Maybe we can find other ways to help lead without him," Janice said. Cathy nodded, and Janice finished her muffin.

On her walk home, Janice thought about her relationships with men. She had angered her father and lost his support. She had failed at her marriage, not feeling understood or loved. She saw the possibilities with Ben, but he wasn't ready to commit. When she entered her apartment, her head was down, and she felt empty and alone. She started to pack for the next day's trip to Chicago, but she stopped and sat down. Her failures with men were all over the place, but ultimately, her thoughts turned to how Grandpa had taught her to focus on the process of playing the game, not on winning or losing. She remembered the one time he had judged her play in a basketball game.

It was at her final game in the state tournament. Janice had held the other team's star player to only four points, preventing her from making her last shot at the end of the game when Janice's team was ahead by one point. Unfortunately, the star's teammate caught the rebound and put the ball in the basket for the winning score as the buzzer sounded. Janice came off the court in anguish, using her towel to wipe away tears, while the other team screamed and hugged each other to celebrate their victory. Janice looked into the stands at her grandpa and her parents, and Grandpa smiled at her. He then raised his hand and gave her a strong fist pump. He was silently cheering her on, showing his pride in her and love, telling her she had done all she could.

Janice finished packing for the Chicago trip and slept well that night. Early Sunday morning, August 25, she picked up Cathy and drove to the Iowa City starting point for the four-hour drive to Chicago. When Ben and Liz arrived, Ben confirmed that, given Janice's knowledge of Chicago, she would lead their caravan of five cars transporting about twenty students.

Janice didn't meet Ben's eyes during the conversation; instead, she looked toward the river. But she did notice a red welt on his cheek. When Liz said, "This is exciting," Janice gave her a cutting look that made Liz step back behind Ben. Cathy ended the conversation, moving Janice to the car. "You okay?" she asked.

Janice nodded. "Just keep them away from me."

12

Cathy got into the passenger seat of Janice's car, and three undergraduate women slid into the back. The caravan left shortly after seven. It was an uneventful ride, with the talk in Janice's car dominated by the undergrads' questions about things to see in Chicago. "Our priority is to make a statement against the war," Janice finally said, when she'd had enough of their happy chatter.

After they parked outside of Susan's place, Janice hurried up the stairs to drop off her bag. She and Susan embraced, with squeals of delight in seeing each other. "Can't wait to catch up later!" Susan called after Janice as she hurried down the stairs.

"Me too!" Janice yelled back.

Janice walked the Iowa students to the Fullerton L station. They rode it to a downtown station and then walked toward Grant Park and Lake Michigan. The undergrads who had never been to Chicago kept saying, "Far out," as they walked down narrow street corridors lined with tall skyscrapers amid noisy crowds of people and clanging L cars. Janice noticed Ben looking at her, but she ignored him.

They arrived at an older hotel, where many of them had reservations, three or four people to a room. When everyone was checked in, Janice led them up Michigan Avenue, and they saw the Hilton, where they were to meet for the MOBE march that afternoon. Ben split off from the group to find the MOBE leaders, and the rest of them sat on lakeshore benches and waited, watching the boats sail far out into the huge lake. Janice was satisfied, feeling she had done her job. With Ben gone, she could enjoy the familiar energy of downtown Chicago. She smiled at Cathy and said, "Here we are."

Shortly before two, Ben returned and gathered them around him to go over the plans for what MOBE called the "Meet the Delegates" march that afternoon. The intent was to welcome Democratic Party delegates arriving at the Hilton with an antiwar message before their convention started the following day.

"We don't want to provoke the police," Ben said. "They seem edgy after last night."

"What happened?" Cathy said.

"They kicked campers out of Lincoln Park, and the crowd got angry. Allen Ginsberg tried to calm them with 'Om' chants." Ben's eyes grew wide.

"Did it work?" Cathy asked.

"For a while, but the police started pushing, and the crowd threw stones at the police cars. They arrested eleven people."

Janice looked at the Iowa students. Like her, they were quiet, with the alarm she felt herself showing on their faces. When Ben led them to join others near the Hilton, their eyes focused on the police line. The officers were all wearing batons on their belts. "Choose from the signs over there and join the picket line," Ben instructed.

They all marched on the sidewalk, with protesters often calling to delegates to stop the war as they entered the Hilton. Janice stayed close to Ben and Cathy, her anger at Ben replaced by her fear of what the police might do.

As more people joined the marching and chanting, Janice watched additional police arrive in vans. A police officer using a bullhorn said, "Move into Grant Park, or you'll be arrested." The protesters moved away from the street into the park near a stage that had been placed for speakers. MOBE leaders stepped up onstage, with Tom Hayden and Rennie Davis in front and Ben and others behind them. Hayden spoke using a microphone, saying that the day had been a success and their march was sure to be on the evening news, helping educate the American public about their opposition to the war. He told them the next event would be in Lincoln Park, where the "Yippies" had planned a music festival. The crowd dispersed, and Ben told the Iowa students to follow him if they wanted to attend the festival.

Janice was relieved they had completed the march without any violence. She didn't feel like following Ben to listen to music, and Cathy agreed. They decided to eat at one of Janice's favorite restaurants in Greektown. They were soon sitting at a table in the noisy, bustling restaurant with a bottle of red wine in front of them.

"This is great," Cathy said. "You must miss Chicago."

"I do. But I don't miss the police we saw today."

A Greek waiter yelling, "Opa," delivered a platter of flaming cheese to the table next to them. Janice and Cathy smiled, but not for long.

"I'm nervous about these protests," Cathy said. "It seems like a powder keg."

"I agree," said Janice. "I admire Allen Ginsberg trying to keep the peace."

"He reminds me of a Zen Buddhist priest from my days at the monastery."

"Really? Tell me about that."

"Well, I'd just dropped out of college . . ." At this Cathy looked up at Janice. "I was confused and depressed, not knowing what to do. Decided to hitchhike to the West Coast, and a Zen Buddhist residence program at a monastery in California was where I ended up. After weeks and weeks of silence and meditation, the answer came to me—I decided I would pursue social work."

"I'm envious," Janice said. "While you were on a spiritual exploration, I was helping advertise products people didn't need."

"Yeah, but you might have learned as much as I did."

"I did learn about the need to leave a bad marriage."

They took a cab to drop Cathy off at her hotel after dinner. Then Janice rode the L to the Fullerton station and walked toward Susan's apartment. People were walking rapidly toward her as she got closer to Susan's. She learned from a woman that the Yippies and police had argued over a flatbed truck for the rock bands. The police wanted it out of the park, and the crowd was angry.

Janice continued walking and saw police officers ahead of her getting out of a police van, batons in hand. An officer on a loudspeaker told people to clear the area. Suddenly, the crowd surged toward Janice, and she ran to Susan's apartment, a block away. Susan let her in, and Janice collapsed on the couch, breathing heavily.

"Are you okay?" Susan said.

"I could've been clubbed by the police."

"I almost was last night. The police in the park were aggressive, and people threw rocks at them."

"I don't know who is worse, the protesters or the police," Janice said.

"The police are out of control—so much anger—and Daley's bringing in more National Guard troops," Susan said.

"The military presence is new to me," Janice said. "We only have to deal with a few campus cops in Iowa City." Susan wanted to hear more, and Janice described her growing role as a protest leader, starting with the demonstration at the Regents' meeting.

"You've come a long way since we first met at the ad firm," Susan said.

They talked late into the night, trading memories of their days in Chicago together—making fun of managers, listening to blues music at bars, staying overnight at Susan's, and laughing uncontrollably after smoking pot.

———•••———

Monday morning was crowded and noisy. Susan's two friends who'd planned to camp were staying in the apartment. Susan told Janice she would be free the entire afternoon the next day, and Janice smiled. "We'll need all that time," she said, "because one topic I want to talk about is men." Susan laughed and left for work.

Janice relaxed at Susan's after everyone left. She devoured the articles in the *Chicago Tribune* about the protests, learning that there were 10,000 demonstrators in town and 23,000 police and National Guard troops. The MOBE march on Sunday received coverage in the *Tribune*, with quotes from Hayden and Davis. Janice was intrigued to read about political leaders, like Senator McGovern and Senator Ribicoff, speaking against the war.

That afternoon, Janice and Cathy traveled to the Democratic Convention at the Amphitheatre, where Ben had led the Iowa City group that morning. He walked up to them, his eyes wide.

"You wouldn't believe what happened here this morning," he said.

"What?" Cathy asked. Janice took a step back, not wanting to engage with Ben.

"More and more police kept arriving, with National Guard troops lined up on the other side of barbwire, like they are now. Some reporters tried to go inside and were stopped by the police. The reporters argued with them and the police suddenly started pushing them, so hard that three of them fell to the ground."

"This is a war zone," Cathy said. Ben nodded.

"We'll probably see tanks next," Janice said. She felt small and helpless in the face of all the military power. Was what she was doing there really making a difference? And was there a significant value in the protests, particularly if they became violent? Maybe her time would be better spent supporting elected leaders? She didn't have any answers yet.

———•••———

On Tuesday morning, before meeting Susan for lunch, Janice walked around downtown, visiting sites that brought back memories of her love for the Chicago Loop. She was tempted to stop by the advertising agency to see old friends, but her days of working there in a meaningless job seemed like decades ago; plus she didn't want to answer questions about why she was in town. Janice kept a distance from the Monsanto offices, not wanting to run into Jim. But she was reminded of how she would meet him at the plaza every night to walk to Union Station and catch the train home.

Janice crossed the river near the beautiful Wrigley Building, remembering St. Patrick's Day when the river was dyed green. She was in a reflective mood when she sat across from Susan for lunch at the sidewalk café Susan had chosen north of the Loop.

"You want to talk about men," Susan said after they ordered wine and food. "Have you figured them out?"

"Are you kidding?" Janice said.

"I haven't either, but I'm through with seeing more than one at a time. I've been going with this guy, John. He's so sensitive—we haven't even been to bed yet. We'll see where it goes."

"I can't imagine ever seeing two men—I have enough trouble dealing with one. I've been on a roller coaster with our protest leader, Ben."

"Are you falling in love?"

"I thought maybe at first. Charming, funny . . . the whole bit. Then I caught him in bed with a nineteen-year-old."

"Too bad, but it sounds like you had some fun, even if he's not your soulmate," Susan said.

Janice was silent for a moment. "Are we ever going to find our soulmates?"

"I don't know, but it would have to be someone who respects us—who sees us as equals."

Janice thought about Ben. He related well to women, but did

he respect them? Probably not, given how he had treated both her and Liz.

"I keep following Betty Friedan," Susan said. "I've helped her NOW organization write letters to Congress supporting the Equal Rights Amendment."

"I've been wondering about political action versus protests. It sounds like you're moving to more of a political role."

"Yeah, I am, I suppose."

The waitress brought their food, and Susan told Janice about her work at Amnesty—compiling and editing stories for its newsletter. "Incredible stories," she added.

"I'm more and more interested in organic farming," Janice said. "Perhaps someday I can influence the farming practices my Iowa relatives use. Though, let me tell you, they are a stubborn bunch!"

Susan grinned. "Yeah, I wonder how Aunt Rose would react to that."

Janice laughed. "She'll probably peg me for a communist."

After their second glass of wine, they decided to walk south on Michigan Avenue. They looked into windows of department stores and passed the Chicago Tribune Tower. They entered the park's northern end and sat on a bench at the lake's edge, silently watching the vast body of water. It was warm but breezy, and the choppy waves produced small whitecaps. Janice thought it wouldn't take much for those whitecaps to turn into larger waves—for this beautiful lake to turn into a destructive force.

"Let's see what's happening at the Hilton," Susan said. They continued walking south and saw masses of people demonstrating in the park. There was no violence, but police and their vans were everywhere. Janice and Susan walked until they could see the Hilton but stopped short of joining the crowd. The front of the Hilton looked like a fort, with police behind barricades, wearing helmets and batons on their belts. A constant din filled the air—chanting by protesters,

bullhorn commands by police, speeches by protest leaders. Occasionally the breeze brought whiffs of marijuana smoke, especially when a
group of long-haired protesters danced near them, beckoning them to
join in their celebration.

Janice turned to Susan, moving close to her ear to be heard above
the noise. "Tomorrow is a big day. Everyone will march while the
delegates debate the party's platform."

Susan became serious as she watched the protesters, her squinted
eyes no longer sparkling as they did during their banter at the sidewalk café. She turned to Janice with a somber look bordering on fear.
"You need to be careful," she said, making Janice wonder again why
she was there.

13

Janice took the L downtown on Wednesday afternoon and walked to the hotel to meet Cathy, where they would join the Iowa City group for the march to the Amphitheatre. Cathy was seated in one of the oversized stuffed chairs scattered around the lobby. Faded drapes hung down in front of tall windows, and worn carpet showed threadbare spots inside the entry.

"I missed you yesterday," Cathy said.

"Anything happen?"

"We didn't have any direction. Ben was with MOBE, and our guys got rowdy." Janice could tell that talking about it was upsetting Cathy.

"What did they do?"

"They chanted in front of the Hilton. They were only a few feet across from the police line. I thought they were going to provoke them."

"What did the police do?"

"When they saw me trying to get our guys to leave, a policeman yelled at me to get the students back in the park or they would arrest them. I finally got them out of there." Cathy shook her head, her lips pressed together.

"It must have been scary," Janice said. Cathy's eyes looked over Janice's shoulder, and Janice turned to see Iowa students gathering near them. Some had water bottles in preparation for the march, and others seemed like they just rolled out of bed.

They looked at four male students laughing in the lobby corner. "I bet they're already high," Cathy said. "I'll be glad when today is over."

"Me too." Janice felt guilty she hadn't been there to help Cathy. But she was glad she spent her day with Susan instead of protesting in a dangerous environment. She wondered what they were going to face today.

Ben arrived and raised his arm for students to gather around him in the corner. He cleared his throat and spoke loudly above the noisy hum of other groups gathering for the march. "You'll follow me to the Hilton, where we'll start the march to the Amphitheatre. We're expecting about eight to ten thousand protesters today."

Cathy took Janice's arm as they followed Ben. When they reached the Hilton, they joined the rapidly growing crowd chanting, "Bring the troops home! Bring the troops home!" Soon the crowd started to move, but the direction was unclear. They stopped and stood for several minutes, joining in chants periodically. Ben said he would go find out what was happening. When he returned, he told them the police and National Guard weren't allowing them to use the road for their march. Liz came to Ben's side as he talked, holding his hand and looking nervous.

"The MOBE leaders are pissed that we can't use the road to march to the Amphitheatre. So, we're going to move the march to the sidewalk and obey all the traffic signals."

"We'll never get there," Cathy said.

"That's the point," Ben said. "It's similar to what's been done in civil rights marches. The MOBE leaders are frustrated that the Democrats picked Humphrey to run for president, with a platform that supports the war. They want us to slow down and have our march be a statement of resistance."

"What happens if the police don't want us on the sidewalk?" Janice asked. But a roar from the crowd drowned her out, as everyone slowly started inching toward the sidewalk. Janice could see National Guard troops blocking the road that ran south from the Hilton. They carried rifles with fixed bayonets and wore gas masks, forming a threatening line ready to stop anyone from using the road. Military jeeps were behind the troops, with frames of barbed wire attached to the jeep fronts. Janice grew anxious, fearing what this armed military force might do to marching students. The number of Chicago police with white helmets had increased in front of the Hilton.

"I don't like this. I don't like this at all," Cathy said to Janice. Janice nodded as the front of the crowd started to move down the sidewalk. They advanced about a block until they stopped at a "Don't Walk" sign at the intersection. A police chief spoke to them using a bullhorn. "We want you to clear the streets and sidewalks. Do it now." The march leaders waited. Janice turned around and saw an unending crowd behind them. Nobody moved. A few people at the front started chanting, "Stop the war; stop the war." Everyone soon joined in, making a loud roar.

A TV camera operator walked to the edge of the crowd filming, and a middle-aged, professionally dressed woman talked to protest leaders and took notes. The police chief used the bullhorn again. "Clear this area! Clear this area, or we're going to clear it!" The march leaders sat down on the sidewalk. Ben and others turned to the crowd and told everyone to sit down, and everyone did. Janice sat, and Cathy took her arm again. The leaders at the front started a new chant:

"The whole world is watching! The whole world is watching!"

Janice, Cathy, and thousands of others joined in. The police captain tried to speak above the deafening noise, "Clear out, right now!" but he couldn't be heard over the crowd's chanting. Suddenly, the American flag outside the Hilton was pulled down; Janice couldn't see who did it. The police seemed to take that as a signal to clear the crowd. They advanced in a loosely organized line from behind the barricades, waving their batons ominously. Some people stood up and moved away, while others sat and chanted. The police grabbed the sitting protesters by their collars, dragged them to police vans, and pushed them inside. When people resisted this rough treatment, police clubbed and dragged them to the vans.

"The whole world is watching!" the crowd continued to chant.

Janice and Cathy stood with the others and turned to leave, but they could only move slowly in the middle of the packed crowd. They found an opening to the side of them where people were beginning to run, fearful of being clubbed and taken to vans. But Janice and Cathy stepped back when the white-helmeted police broke ranks and pursued the running protesters. When the police encountered clusters of protesters, they swung their batons up and down, clubbing people indiscriminately. Janice was horrified to see the middle-aged reporter get clubbed in the back; she fell to the ground and two officers dragged her to a van.

Ben, who was nearby with Liz, kept saying, "We need to get out of here."

They all moved with the crowd as fast as they could. Liz clung to Ben and began to cry.

A new noise replaced the chants. People yelled and screamed, and the police shouted nonstop bullhorn commands, creating a chaotic din. Cathy tried to say something to Janice, but Janice couldn't hear her. Cathy's eyes widened with fear, her head turning rapidly like Janice's, searching for a way out. The TV camera operator moved with the crowd, filming the altercations and quickly moving away, staying out of reach of the police, who kept coming, running like bulls, batons swinging. The police drove vans filled with protesters away and replaced them with empty ones.

The police scattered into groups of three or four in pursuit of the protesters. Young male protesters, many shirtless and wearing sashes around their long hair, began to fight back, especially if a couple of police officers were left behind as their fellow officers dragged protesters to the vans.

A fierce fight erupted in front of Janice and Cathy. Four young men punched two police officers trying to protect themselves with their clubs. The crowd stopped running momentarily and cheered the fighting protesters, blocking Janice and Cathy from moving. A woman with long frizzy hair held in place with a sash around her forehead started screaming, "Off the pigs! Off the pigs!" Others joined in. Police reinforcements quickly arrived and waded into the fight, clubbing the protesters on their heads and backs. One police officer held his baton palms down and swung the end into the stomach and ribs of a protester near Janice. He crumpled to the ground in pain. Janice feared the police, but she also felt something else—an intense anger over their brutality.

The police dragged the fighting protesters to the vans while the remaining police looked for other protesters to pursue. They moved toward Janice and the Iowa group. The frizzy-haired woman and her friends continued to scream. Janice and Cathy turned to run and saw Liz trip and fall.

A police officer caught up to Liz, swung his baton, and split open her forehead. Blood poured down her face. Ben yelled, "You motherfucker!" and punched the policeman in the side of his head, knocking him to the ground. Two other policemen descended upon Ben, raining blows with their clubs on his head and body. He held up his arms to protect himself and shouted in pain as a club came down on his forearm.

Cathy screamed, "My God—no!"

Furious, Janice leaped on the back of one of the police officers, shouting, "You assholes!" The officer threw her to the ground and raised his club, but before he could strike her, one of the men with the frizzy-haired woman tackled him. Janice stood up and joined the woman, screaming, "Off the pigs!" at the top of her lungs.

"Janice, you have to come with me!" Cathy yelled. She turned away and began to run.

Janice started to follow, but the police quickly overwhelmed her and the woman. They dragged them along with Ben and Liz to a van and pushed them inside. Ben used one arm to clean the blood from Liz's face with his shirtsleeve while holding his other arm against his side in pain. Janice sat infuriated, glaring at everyone but not seeing them, her breaths deep and rapid. Her rage was all-consuming and relentless.

When the police unloaded their prisoners from the vans at the Cook County Jail, city medical staff asked if anyone was injured. Ben and Liz, along with a couple of others, stepped forward. Liz's head was still bleeding, and they said she needed stitches. Ben's misshapen forearm was broken. The medical staff walked them to a nearby ambulance. "Where are you taking them?" Janice asked.

"Cook County Hospital," a medic told her before slamming the ambulance door closed behind him.

The jail officers fingerprinted Janice and the others and charged them with disorderly conduct. They led them to a room in the jail used for arraignment hearings, where all the protesters pleaded not guilty to the judge, who set their bail. Before being led to their jail cells, the jailer told them they could make one phone call. Janice called Susan.

"I've been so worried!" Susan said, making Janice cry at hearing her voice.

"I'll call you when I get out of jail—I heard they might be releasing us."

The jailers locked Janice in a jail cell with ten other women. They sat on a concrete bench that ran around the three sides of the cell, their heads resting against the concrete walls. The women talked for a while, finding out where each was from. They were all angry at the police, sharing stories of the uncontrolled violence. Some showed bruises on their backs and arms where they were clubbed. As the evening went on, they dozed off. Janice fell in and out of sleep, frequently awakened by the uncomfortable benches and the fluorescent lights.

Sitting awake in the middle of the night, Janice felt worn out and ragged, a far cry from the relaxed time she had experienced with Susan the day before. She looked at the sleeping women—beaten, bruised, and jailed. Never again would she participate in a protest where there was the risk of such senseless violence. She couldn't wait to get back to Iowa City. She needed time alone to recover and to figure out how to protect herself, whether from dangerous romantic relationships or violent political protests. She thought a lot about her anger. She needed to change. She couldn't have her behavior be driven by blind rage.

14

Janice was dozing when a jailer shouted, "Janice Wagner?" His voice reverberated off the concrete walls. Several women lifted their heads. Janice raised her hand, irritated that he had been so loud, seeming to purposely wake everyone.

The jailer motioned for her to come, and they walked down a poorly lit corridor. He told her that her bail had been paid and that she was free to leave. She asked who had paid the bail, but he didn't know—some guy. He led her to a counter to pick up her bag of possessions. She found her watch—it was eight o'clock in the morning. The jailer handed her over to a police officer with a holstered gun and other equipment jutting out from his hips.

Swaying from left to right with each step, the police officer walked her out of the building, saying that he hoped she'd had a lovely night—he looked directly into her face with a grin. Janice didn't react, ignoring him. She thought again of the riot, when she had leaped on a policeman's back; she was amazed she had done that. She felt far away from it now. Still grinning, the police officer opened the exit door for her and told her to have a nice day. She walked out into the warm, welcoming sunlight without looking at him.

The first person she saw after she left the building—leaning against a sports car in the drop-off circle with his legs crossed—was her ex-husband, Jim. Her mouth opened and her eyebrows rose. He was heavier than the last time she had seen him, wearing a three-piece suit that signaled success. He tried to act reserved and in control, but she could tell he was nervous, with an uncertain look in his eyes.

"What are you doing here?" she said.

"I saw you on the news last night and figured you were arrested."

"On the news? What was I doing?"

"You were screaming, 'Off the pigs!'"

"My God." Janice couldn't believe that she had screamed that, much less that it was caught on camera. She wondered what Jim was planning.

"You bailed me out?" she asked.

"Yeah."

She shook her head, her eyes looking to the side. Her ex-husband had bailed her out, another unexpected development joining the series of absurd events in the past twenty-four hours.

"I'd like to take you to breakfast," he said.

"I need to go to Susan's."

"It's early. She'll still be there when we're done."

Janice didn't think accepting his offer was a good idea, but she was famished. She got in the car, and Jim drove, telling her they were going to a business club near his Monsanto office. Janice protested, saying she wasn't dressed for such a place, but Jim said he didn't care. She rode in his sports car's plush leather seat, quite a contrast to sitting on the jail's concrete bench. When they arrived at the club, Janice quickly called Susan, saying she would come to her apartment that morning. She then ordered fresh orange juice, an omelet, a muffin, and coffee.

Janice relaxed in the dining room's luxury while waiting for her food. It had oak-paneled walls and large windows with views of the Chicago skyline. She waited for Jim to initiate a conversation.

"I'm glad you're okay," he said. "I can't believe how stupid the Yippies were to provoke the police."

Janice looked out the window, pushing his words out of her mind.

"My Guard company is on alert. Don't these protesters know they will be crushed if things get violent?"

Janice ignored him again, looking at a painting on the wall. He stopped talking. After a couple of minutes of silence, he took a deep breath.

"I'm sorry our marriage ended the way it did," he said.

Janice was surprised and looked at him intently. "It wasn't all your fault."

"I pushed you too hard to get what I wanted. I apologize."

Janice looked at him silently. She felt a pang of sadness, seeing in him the college boy who first attracted her and remembering their enjoyable times before they moved to Chicago.

"Thanks," she said. "I wasn't the greatest wife."

"I still love you."

She looked at the table of people behind Jim, trying to stop her eyes from watering. "Jim, we're completely different people—there's no future for us."

"I know." He smiled. "So . . . how do you like my new car?"

She smiled back, realizing he had accomplished his mission. "It's nice," she said. "The kind of car an executive would drive." She didn't add, *Or the kind a corporate wife would drive.* If she had stayed married to him, that was what she would have become—living a completely different life from her current one.

They finished breakfast and drove to Susan's. Jim got out of the car when she opened her door at Susan's, coming around to hug her and wish her the best. She wished him well and quickly turned to walk through the gate to Susan's apartment. Once inside the front door, Janice exhaled deeply, the tension in her shoulders and neck releasing.

"I was worried until you called," Susan said. "How did you end up in jail?"

Janice told Susan about her leap on the back of a police officer,

Ben's and Liz's injuries, her jailing and being bailed out, and her breakfast with Jim.

"Wow! What an adventure!"

"Yeah, as long as I'm still alive." Janice reached out to put her hand on Susan's arm. "I'm glad I had you to come to."

Janice called Cathy at the hotel, who was glad to hear she was out of jail. "I heard from Ben. He said the police were going to drop charges later in the morning and release them."

"I can get them at the hospital and drive them to the pickup location in Lincoln Park." She put aside any feelings she had about helping Ben. Her goal was to get back to Iowa City.

Janice made one more call—to her family in Iowa.

Her father answered.

"Dad, I'm calling from Chicago. I wanted to let you know that I'm okay."

There was silence on the phone. "Dad?"

"Here's your mother."

"Janice, I'm glad you called," her mother said. "We've been so worried about you."

"Why didn't Dad talk to me?"

Her mother sighed. "He's upset, honey. He saw you on the news last night and said you were screaming to kill the police."

Janice was silent. She looked down and closed her eyes, thinking again of how stupid she had been. She returned the phone to her mouth and saw Susan looking at her with concern.

"I'm sorry, Mom. I was so angry I didn't know what I was doing. The police were clubbing my friends."

"I wish you wouldn't have used those words," her mother said. "I wonder if others recognized you when they watched the news."

"I hope not." Janice knew her mother was most likely thinking of Aunt Rose. She'd disappointed her mother, as well as her father. Her mother was silent. "I just called to tell you I'm okay," Janice said. "I'll be driving back to Iowa City this afternoon."

"That's good to hear. I'm glad you're safe."

"Thanks, Mom. I love you. Give my love to Dad and Timmy."

"I will."

Janice sighed when she hung up the phone. Usually, her mother would have given her love at the end of a call. Maybe she was as irritated at Janice as her father was. Susan looked at Janice with sympathy.

After Cathy called to say Ben and Liz were ready to be picked up, Janice gathered her things and turned to hug Susan. They held each other for a long time, and Janice began to cry, deep sobs shaking her shoulders.

"I don't know what I'd do without you," Janice said. "You and Cathy keep me sane."

"And you, me. Remember, women can make a better world."

Janice agreed. But when she drove down Lake Shore Drive to the hospital, she felt abandoned. She had angered her father again, who had made no attempt to understand what had happened to her. She had upset her mother, who was more concerned about what their family would think than about her.

Janice looked to her left at the enormous Lake Michigan. It sparkled in the bright sunlight, and she felt small and alone next to its majestic presence. She was less connected than ever to her family and Iowa relatives, who had been such a critical source of support for her.

Janice found Ben and Liz waiting in wheelchairs at the hospital entrance, as required by their nurses. She listened politely to Ben expressing his gratitude to her. "Not only for picking us up," he added, "but also for trying to protect us from being beaten by the police. It was very brave." He was charming as usual, but all Janice could feel was her disappointment in him. She looked at Liz, silent and withdrawn, seeming to be in shock over the events of the past twenty-four hours.

Janice drove them to Lincoln Park, where Cathy and the students were waiting. The students greeted Ben and Liz as wounded heroes. Eager to get started, Janice told Ben and the other drivers to follow her—she would lead them to the highway. The three undergrads crawled into the back seat of Janice's car, and Cathy joined Janice in the front.

The undergrads peppered Janice and Cathy with questions about the riot. They had been marching at the Amphitheatre at the time. "We heard about you jumping on the police officer and spending the night in jail—so cool," the girl sitting in the middle said.

"Yeah, what was jail like?" the guy sitting directly behind Janice asked.

After several more inquiries, Cathy laughed. "You're going to become a legend," she said.

"Cathy was the smart one in all this," Janice replied, keeping her eyes focused on the road. "She knew enough to lead the others away so they wouldn't be thrown in jail." Soon the three undergrads dozed off, exhausted from sleepless nights in an exciting city. Cathy turned to Janice and asked her how she was doing.

"I can't even tell you—I'm so burnt out."

"It's no wonder. You've had a lot happen."

Janice looked at Cathy, and her eyes filled with tears. Cathy reached over and put her hand on the back of Janice's neck, giving her a small massage as Janice turned her eyes back to the road.

15

They drove in silence for several miles through the flat Illinois farmland. Janice grew tired from her lack of sleep and asked Cathy to drive. Janice dozed and then woke with a start at the image of the policeman striking Liz on her forehead, causing blood to flow down her face.

"Are you okay?" Cathy asked.

"I was dreaming about the police clubbing us, with blood everywhere."

"I keep thinking about the violence, too. There has to be a better way."

"I loved it when Senator Ribicoff confronted Daley. I could see working to help elect more leaders like him."

"Yeah—I agree."

Janice dropped her passengers off and returned to the solitude of her apartment. She ate her favorite shrimp pasta meal and soaked in a hot bath while listening to classical music records on her small stereo system. She slept late the next day and, after breakfast, sat on the landing to read back issues of the *New Yorker*.

When the sun grew too warm, she went inside and lay on her couch, her head propped up by a pillow. She opened a novel Cathy had given her, *Trout Fishing in America*. She read for a while, letting herself doze off several times. In the afternoon, she walked through the neighborhoods of beautiful homes and tall trees, passing the house where the artist Grant Wood lived before his death. Whenever she saw his famous *American Gothic* painting, she thought of her Iowa farm relatives— the woman in the painting could be a young Aunt Rose.

On Saturday, Janice spent time reviewing the courses she was tak- ing in the upcoming fall semester and considering course options for the spring, thinking about how her choices fit potential career plans. She controlled her pace, reading course descriptions carefully and keeping her thoughts slow and deliberate, trying to put any memories of what she went through in Chicago behind her.

———•••———

Janice's first week of classes was a welcome change. She'd forgotten how much she loved being in a classroom. A course on the politics of environmental protection intrigued her, taught by Ann Bruhn, an assistant professor and one of the few female faculty members in the program. Professor Bruhn skillfully drew out Janice's views in the dis- cussion on the first day, and Janice felt more encouraged by her than by her other professors. By the third week of classes, Janice asked Professor Bruhn to be her advisor on her master's thesis.

"I want to conduct research on the politics of organic farming," Janice said after Professor Bruhn motioned for her to sit in her office. The professor's doctorate diploma from the University of Michigan hung on the wall behind her desk, and well-organized shelves of books lined another wall.

"Good, but what else is important besides the politics?" Professor Bruhn spoke with an intensity that made Janice alert.

"The culture—society's readiness?"

"Yes. But also economics. Changing the farming business is dif- ficult if the alternatives can't compete."

The thesis wasn't due until the end of the spring semester, but

Janice began spending long hours in the university library, collecting articles related to her topic. She also read several publications by Professor Bruhn. She wondered whether she might follow the professor's academic path. Janice had recovered from the traumatic events in Chicago and felt more focused than ever.

She saw Cathy at least once weekly, often having a meal together on the weekend. Cathy informed her that Ben was planning an antiwar meeting during the fall semester to welcome students and report on the demonstrations in Chicago. Ben wanted Cathy and Janice to join him in describing what had happened—some national media and political leaders were now calling the event a "police riot."

"I don't know. Why should I do him a favor?" Janice said.

"I think you should join us one more time—the students will want to hear what happened in Chicago."

"Has Ben said anything about me?"

Cathy smiled. "He's admitted he made a mess of things with you. He also told me he's no longer with Liz—he hadn't handled that whole thing well either, apparently."

Janice nodded, thinking how predictable that was.

"I think he wants another chance," Cathy added.

Janice just looked at her, shaking her head.

———••———

Janice and Cathy attended the meeting together. Janice was amazed at the number of students present, many of them new. It was the same room in the student union where she had attended her first meeting. So much had happened since then.

Ben gave a passionate speech as usual, welcoming the students to an important cause and saying how critical it was to continue protesting the war. Janice understood how his passion once had attracted her, but now it seemed like a shallow performance. Ben summarized the protests in Chicago, saying he believed they showed the nation, through the out-of-control police violence, that change was needed.

He then turned the program over to Janice and Cathy. Janice kept her talk factual, even when she spoke about the police clubbing the protesters. Cathy spoke about her fear of the police and the widespread panic shown in the media coverage, which she hoped would help the country avoid that kind of violence.

Many students asked questions. They wanted to know what to do next—what were the plans to keep the pressure on? Ben was prepared for that question. He invited everyone to an organizing meeting on Saturday.

"I'm glad you both came," Ben said after the meeting ended. "The younger students were spellbound listening to you talk about Chicago."

Janice nodded. She could feel his familiar charm but found herself indifferent to it.

"I'd love to have you help me at the Saturday meeting," Ben said.

Janice was ready with her response: "I'm sorry—I can't. My priority this semester is to do well in my classes."

"I'd be glad to help one more time," Cathy said. "But I'm going to focus more this semester on Governor Hughes's campaign for the Senate."

They parted, and Cathy and Janice decided to stop at the coffee house. "I'm interested in your support of Governor Hughes," Janice said.

"He's great. Bobby Kennedy encouraged him to run for the Senate before he was assassinated."

"So, he's spoken against the war, like McGovern and Ribicoff?"

"Definitely. He was one of the first Democratic governors who disagreed with President Johnson over the war."

"I'd love to help you support his campaign," Janice said.

"All right!" Cathy said. "Let's visit his Iowa City office next week."

———————

Later in the semester, Janice called to give her mother an update.

"I like my classes, and I have a really terrific professor advising me on my thesis."

Her mother said they were all doing well at the farm. "Tim's just started his junior year, and he's been letting his hair grow—you can imagine how your father feels about that. Oh! He passed the test for his driver's license."

"That's great—tell him I said congratulations," Janice said. "How's Dad?"

"He's keeping to himself, spending time on farm projects." Janice could tell her mother knew the intent of her question: whether he was still upset about her Chicago trip.

"How about Grandpa Cole?"

"He's still going strong, although he's hard to understand sometimes because of his stroke."

"I've started a letter to him. I'll try to finish today and get it in the post by tomorrow. And I'll talk to Dad more over Thanksgiving. I'd like to explain what happened in Chicago."

At this, her mother was silent, and Janice bit her lip. They ended their call with Janice still feeling she lacked her father's understanding and support. It seemed to be an intentional withholding of his love, which made her stomach ache.

———————

October was a busy time for Janice. It was her favorite season, with the temperature cool and crisp and the leaves bright red and orange. She worked on assignments for her classes, making time for meals with Cathy. She also knocked on doors in her neighborhood and left pamphlets promoting Hughes for Senate.

One Sunday, she spent a sunny afternoon in the city park, walking along the path by the river and sitting alone on a bench to meditate, letting her thoughts leave her mind as Cathy had taught her. She also returned to working out regularly at the campus fitness center, often the only woman in pickup basketball games.

Janice wrote to her grandpa, describing her thoughts about organic farming and proposing they discuss it at Thanksgiving. Her mother's calls increasingly focused on Tim, who was doing well in school but who was getting more challenging to live with, often arguing with his father over driving the car and the pickup.

In mid-November, Janice's mother called her, and they went through their usual ritual of updating each other. Her mother hesitated, and Janice sensed she was preparing to say something serious.

"I want to talk about Thanksgiving. It's your aunt Rose's turn to host the meal. Then we'll host Christmas."

"And? Is there something specific she'd like me to bring?"

"Janice . . . Rose doesn't want you to come to her house on Thanksgiving."

"Why?" asked Janice. She tried to calm her breathing.

"She heard you were on TV during the Chicago riots. She doesn't want anyone in her house who believes police should be killed."

Janice closed her eyes, picturing Aunt Rose's righteous look and words. She was the last person Janice wanted to know about what happened in Chicago. "How did she find out? Did Dad tell her?"

"No. She found out from Jim."

"Jim! I can't believe he would do that." Janice remembered him hugging her when he dropped her off at Susan's apartment. But she also knew Jim and Aunt Rose had stayed in touch after Janice's divorce and had celebrated Nixon's nomination over the phone.

"I was surprised, too—I didn't realize they were even in touch."

"So, what does this mean?" Janice asked.

"Your father suggests you come home but not go to your aunt's."

"He didn't stand up for me?"

Her mother was quiet for several seconds. "I had a huge fight with him." She stopped, and Janice could sense she was trying not to cry. "You know how stubborn he is."

Janice nodded, pressing her lips together. "You're caught in the middle," she said. She grew silent, absorbing the news that she couldn't join her family for Thanksgiving.

"I'm sorry. I love you," her mother said. "Your father does too, but he can be impossible."

"Love you too," Janice said, tears welling in her eyes. Despite her mother's words, she felt unloved and insignificant.

16

Janice lay on her bed and stared at the ceiling, thinking about Aunt Rose. Everything felt mixed up. She was angry at Jim for being an informer after wishing her well. She felt sorry for her mother, who'd been put in a difficult position. She couldn't believe her father would take his family to Thanksgiving dinner and leave his daughter home, as his sister had commanded. But she also felt embarrassed that her rage over the police violence had taken control of her. It would be hard for her family to understand that.

She decided to get Cathy's thoughts at their weekly dinner. "Can you believe I've been banned?"

"Your father is something else. Families are crazy."

"What do you think I should do?"

"This reminds me of how the Amish shun a family member who goes against their rules. It's cruel and can be tragic for the entire family."

Janice nodded repeatedly. "That's exactly how I feel."

"Are you thinking of not even going home?" Cathy said.

"Yeah. I can't see myself sitting in our house while everyone goes to Aunt Rose's."

"That's probably how I would feel," Cathy said, reaching across the table to hold Janice's hand.

Janice nodded again, her eyes glistening. She thanked Cathy and walked home in the dark. A cold wind blew through the leafless trees. She zipped her jacket to the top and pulled her stocking cap over her ears.

———————•••———————

Janice called her mother on the weekend before Thanksgiving and said she wouldn't be coming home. She tried to keep herself from becoming emotional, limiting herself to the facts of her decision. Her mother said she had been afraid of that, but she felt powerless; Janice's father wouldn't budge. Janice said she would come home at Christmas and hung up before starting to cry.

On Thanksgiving Day, isolated and lonely, Janice tried to find a positive side—she took advantage of having a free weekend. She caught up on her assignments and collected publications for her thesis. She worked out each day at the rec center. But it wasn't enough to keep her from feeling depressed. She gave up trying to read a textbook assignment on Saturday and collapsed on her bed for two hours. The lack of support from her family devastated her. She was shunned, as Cathy had said. She had no idea what the future looked like.

On Sunday afternoon, Janice's doorbell rang. She opened the door to find her brother standing there. She noticed he had filled out and his hair had grown longer, covering his ears. However, the look on his face reminded her of him as a vulnerable young boy. She embraced him, saying, "Timmy, you've made my day!" She took his coat, offered him some water, and motioned for him to have a seat. "So, what's going on?"

"I've been angry ever since Thanksgiving dinner. I got into a huge fight with Dad after church this morning," Tim said. "I told him he was a hypocrite for listening to a sermon about forgiveness while punishing you. He yelled at me, so I jumped into the pickup and drove here."

Janice thought of her father's anger when he had slammed the counter with his hand. "Dad can be pretty intense," she said.

"I can't believe he didn't stand up to Aunt Rose. It's bullshit!" He stopped for a moment, looking out the window as tears welled in his eyes. "He could have told her we'd have Thanksgiving at our house if she didn't invite you."

"I thought the same thing, but you know how stubborn he is."

"I'm tired of it. I can't wait to get out of that house. I even got into it with him over Vietnam."

"You did? I didn't even follow the news when I was your age." She smiled at him. "I'm proud of you!"

Tim beamed at her. "I think I got Aunt Rose's attention, too. I didn't talk to her at Thanksgiving—I think she may have felt guilty. And Grandpa kept asking where you were. Mom made something up about your schoolwork, but I think he knew what was happening."

"I'm sure he knows everything by now," Janice said. "I'm going to write him—I want to spend a lot of time with him at Christmas."

Tim was silent, and she sensed he was waiting for her guidance.

"I'm going to call Mom, and then I'll take you out to dinner," Janice said. "How about staying here tonight and driving back in the morning?"

He took a deep breath and nodded.

Janice called her mother, who was glad Tim was with her.

"Mom said she thought you might be here," Janice told him.

"She did?" Tim said.

"She's smart. She knows us pretty well."

"Well, I wish Dad was as smart."

Before Tim got into the truck to leave the next day, Janice gave him an extra hug. "I'm really glad you came to see me!" She waved as he drove off, feeling the crisp air enter her lungs with each breath. She was so proud of her brother, maturing rapidly and developing his own sense of right and wrong.

Janice concentrated on her studies between Thanksgiving and Christmas, including a stimulating meeting with Professor Bruhn about her thesis. Cathy kept her up-to-date on antiwar activities, which were energized by the election of Richard Nixon. The media anticipated he would accelerate the war before trying to negotiate its end. Ben led a march through the center of Iowa City on the day of a Hawkeye football game, snarling traffic and receiving national media attention. Janice decided not to participate, but she did walk down after the march to join the crowd that had gathered and show her support for the protest.

She put her energy elsewhere, participating in an antiwar rally led by Senator-elect Harold Hughes. His staff invited campaign volunteers to meet with him in a hotel conference room before the rally. Cathy went with her, and Janice was honored to have him shake their hands and thank them for their help. He said they needed to keep the pressure on to end the war. When he moved to greet other people, Ben joined them.

"You two must feel good, given all the work you did on his campaign," Ben said.

"Yeah, it's great," Cathy said. Janice nodded. She agreed it was great but didn't want to join the conversation with Ben.

"The antiwar movement is continuing to grow—I can't believe how many students want to participate," Ben said.

"Nixon is a motivator," Cathy said.

Ben moved closer to them. "I'm going back to law school this spring. I'll stay involved with MOBE, but I want to make room for new leaders. Maybe we can stay in touch."

"Sure," Cathy said. Janice nodded, not knowing what to say. She looked across the room to where pictures were being taken with the senator. She didn't want to stay in touch. She was reminded of her disappointment in Ben whenever she was around him.

When Ben left, Cathy looked at Janice and said, "I think he means to stay in touch with you, girl—I'm an afterthought."

"Maybe, but that's over for me. I'm going to spend time helping Senator Hughes end the war."

17

Janice woke early to drive to the farm to celebrate her 1968 Christmas with her family. She grew uneasy as she drove, unsure how things would go with her father and aunt. She had made plans with her mother to arrive a day early to help prepare the meal and to stay through New Year's Day. She wanted to talk with Grandpa Cole about organic farming and see Tim play basketball in a holiday tournament. Those were her priorities. But her mind whirled as she drove, remembering her father's anger and aunt's shunning.

After exiting the car, she hugged her mother and Tim and turned to her father. He was quiet and expressionless, but he reached out to hug her—she didn't see any sign of anger on his face. She spent the afternoon and evening helping her mother bake Christmas cookies and cleaning the large turkey for roasting the following day. In the morning, she stuffed the turkey with dressing before they put it in the oven, and she set the dining table and the extra table borrowed from the church with dishes, glasses, and silverware. The smell of roasting turkey filled the house.

Janice anxiously waited for their relatives' arrival—she didn't know what would happen when she and Aunt Rose saw each other. *Control your temper*, she reminded herself. She was determined not to let her aunt provoke her.

One of the two Cole families arrived first, including her cousins Laura and Steve. They all greeted her with big hugs. After Janice took their coats upstairs, she stood and joked with her cousins in the living room. "It's nice that you stooped so low to be with us on this holiday," Laura teased, and Janice rolled her eyes.

The doorbell rang, and the Wagners entered. Aunt Rose led the way followed by Uncle John and his family from Des Moines. She took the measure of the room, her eyes resting briefly on Janice, with a slight nod. Tim took their coats, and Aunt Rose went into the kitchen to give Janice's mother the dish she had brought, saying, "Barbara, this is going to be a feast."

Janice felt some of the tension release from her shoulders. First, her father, now her aunt, had been civil. Were they ready for a truce? How would she know?

The other Cole family arrived with Grandpa Cole. They had brought a wheelchair from the nursing home and used it to wheel him to the front steps. Steve and Laura's husband lifted the wheelchair up the steps and rolled Grandpa into the living room. Janice watched him as her mother and father helped him out of the wheelchair and into his favorite reclining chair. He had aged considerably since Janice had seen him last.

Grandpa's eyes glanced around the room, somewhat lifeless and a little confused. Janice's mother fussed over him, helping him recline partway to support his feet off the floor. He lay back weakly and rested his head on the recliner pillow. Janice noticed that his eyes suddenly came alive, riveting on her mother, who asked whether she could get him anything. He ignored her words and looked at her intently as he said something. The crowd of relatives had directed their attention to him as he got settled, but even though it had quieted, Janice's mother couldn't understand him as he tried to speak to her.

"What would you like, Pa?"

His lips moved again, but she still could not make out what he was saying—Janice and the others couldn't, either. He looked up at Janice's mother, his jaws clenched and his eyes glistening.

"Janice!" he said.

Her mother looked around the room. Janice was already walking toward them after she had heard Grandpa say her name. She walked by Aunt Rose, who stared at her. She ignored her—her stare meant nothing—as she walked toward her grandpa. He finally saw her, and they locked eyes. She pushed her hair away from her face and bent down to his level. Without words, he slowly raised his arms to hug her. She kissed him on his cheek, rested her hands on his shoulders, and put her face against his. He circled his arms around her and drew her closer. She returned his hug, moving her hands behind his shoulders. She suddenly felt like a little girl again when she fell off her bicycle. Her grandpa had held her, saying she would be fine.

Grandpa kept hugging her, and she felt tears well in her eyes. The room became quiet. He tightened his embrace of her, and she began to cry, her shoulders shaking with silent sobs. They held each other for several seconds until Grandpa loosened his arms. He smiled at her and raised his hand when she looked at him. He looked at her intently and then gave her a strong fist pump. She half laughed and half cried. Grandpa lowered his arm and then turned his attention to her mother, saying, "Coffee?"

His request for coffee triggered a flurry of activity as her mother asked people what they would like to drink. Aunt Rose joined her, asking everyone if they would like wine. Conversation filled the house again.

Aunt Rose moved toward Janice, who was drying her eyes with a napkin.

"Honey, would you like some wine?" Aunt Rose said with a smile.

"Yes, please," Janice said, accepting the peace offering.

Janice moved to help her mother and ran into Tim, who surprised her with a hug. When they pulled apart, she laughed and reached to mess up his hair. She turned to go to the kitchen when her father approached her. Her smile slowly disappeared as she wondered what he was going to say.

"Hi, Dad," she said quietly.

"Janice, it's good to have you home."

Standing awkwardly, her father didn't move. "I better help Mom," Janice said. She approached the kitchen, and her mother was in the doorway. Her mother probably had taken it all in: the hugs from Grandpa and Tim, her aunt's offer, and her father's words. She gave Janice a knowing look and asked her to uncover the dishes in the buffet line.

Conversation and laughter filled the house as people ate the delicious meal and socialized over coffee. When everyone left in the late afternoon, they thanked Janice and her family for being such wonderful hosts. Aunt Rose gave Janice a quick hug and said, "Now, you take care of yourself." Janice noticed that her aunt rolled her eyes slightly when she approached her father to say goodbye, but Janice ignored it— she would never let her aunt bother her again. Janice hugged Grandpa tightly and told him she would visit him to discuss farming. After everyone left, Janice joined her parents and brother in cleaning the dishes, putting leftovers away, and stacking the church's chairs and table in the back of the pickup.

When they were done cleaning, her mother asked Tim to set up TV trays in the living room. She put leftovers from the meal on the kitchen counter for them to snack on for supper. They filled their plates and sat in the living room. Her father surprised Janice by not turning on the TV.

"How's graduate school going?" he asked.

"Great." Janice was pleased with her father's interest, but she was amazed that he asked her.

"What kind of job do you think you might get with that degree?"

"I'm not sure, but I'm interested in organic farming." She didn't know how he would react to this and wouldn't be surprised if he ridiculed it.

"Your grandpa mentioned that. I've read some Extension newsletters about reducing pesticides and herbicides. You'll have to tell us what you learn."

Janice was surprised, never thinking that her father might be open to changing how he farmed. She sensed he had something else to say, even though he had already talked more than usual.

"I think we're going to continue to be on different sides in politics," he said.

"That's probably true." She was again surprised, not believing her father would touch such a loaded topic. But she wasn't going to get into an argument with him.

"Let's agree to disagree. Is that all right?" he said.

"Yeah, that sounds good."

He breathed deeply and looked away from her. She sensed he still had more to say.

"I also wanted to tell you that the Chicago police were out of control. I'm glad you got out of there without getting hurt."

Janice looked at him with gratitude. "Thanks. It was difficult, and I was way too angry."

Her father let out a long breath and turned to Janice's mother. "I think there's some pie left. I bet Tim and maybe others would like to have a piece." He then turned on the TV and found a basketball game to watch.

Janice knew her father's words were as close to an apology for Aunt Rose's and his behavior as she was going to get, which was fine. She turned her attention to the game.

She had a good week on the farm before returning to Iowa City. She saw Grandpa several times, and he listened closely to her ideas. He was intrigued with the politics of organic farming, nodding when she described the alliances for and against it.

Tim's Blairsville team came in second in the holiday tournament, and she was proud of his play as a starting forward. After the game, when she said, "Good defense," he replied, "Guess who I learned that from?"

Janice woke up early on the day she was returning to Iowa City. It was cold and dark outside, and the farmhouse was quiet—her father had not yet started his chores. She walked to the bedroom window and looked at the stars in the cloudless sky, bright and distinct against the blackness. As it began to get light, she could make out the trees in the grove across the road. She thought of all that had happened to her since she had left the farm six years earlier. She had struggled and learned and was aware that she would face challenges in the future.

Her greatest awareness, though, was how vital support from her family was, support that was tied to the Iowa farm culture and nature, to steadiness and caring. She had almost lost her family, but Grandpa had not allowed her to leave, nor had he allowed her family to let her go.

After her return to Iowa City, Janice plunged into her second-semester coursework and thesis. She still had her weekly meals with Cathy, but she expanded her friendships by attending Friday night happy hours with fellow students in her graduate program. She also started looking into potential employment at the Iowa State Extension service, instigated surprisingly by her father's interest in its newsletters.

———•••———

In March, her mother called her with sad news: Grandpa Cole had passed away in his sleep. Janice immediately drove to the farm, and her father greeted and hugged her as she exited her car. "Your mother isn't doing well," he said as they climbed the porch stairs. Her mother was dabbing her nose and red eyes with a handkerchief as Janice entered the house and embraced her, realizing she had rarely seen her mother cry. Tears quickly came to Janice's eyes, and they hugged and cried together while her father watched.

They drove to the funeral service in bright sunshine, almost blinded by the surrounding snow-covered fields. The intense whiteness, starkness, and peacefulness struck Janice, in contrast to the warm church filled with friends and family of Grandpa Cole, conversing and celebrating the life of one of the stalwarts of their Iowa farm community.

A room to the side was reserved for Cole family relatives. All her cousins were there. Janice thought that members of her generation were products of a farming way of life even though many, like her, were pursuing other careers. She was proud to have farming in her blood and glad to have the Iowa heritage that Grandpa and her ancestors had given her.

The service started, and she tried to relax as tears reappeared. She stared at a tree branch outside one of the church's windows, black and barren, silhouetted against the blue sky. It moved back and forth in the wind. She tried to empty her mind and concentrate on its beauty. The minister preached about her grandpa's life—his community leadership, innovative farming, and interests in education and sports. She silently added her memories of Grandpa—his support in everything she tried.

She particularly remembered his hug on Christmas Day—eighty-five years old, sitting in a recliner, still alert and strong, knowing everything about her and why she needed his hug. He never spoke of her divorce or protests in Chicago, but she knew that he knew everything. He dealt with it like the tree branch in the wind—shifting, adjusting, and returning to its place. He accepted her changes with support and love—a love that helped her become who she was, and who she was going to be.

The
Fighters

1

Pat Stevens ran into Dave around midnight on the sidewalk near Tony's Pizza as they walked toward their parked cars. Tony's was a popular hangout, and it was a coincidence that they were both heading out at the same time. It was dark, but Dave's muscular frame—he was a football lineman, a head taller than Pat, and the toughest fighter in Central High—was easy to pick out as Dave approached him. They stood talking for a bit, and Dave asked Pat about his plans after high school.

"I'll need to make a choice soon," Pat said, tossing the empty glass cola bottle he'd been carrying into a nearby trash can. "I've been accepted by three colleges." Dave talked about becoming a Marine, then circled back to asking about which schools Pat had applied to.

Pat was flattered to be asked about his plans by someone who fascinated him. He tried to read Dave's emotionless face and squinted eyes. Maybe Dave respected him because he was a fellow athlete—Pat's sport was wrestling—and he'd been voted most likely to succeed in their class of '67. Either way, he was eager to continue the conversation when Dave said, "Look who's here." Walking toward them were a couple of students from Kennedy High. They were friends of Beck, Dave's crosstown fighting rival.

"What are you doing on this side of town, Miller?" Dave asked. "And where's your buddy, Beck?"

"None of your business, asshole," Miller said. He was the larger of the two, and wore a tight black T-shirt to show off his bulk.

Dave turned to face him. "So you're calling me an asshole? Do you want to go right now?"

"Whenever and wherever."

"Follow me." Dave led them to the alley behind the restaurant.

Miller's friend walked next to Pat and said, "This is so stupid." Pat shrugged in response, silently agreeing.

Dave stopped in the backyard of Tony's Pizza. Weeds and dirt covered the yard, and a tree with several dead branches stood near the back of the building. The restaurant's exhaust fan ran continuously, its high-pitched whirring muffling their voices. They were alone, separated from a row of houses on the other side of the alley by a seven-foot wooden fence.

Before Dave turned, Miller rushed at him and swung wildly at his head. Surprised, Dave sidestepped the swing and punched Miller in the ribs, the thuds followed by Miller's grunts. Miller tried to tackle Dave, and Dave smashed him with each fist. They both fell, rolling in the dirt. Miller got on top and hit Dave with a glancing blow on the side of his head.

Dave reacted furiously, more enraged than Pat could have imagined. "Motherfucker!" he yelled. He turned Miller on his back and sat on him, repeatedly striking his head and body. Miller used his hands to protect himself and curled up. Pat could see a bloody swelling form under Miller's eye.

"Are you done?" Dave asked. Lying in the dirt, Miller tried to swing up at Dave. Dave hit him again, his fists smacking against Miller's head. "Are you done? Are you done?"

"Hey, that's enough!" Miller's friend yelled. Pat was startled to see him rush to push Dave off Miller. The unspoken rule was you didn't interfere in a fight. Everybody knew that.

"What the hell?" Pat shouted. He moved quickly and punched

Miller's friend in the face, hearing a crunching of bone and carti-lage. Miller's friend fell to the ground, holding his bleeding nose and moaning. Pat smelled the coppery odor of blood on his fist.

Dave stood up, glaring at Miller. "This is what happens if Beck or his buddies come to this side of town!"

Miller helped his friend to his feet, and the two of them staggered away.

Pat looked closely at Dave, who was breathing heavily and touch-ing his ear. "Are you okay?" he asked.

"My ear is ringing, but I'm fine," Dave said. "How about you? You about killed that guy."

Pat was nervous, thinking he had gone overboard. He should have just taken the guy down to the ground instead of breaking his nose. He didn't know how Dave felt about what he had done. "I shouldn't have hit him so hard," he said.

Dave looked at him and started laughing. "This was a fight, man! You don't hold back! I'm glad you pasted the sucker. You can come to any of my fights."

Pat nodded, matching eyes with Dave's warm gaze, absorbing Dave's approval.

They walked quietly. When Pat's heart stopped racing and Dave's ragged breathing quieted, they talked again about their plans after high school. Pat said he might major in history and asked about Dave's idea to join the Marines. Dave wasn't interested in college and might not be accepted anyway. After talking with his brother's friend, a Marine on leave from Vietnam, he had begun to think that fighting communists might be a better cause than fighting Beck and his friends. But enough about fighting, he said—it was time to see his girlfriend.

After they parted, Pat couldn't stop thinking about what had happened. He was glad Dave approved of his actions but was still unhappy about the punch he had thrown. It hadn't been necessary.

2

Over twenty years later, Pat turned on his side to face the digital clock on his nightstand. The bright red numbers told him it was after two. He'd been lying awake thinking of his competitor, Jack Eastman, while listening to the leaves rustling in the oak tree next to his house. Otherwise, it was quiet in the uncluttered room with its dark wooden floor as he deliberated over what he was going to do. He was glad his son had stopped coughing in the bedroom across the hall—at least there was that.

Pat didn't consider himself a boastful person, but he knew he was the best candidate for county administrator, the top job in county government, especially when he had learned that his only competition was Eastman. Pat had worked hard for years as a county employee in the western suburbs of the Chicago metropolitan area, steadily advancing and helping build an organization he loved. He felt well prepared for the interviews that would evaluate applicants, confident that he was more qualified than Eastman.

But Pat had heard surprising information about Eastman, news that had caused him to hit his steering wheel twice with the heel of his hand on his drive home and say, "What an asshole!" He hadn't recalled feeling this rageful since he was in a fight in high school, where he witnessed his classmate Dave pummel a fighter from Kennedy. Pat wanted to take Eastman to an alley and beat him like Dave had battered his Kennedy rival.

That afternoon, Pat had heard from a friend that Eastman was conducting a smear campaign against him, meeting with the elected county commissioners to tout his experience and criticize Pat. Eastman had informed commissioners he would resign from his finance director position if they appointed Pat county administrator—he wouldn't work for someone so incompetent. Eastman told the commissioners that Pat didn't have enough experience, being ten years younger than himself, and reminded them of an internal audit of Pat's planning department that had resulted in an employee's firing.

Pat couldn't believe Eastman had used the audit as an example of his incompetence. Pat had requested the audit because he suspected an employee was sharing confidential information. The audit confirmed this, giving Pat grounds to fire the employee. His boss saw it as an example of successful supervision by Pat, not the failure portrayed by Eastman.

Feeling blindsided, Pat thought of Dave's powerful punches to counter attacks by his high school adversaries. He had first become aware of Dave's fighting skills in the locker room after gym class, listening to boys talk to Dave about a fight where Dave had knocked out four of a Kennedy fighter's teeth. Dave sat silently in front of the lockers, a towel draped over his muscular shoulders in a room smelling of sweat. A football player asked Dave how he had avoided getting tackled and taken down, a well-known move by the Kennedy fighter. Dave looked up calmly, silent and expressionless, with his square chin lifted in the speaker's direction. "I hit him," he finally said. Another football player whooped, "Yes, you did, brother!"

A gust of wind caused the tips of tree branches to scrape against the house. When the scraping stopped, Pat heard Billy cough twice. Billy had come down with a cold after a birthday party with other seven-year-old boys. Pat thought of Billy's joyful enthusiasm—he loved playing with his friends. When he coughed again, Pat silently got out of bed, took the humidifier out of the closet and into the bathroom, filled it with water, and carefully set it near Billy's bed. The night-light allowed Pat to see the Chicago Bears team poster above Billy's head-board. What a fan that boy was. Pat looked at Billy's thick brown hair. Billy had asked to grow it long, and Pat had let him.

Pat returned to his bed, where he continued to lie wide awake, his eyes exploring the dark ceiling. For some reason, he was stuck on high school stuff.

One Saturday night in his senior year, Pat had entered Tony's Pizza and felt lucky to find a seat across from June in a six-person booth. A noisy crowd having weekend fun surrounded them, and the waitress struggled to get through to take his order after delivering a steaming pizza to the adjacent booth. Pat looked at June, intrigued by her short brown hair that accentuated her lively eyes. He had vague plans of asking her out, but a football player interrupted them, asking loudly over the din if anyone had seen Dave.

They hadn't, but another player arrived and said Dave was going to a dance near Kennedy, where he might fight Beck. Both of them left to join Dave. Pat stayed sitting with June and the others. They all started talking at once, wondering and guessing what might happen at Kennedy. "How ridiculous," June had said.

Pat had debated whether to follow the football players. Why didn't he? Was he afraid of what might happen? When June had looked at him and said, "I'm sure glad you're not going," Pat ignored her, even though those were the warmest words she'd ever said to him. Although the potential fight at Kennedy that night never happened, Pat was annoyed with himself, suspecting his avoidance of high school fights was a sign of cowardice.

Pat's uncertainty about how to counter Eastman felt similar to that reluctance in high school, although it wasn't because of cowardice. Eastman was wasting his time, requiring him to respond to his dirty tactics to protect his reputation, instead of working to advance the county.

Pat was eager to face the challenges of being the county administrator. He would be appointed by and accountable to the seven elected commissioners. He would lead the departments that carried out the county's programs, such as planning, public works, and human services. It was a big job; each one of the department directors would report to him. He was ready to compete with Eastman and any other candidate for this dream role.

Pat wasn't naive; he had been in difficult conflicts in his career. An unhappy contractor had wanted Pat's boss to fire him. A land developer had objected to the zoning recommendations by Pat's office and sued the county. He'd responded professionally and defused both situations, receiving praise from the administrator for resolving these issues independently.

But he hadn't faced a situation where someone on the same team had gone behind his back to criticize him to his superiors. Would the county commissioners see through Eastman and discount his attacks? Who knew. Eastman's experience was narrower than Pat's, but he was valued and successful, with a master's degree comparable to Pat's. Except Eastman was playing dirty, pursuing his goal of becoming administrator with whatever tactics worked. He was violating the professional norms that Pat—and the people Pat admired—lived by.

When Pat looked ahead at where the conflict with Eastman might go, he had trouble seeing a constructive resolution. Eastman was trying to destroy him, and he had to respond, just as if a person had thrown a punch at him. It was like a high school fistfight, with the potential to become raw and brutal.

Pat didn't know what influenced boys in high school to fight. Maybe it was comic books of U.S. soldiers fighting German and Japanese World War II enemies. Maybe it was TV westerns where fistfights were won by good guys over bad guys. Or, perhaps, it was stories from their fathers about how they helped lead the U.S. to victory. Pat's father had entered the U.S. Navy shortly before the end of the war and hadn't seen action. Still, he was proud of his contribution and would let Pat know as much. His satisfaction and confidence—and that of all the other guys who fought in the war—created high expectations.

Whatever led his classmates to become fighters, Pat looked up to them, seeing their victories as an acceleration toward manhood. Pat had wanted to be seen as they were seen—a silent leader, unafraid of conflict, and ready to engage and dominate enemies who threatened him. He remembered thinking of Dave as a man among boys, a fierce warrior confident of his ability to face dangerous conflict. He'd wished that he had the confidence that Dave exuded, and he wished for it now as he puzzled over what to do about Eastman.

Pat glanced at the clock. It was too early to get up and risk waking Billy. The wind continued to blow the tree branches; it was a pitch-black night. What could he do to respond to Eastman's smears? He didn't want to use dirty tactics like Eastman had. Could he win over the county commissioners by taking the high road—ignoring Eastman and maintaining his professionalism? He doubted it, because Eastman's criticisms of him were becoming known by county staff. He suspected the commissioners and the staff would be expecting a response from him, and the type of response he made could influence the commissioners' view of him. How could he continue to show strong leadership while defending himself?

Pat thought about the one high school fight he was in, where he and Dave fought Miller and his friend. Pat's feelings about fighting hadn't changed. Whether he was responding to attacks by Eastman or Miller's friend, he saw fighting as a risky distraction. He'd rather avoid emotional personal attacks and use rational problem-solving to address conflicts. He also didn't trust his emotions if he did participate in a fight. He was afraid of overreacting and possibly hurting his opponent.

Pat could hear Billy stirring. It was getting light outside, and it was time for them to get up. Pat got out of bed and looked in the bathroom mirror. He saw an overweight person under stress—wrinkles in his forehead and graying hair flopping toward his bloodshot eyes. He'd been working long hours, and the news about Eastman added unexpected tension.

Pat's worries stopped momentarily when Billy came into the bathroom. "Can we play catch with my football after school today?" Billy asked.

"You bet, buddy."

Billy gave him a high five, and Pat laughed at his exuberance.

While Billy dressed, Pat let the warm water from the shower stream onto the back of his neck, still thinking about his next steps with Eastman.

Pat dropped Billy off at school and drove to work. He had two priorities in his life: Billy and his job. He was glad the joint custody arrangement with June finally seemed to be working. But Eastman's attacks had created uncertainty about the future of his job. He was calmer, not striking the steering wheel in a rage. But he still shook his head in anger when he thought of Eastman's aggressive move, a sneak attack that he had to respond to. He thought again about punching him, like he did to Miller's friend. He knew it wasn't the solution, but what else would he do? He thought about the nonphysical equivalent of hitting back. He wasn't sure what that would be, or whether he wanted to do it, but he knew he needed to do something. He couldn't just stand still while Eastman took his dream job away.

3

"You're kidding!" Gary said. "It's one thing to lobby for the job, but bad-mouth the other candidate?" Pat had invited Gary to lunch at a small, family-run café with dark wooden booths. Gary and Pat used to eat there at least once a week to update each other on county issues. Gary was Pat's former boss in the planning director position that Pat had been promoted to after Gary retired. He was as close to being Pat's mentor as anyone.

"I've heard it now from two staff who support the commissioners," Pat said. Gary had gained weight and seemed relaxed in retirement, but he became alert, the skin around his eyes crinkling at this news, just as it used to when he had to deal with political issues involving the county board.

"There are only two commissioners left who served when I was doing your job: Bill Jones and John Larsen," Gary said. "Jones got what he always wanted after I left—board chairman. He's slippery. Larsen, though, is a stand-up guy. Have you thought of talking to the commissioners?"

"Yeah, but it seems awkward—they know I can talk to them when they interview me."

"It didn't stop Eastman."

Pat frowned and looked out the window at a man hurriedly walking by.

"I know you don't want to stoop to Eastman's level," Gary said. "It's early, so you probably should keep your powder dry. But if Eastman keeps dragging your name through the mud, you may need to do battle with him."

Pat grimaced, his eyes half-shut. "It's unbelievable what this jerk is doing."

"I know, but it happens. You might talk to Mary Beth—she may have some advice."

Pat looked at Gary and smiled. "That's a good idea." Mary Beth was the county's lobbyist. When Pat had seen her at county board meetings, she'd always arrived early and seemed to float around the boardroom despite being a large woman, smiling and tossing her thick black hair as she greeted people, never failing to shake hands or hug each commissioner.

Pat promised to keep Gary up-to-date, and they changed topics, talking about Gary's family and retirement activities. After lunch, they walked to their cars.

"How's that son of yours doing?" Gary asked. "How old is Billy now?"

"He's seven and doing well. He's become quite the sports fan."

"Well, Pat, just remember that Billy is more important to you than all of the Jack Eastmans in the world."

Pat nodded and smiled. Although he still had challenges with Billy's mother, he felt he had successfully taken on single-parent duties after his divorce. It was hard to believe three years had already gone by without much of a hitch.

Pat drove back to work and his thoughts again turned to Eastman. Gary's idea to talk to Mary Beth was a great suggestion, but their lunch hadn't made Pat any less anxious. Gary had confirmed that Eastman was putting Pat in a risky position and that it may require Pat to do battle with Eastman to resolve it. Pat had difficulty imagining what that might mean.

After he returned home from picking Billy up at school, Billy ran to get his football, ready to play catch, over his cold and cough. Pat laughed and put aside his worries. He loved being with his son and helping him grow, making sure he followed Billy's lead whenever it made sense to. His father wouldn't have waited for Pat to suggest playing catch with their football. He would have found the football and ordered Pat to go outdoors to throw it to him. Proud of his athletic success, his father never let Pat forget he was a starting linebacker on his high school football team. He related winning in football to succeeding in the private sector, as he'd done as a regional corporate manager.

After changing clothes, Pat went through the mudroom to the backyard. Billy had dug out his football from the mudroom shelves and left sports equipment scattered—a soccer ball, baseball glove, and basketball. While he waited for Pat, he tossed the football in the air and caught it. He moved to the open side of the yard, opposite of the two oak trees, where he and Pat had often played catch or dribbled the soccer ball. Each time, his slender body seemed taller and more coordinated.

"I'm going out for a pass," Billy said as he lined up next to Pat.

"Okay, fake to the right and then cut left like you were a Chicago Bear," Pat said.

Billy cut across in front of Pat, his long hair flopping as he ran, and dropped the first two passes. He caught the third and yelled, "I did it!"

Pat had often heard from his father that a man needed to be tough to survive in a dog-eat-dog world and that football provided valuable training. Pat enjoyed pickup football games in their neighborhood in grade school, but once he started organized football in junior high, he grew to resent the constant pressure from his father to play well.

"Now I want to be the quarterback," Billy said and motioned Pat to go out for passes. Billy did well at throwing short passes and told Pat to go out farther. Pat remembered playing defensive halfback in a junior high game on a cold and cloudy afternoon when the opponent's fullback smashed into him, dragging him for yards and almost escaping until his teammates helped tackle him. His father had yelled from the sideline, "Hit him, Pat! Hit him!" Pat tried to live up to his father's expectations, but by the end of ninth grade, he was sick of football and chose wrestling as the sport he would pursue, which his father knew less about than Pat did.

"You're getting better every time we play," Pat called to Billy across the yard. "Let's end and you wash your hands while I grill some chicken. But first pick up the mess you made in the mudroom. No chicken for you until you do!"

"What if I don't want chicken?" Billy said, hugging the football. He smiled defiantly, showing off the gap where he'd lost his upper front teeth.

"Guess you don't eat then—more for me." Pat grinned back. "But you'll still need to pick your stuff up off the floor either way."

After heating the charcoal and putting the chicken breasts on the grill, Pat poured frozen green beans into a pan to cook. Billy played his toy record player while they waited for the food to be ready. After dinner, Pat and Billy played a couple games of checkers before Pat asked Billy to shower. He tucked him in bed and read a Sesame Street book to him—the one about the monster at the end of the book, Billy's favorite—before turning off the lights and closing the door, leaving a night-light on, as Billy wanted, near his bed.

Pat sat down on the sofa and flipped TV channels to find a sporting event or movie to watch, but his mind continued to grapple with what to do about Eastman. What a disruption, an obstacle he was! Pat's decision to apply for the administrator position was natural and inevitable. He had advanced at every level in the county to become the planning director. His next step up was to become the administrator.

As Pat headed off to bed, he stopped to look at the plaque that

hung on the hallway wall. Even in the dim light, the bronze letter-
ing stood out. On tough days, kind of like the ones he'd been having
of late, the plaque reminded him that his efforts were noticed. He
had received it for being county employee of the year, celebrating
a successful zoning and economic development project he had led
under Gary. He thought about the values he had helped establish over
many years of working for the county—he'd worked hard to create a
positive and innovative culture. Eastman's lack of professionalism not
only hurt Pat's candidacy for the administrator position. It was also
destructive to the county organization Pat loved.

Mary Beth walked toward Pat's booth in the restaurant, but stopped at
two tables where people had called out to her. She smiled and talked
briefly to each group of people before waving and heading toward
Pat. She sat across from him, filling her side of the booth with her size
and personality.

"What can I do for you, Pat?" she asked, with a smile. "Have you
gotten yourself crossways with a legislator? Or do you just want to
hear about my problems with our crazy commissioners?"

Pat laughed. "Thanks for seeing me," he said. "I'll get right to the
point. I want to be county administrator and would like your advice."

Mary Beth looked at Pat intently. "I'd be glad to give you my perspective, but I know you're already a favored candidate."

Pat smiled, pleased to hear that news. "That's great, but I've got an
obstacle. Jack Eastman is bad-mouthing me to the commissioners."

Mary Beth took some time to absorb the news, raising her eyebrows. Before she could respond, a waitress interrupted them, asking
for their orders.

"So, what's going on?" Mary Beth asked after they each ordered a
sandwich.

"Eastman is scheduling meetings with commissioners to tell them he will resign if I'm appointed administrator, and to falsely blame me for an audit finding."

Mary Beth frowned. "I don't know him well, but my opinion of him just dropped," she said. "I've seen him in Chairman Jones's office. Do you think he was lobbying for the job?"

"Probably."

"Let me ask you a question. We haven't worked together much, but I know you have a good reputation with your staff. Why do you want to be county administrator?"

Pat was surprised by this question, but he knew Mary Beth would report to him if he were the administrator. Maybe she was testing him to see if she would want to work for him.

"Here's what I'll say in the county board interviews," Pat said. "Our county faces challenges, and I'm eager to address them. I want to involve citizens with the county board to create a vision for our future. We must look at our infrastructure and social program needs." He stopped for a second. "And I hope you'll join me."

Mary Beth grew serious and looked closely at Pat. He wondered if he had overplayed his hand by soliciting her as a partner when they were just beginning to know each other.

"I'd love to work with you to develop a new vision. We have too much closed-door politicking right now, and I'm unsure who benefits."

Pat wondered what Mary Beth meant, but he felt it was premature to ask.

"Let me check on Eastman's meetings with the chairman. I'm close with Jones's secretary, Kathy. Maybe she can share some information with me."

"That would be great," Pat said. When they left, he smiled and shook Mary Beth's hand, glad she seemed to be on his side. He had taken his first action to counter Eastman, through Mary Beth's offer to help. He didn't know where it was going, but action was better than constant worrying.

After employee meetings that afternoon, Pat closed his office door. He rocked back in his chair and shut his eyes. His discussion with Mary Beth about creating a county vision made him think about his decision to work for the public sector many years ago.

He had gone to college at a small liberal arts school out East. Initially, he chose to major in history, but his interests changed when he became active in the presidential campaign, influenced by George McGovern's opposition to the Vietnam War. He switched his major to political science.

Pat remembered struggling to decide what to do after graduation. He was lucky to receive a high draft lottery number and debated alternatives such as teaching or joining the Peace Corps. One night after passionate discussions at the McGovern campaign headquarters, Pat walked around the dark campus for two hours, trying to decide his next steps. Sitting next to the campus pond, he leaned forward and held his head in his hands. He finally looked up and chose his direction—his goal would be to serve the public in a government role. He wanted to improve the country's political and government systems to benefit the lives of American citizens.

After graduating with his bachelor's degree, he had returned to the Midwest to earn a master's in public affairs at the University of Wisconsin. He accepted a county government position in the Chicago area. Since then, he had no doubts about his career goals and direction—and he still didn't, despite the challenge from Eastman.

Pat recalled his father's silence during spring break when he told him he had accepted a county job. His father finally spoke, saying, "The public sector?"

Pat nodded, though his father didn't make eye contact. "Yes," he added. "I know it's not exactly what you had in mind for me, but—"

"It's just fine," his father said. Without more words, he got up and went outside to trim the hedge near the garage.

This lack of approval hadn't surprised Pat. They'd fiercely debated the Vietnam War and the McGovern and Nixon presidential campaigns. But as Pat's career progressed at the county, his father grew to be proud of him, with Pat's well-earned success overcoming their political differences. His father valued hard work and expected success.

Pat's thoughts were interrupted by his phone ringing. It was a call from a contractor friend, who reported that Eastman was criticizing Pat to several of the county's contractors and saying he, not Pat, would be the new administrator.

"Are you serious?" Pat asked the contractor.

"I'm serious. Some of us are concerned about how Eastman will use his power as administrator."

Pat thanked his friend for the heads-up and ended the call. He couldn't believe Eastman's aggression. It was inconsistent with how a public servant should behave.

It was time to leave to get Billy. He picked him up at his after-school care, excited to see him following an exhausting day of work. He tried to put his work concerns aside and focus on being with his son. He cooked him his favorite pasta meal and, after dinner, sprawled out on the floor with him to work on a 500-piece puzzle of a U.S. map, counting the number of states they'd traveled in. When Pat hesitated, though, and looked into the distance instead of trying to fit pieces into the puzzle, Billy grabbed him and hugged him, bringing him back to the moment. Pat refocused and, after a few minutes, was able to get lost in searching for the pieces. It felt good, plugging in one shape after another.

But Pat wondered once he put his son to bed whether his momentary distance was a result of his stress the past few days, and whether Billy hugged him because he felt his father drifting from him because of that stress. That bothered Pat, and he committed to work harder at leaving his job challenges behind when he was with Billy.

The call from the contractor left an impact on Pat. He had yet to hear from Mary Beth, but he thought about confronting Eastman so that at least he'd know that Pat was aware of what he was doing.

He'd first met Eastman a few years ago at a county family picnic soon after Eastman was hired as the county's finance director. After shaking hands, Eastman introduced Pat to his wife. She had wavy blond hair down to her shoulders and an attractive smile. Pat wondered how Eastman—tall, skinny, and stooped—had succeeded in finding such a beautiful wife. Eastman next introduced Pat and Billy to his son, who looked a year younger than Billy. Billy pulled Pat toward the chatter and laughter of kids at the playground, and Pat thought of asking Eastman's son to come with them, but the boy stood quietly behind his father, looking at the ground.

When Pat looked back at these introductions, he realized there were perhaps things about Eastman that he hadn't noticed, mysteries he hadn't detected. Pat now knew he had underestimated him.

He had little to do with Eastman in the years after their introduction, only interacting with him annually during the budgeting process. But Pat wanted to engage him now—to tell him what he had been hearing.

⚬

Later that week, he had an opportunity to do just that when he stayed late and ran into Eastman in the copy room.

"Jack, I hear you don't believe I should be county administrator."

Eastman returned Pat's stare after taking his copies out of the machine. He was taller than Pat but much thinner. Frowning, he looked at Pat over his nose, choosing not to reply. The close space, humming copiers, and bright fluorescent overhead lights added to the ramped-up edge Pat felt, and the words that came next reflected that edge.

"You're telling people you'll leave if I'm appointed," Pat said. "And you're saying I don't have the experience, using an audit I requested as your evidence of that."

"Look, Stevens, I'm the better candidate."

"I don't think so. But, whatever—your way of communicating doesn't reflect well on the county. People wonder whether we have a professional team that can work together."

"We may or may not," Eastman said. "But the cards have been played."

Pat took a long look at Eastman, clenching his jaw. He imagined how it might feel to hit him and flatten his beak of a nose against his skull. Instead, Pat returned to his office, looking out his third-floor window for several seconds. He watched a traffic jam at the intersection near his building, with one impatient driver laying on his horn.

He felt satisfied. Confronting Eastman had confirmed that the stories were true—Eastman hadn't denied them—and he had shown Eastman he was aware and disapproved.

———•••———

Pat's satisfaction didn't last long. Two days later, Gary called.

"I checked with a couple of retired buddies about Eastman," Gary said. "They'd heard about his lobbying."

"How'd they find out?"

"From some developers. In fact, one developer, Doug Kern, met with Chairman Jones recently and pledged his support for Eastman."

"That's not good."

"No."

Pat had first met Kern, owner of Kern Development, during a public hearing on the county's ten-year plan. He was likable, with red hair and a face that always seemed ready to break into a smile. He drove a black Mercedes with vanity plates displaying "KERN."

At a recent hearing, Kern had greeted Pat warmly: "How's my man? Why don't you let me buy you lunch this week?" Pat declined, as Kern knew he would from previous offers, because he didn't want to be perceived as having a conflict of interest when reviewing bids from developers. He liked Kern, though—they often bantered about whether the White Sox were better than the Cubs.

But Pat felt betrayed by Kern's support for Eastman. He didn't understand it, shocked at how bold Kern had been to lobby the county board's chairman so directly.

Pat called Sam Harris, the director of the county's human resources office, to find out the timing of the administrator job posting. He and Sam had worked together many times on personnel actions for Pat's staff. Pat valued Sam's knowledge and meticulous approach to problem-solving, symbolized by his bow tie and wire-rimmed glasses.

"Sam, what's your latest schedule for interviewing administrator applicants?"

"I'm anticipating we would start them in three weeks," Sam said.

"It's just me and Eastman, right?"

"Pretty much. We do have a couple external candidates, but, between you and me, they won't make the cut."

"Thanks, man. I'll be ready."

Pat hung up, deep in thought. He felt an urgency about his need to counter Eastman's attacks. Three weeks would go by quickly.

4

It was Pat's turn to have Billy for the upcoming week. He picked him up on Friday at June's after work. It was a chilly gray day, with a fine mist beginning to fall. June came out to the car with Billy, and Pat rolled down the window to hear what she had to say. Billy strapped himself into his booster seat, and June asked Pat if Billy could come over on Sunday for a birthday party for their neighbor's son.

Pat looked at June, his eyebrow cocked. "You know I'm open to changes if we schedule them beforehand. Why are you just telling me this now?"

"We didn't find out until yesterday."

"I have plans for Billy on Sunday. So, it's not going to work."

"I don't imagine you could adjust your plans."

"That's right."

"Okay, fine," June said, turning away after glaring at him. Her anger was familiar to him, never ceasing to make him uncomfortable. He considered compromising but thought he should stay firm out of principle.

After a few steps, June turned back to look at him, her hair glistening from the mist. "You know, you're really a selfish jerk."

Pat steeled himself. "And who are you? You're the one who broke up our family!"

"No. You're impossible to live with—always right, always in charge."

Pat thought of Billy, who had his head down, taking his gloves off and putting them on again. Pat hated fights with June in front of Billy, and hated himself for rising to her bait.

June and Pat stared at each other silently until Pat finally said, "We need to go." June walked quickly to the house without saying a word.

"Why is Mommy mad?" Billy asked.

Pat smiled, trying to calm down. "She must have had a bad day. Both of us have had bad days. But don't worry—we'll get over it."

But Pat didn't get over it. After Billy went to bed, Pat sat quietly in the living room. The sun seemed to set early, with darkness surrounding the house. He had no energy to read or watch TV. He was upset with himself. He didn't know why June's anger had such an impact on him, and he was frustrated that he had gotten upset at her, especially in front of Billy.

Pat had a couple of serious relationships with women after college, but when he'd reconnected with June at his tenth high school reunion, he felt he'd found his soulmate. They had dated during the summer after high school graduation, but lost touch during college, not seeing each other again until the reunion. He remembered her walking up to him at the bar, still slender with short brown hair, looking at him with her lively eyes as she prepared to speak. They married a year later and rented an apartment near downtown Chicago, where June got a teaching job. But things began to fall apart after Billy was born. They had divorced when Billy was four.

After trying to read a magazine, Pat went to bed early and lay awake for hours, still upset over June's anger. He didn't know how things had turned so negative. He remembered one moment in particular—laughing with her at The Parthenon, a lively Greek restaurant in downtown Chicago. He'd made a joke—what, he couldn't remember now—and her cheeks had colored when she thought the table next to them had heard. But she couldn't help laughing too.

They had enjoyed the delicious lamb kabobs nestled in yellow rice, the red house wine, and each other.

———•••———

Pat was eager to hear from Mary Beth about Eastman's meetings with Jones, but he didn't want to push her. She finally called him at the end of the week and suggested having a drink after work. They met at a restaurant and bar some distance from their offices, not wanting to run into county commissioners or employees.

Mary Beth joined Pat at the table, brushing snowflakes off her coat. "Winter is here!" she exclaimed. "My kids will want to go sledding after this snow."

They each ordered a glass of wine, and Pat asked about her kids. She had a boy and a girl, aged twelve and nine. Her face relaxed as she talked about her family, adding that her husband was a city firefighter who recently had his hours reduced because of a budget shortfall. Pat told her about his joint custody of Billy.

Mary Beth's brown eyes softened. "That must be challenging," she said. "I know men who just contribute child support and see their kids a couple of weekends a month. Are you able to keep peace with your ex?"

Pat smiled and said, "I think so. For the most part." He thought of his recent argument with June. But he also thought of a parent-teacher conference when Billy was in kindergarten. Billy had walked down the hallway with his dad on one side and his mom on the other, holding their hands and beaming from his parents' attention and love. Pat had been glad that he and June were able, for the most part, to put their resentments aside, although he still blamed her for their marriage breakup, now as he did then. They could have worked on it, but she chose not to. She had been the one to file for divorce.

"That's such hard work," Mary Beth said.

Pat nodded, thinking of Mary Beth's skill in connecting with people. What a great listener. He understood why she had so many relationships and why people trusted her.

But it was time to shift topics and hear why Mary Beth had called him. "You must've found some news from the chairman's secretary," Pat said. He leaned forward to be heard over the noise of the growing crowd at the bar, several people standing near the flickering flames in the large fireplace in the corner.

"You won't believe it. Kathy was on guard, but she opened up to me," Mary Beth said. "I'll share it with you if you promise to keep it quiet."

Pat nodded.

"Jones is asking Eastman to help him simplify the purchase and development of the old strip mall property by removing the requirement for bids," she said.

Pat was aware of this mall. His planning staff had suggested using the almost vacant property to meet the county's growing needs. They proposed that the county buy the property, raze the buildings, convert half of the land to recreational fields, and sell the other half for housing development.

"Why would Jones want it simplified?" Pat asked. "And how would Eastman help do it? There's a community development process for handling this."

He thought of the solicitation of bids from developers that was planned for the housing development, which had been approved by the county board. He also recalled how the popularity of this project in the neighborhood had already caused the board to decide to use eminent domain to purchase the land at market value if negotiations with the owner didn't succeed.

"I don't know. Kathy seemed nervous about sharing this. She also seemed more negative than usual about Chairman Jones."

"There must be a benefit to somebody, something behind the scenes," Pat said. He grew quiet, thinking about the land developer, Doug Kern, lobbying Jones for Eastman to be administrator.

"What are you going to do next?" Mary Beth asked.

"I'm not sure. I'm at least going to do some quiet research. I'll let you know if I find anything."

"You better let me know," Mary Beth said with a smile. "I don't want to get caught in the middle of this—it could put my job at risk."

"Definitely!" Pat said. "I appreciate your help. It's time for you to be with your kids, instead of worrying about my dilemmas."

As Pat drove home, he envisioned the research he would do, beginning by looking in the property files. He was glad to act on something that might explain Eastman's motives. But his mind also returned to the conversation with Mary Beth about their families. He envied her.

Pat thought of the happy times when he and June lived in downtown Chicago, independently pursuing their careers, and enjoying urban activities together. He learned to appreciate art shows through her interests, and she became a White Sox fan through his.

They had confirmed their desire to have children and create a family before marrying. They made plans to buy a house and have June take at least a year off from teaching when they had a child. These plans took effect when Billy was born. They bought a starter home in the suburbs not far from Pat's office, and June took pride in decorating it in warm colors, with comfortable furniture and many pillows. He used to tease her about that, because he thought there were too many pillows. Later, it was more like complaining or criticizing, and she responded angrily, telling him to decorate the house himself.

Though there was a reason for their irritation—they were both under pressure. They hadn't ever discussed, or planned for, the changes in their careers that might be needed after starting a family—neither the adjustments Pat might need to make in his work hours nor the impacts on June of taking time off from her teaching career.

After Billy was born, June and Pat argued about the hours Pat spent working, especially on Saturday mornings. Pat relished this time alone at the office to complete things interrupted during the previous week and get organized for the coming week. He was motivated by the possibility of being promoted to Gary's director position after Gary retired. To June, Saturday mornings were a priority for the family to be together, calmly begin the weekend, and appreciate time with each other.

One Saturday, June suggested they take Billy to the petting zoo. Pat said he had to work a couple of hours on an important proposal for the county board and asked if they could go to the zoo in the afternoon. June already had plans to see the neighbor's new baby in the afternoon. Pat said he was sorry, but he needed to finish the proposal and promised to make time the following Saturday.

June was silent, her eyes half-closed. She walked to the kitchen sink, staring out the window as she drank a glass of water. She turned back to Pat, her body looking tense as she prepared to speak. "That's not good enough," she said, her eyes flashing. "It's always something with you. I'm getting tired of this constant battle for your precious time."

Pat backed up slightly, his breaths becoming shorter. "I have a chance to get promoted," he said. "That would be good for us—we could afford a bigger house. Set up the college fund for Billy that we keep talking about."

"That's bullshit! You're working hard to satisfy your ego and have your father see you as one of the great successes of his life."

Pat's face warmed. He stared at her, his lips pressed together. "You think you care about this family, but you can't even support my work for us." He turned and walked out, slamming the door behind him.

Pat grew wary, feeling his attempts to lessen the distance between them just turned into arguments. They tried counseling, but after Pat's promotion, the pressure of his new job and their constant arguments were too much for June. Pat moved to an apartment nearby, agreeing to end their marriage. They decided on joint custody in their divorce, both wanting to do what was best for Billy.

June eventually remarried, to a fellow schoolteacher who was a quiet, slight man with a scholarly demeanor. He was sensitive to the importance of Pat in Billy's life, which Pat appreciated, and June mellowed when he was present. They now owned houses not far from each other, and Billy switched homes each week. Pat realized he had become the involved father June had always wanted him to be, although it was without her.

Pat started his research on Monday morning. He stopped by the property records office and asked the clerk for the strip mall property file. She seemed to think nothing of his request, given the county's plans for the property. She checked the file out to Pat and offered him a conference room to review it. Recent additions to the file immediately intrigued him. They included an appraisal of the land, anticipating the county's purchase, and transaction papers that showed the property had recently changed hands. The new owner was Doug Kern of Kern Development, who had paid the previous owner an amount equal to the county's appraised value of the land.

Pat stared at the file, trying to make sense of this new information. Clearly, Kern might benefit when the county purchased the land from him. At the minimum, he would break even, assuming he couldn't negotiate a price above the county's appraised value, but that value could increase depending on timing. Kern's touching base with Jones made sense to Pat because Kern was now involved in the county's plans. But Pat couldn't figure out why Jones wanted the county's purchase and development process simplified, and what role Eastman would play.

Pat decided to update Gary. When he told him that Kern was the new strip mall property owner, Gary became silent and then suggested they meet privately at his house the following morning.

Pat drove by the strip mall property on his way to Gary's. Only a few shops remained open in the mall; most of the space was abandoned. The parking lot looked larger than he remembered. He envisioned athletic fields for children, their green grass replacing the deteriorating blacktop pavement and its oily smell. Students from the nearby middle school would be able to reach the new fields with an easy walk on residential streets. He could imagine the part of the property devoted to housing, too, aimed at low- and middle-income families. This project benefited the county, and Pat was proud of his staff who had planned it. He wanted to make it happen without corrupt politics getting in the way.

After serving Pat coffee in his kitchen, Gary shared his thoughts. He didn't know why Jones would want to simplify the purchase and development of the property. Still, he could see Jones asking Eastman to help him, since Eastman was most likely lobbying Jones for the administrator position. Eastman probably had jumped at the opportunity to pledge to help Jones if he were administrator. But Gary wondered what motivated Jones to push for a process without bids.

"Kern owns the property now," Pat said. "The county board voted that the owner will have to sell it to the county at its appraised value."

"So Kern probably will benefit when the county buys the land," Gary said.

"Yeah. The file showed that the property has already been appraised, so he knows the minimum he'll be paid if he can't negotiate more. There's nothing wrong with that."

Gary looked down for a few seconds and then raised his head. "Once the county owns the land, the plan is for the county to keep its ownership of half of the land for recreational fields and sell the other half to a developer for housing development, right?"

Pat nodded, beginning to smile. "You're thinking that Kern could be positioning himself to be that developer."

"Right," Gary said. "He could make the case that the county wouldn't need to buy the housing half of the property from him—the board could just let him develop it instead. That could be much more profitable for Kern than selling the property to the county. Millions of dollars might be at stake."

Gary got up and brought the coffee pot over to the table to refill Pat's cup. Pat took a sip, thinking about Gary's words.

"But the county board approved the purchase of the entire piece of land, not just half," Pat said. "And our policy is to require a request for proposals for developing public land owned by the county. Other developers would be expecting an RFP. How would Kern get around these plans?"

"Chairman Jones wields a lot of power on the board," Gary said. "If Eastman were county administrator, he could join Jones in convincing board members to reverse their vote and let Kern develop the land instead of going through a drawn-out bidding process, even though it might risk a lawsuit from other developers. They could argue that this approach would be more efficient. It would not only be simplified by removing the requirement for bids—it wouldn't even require the housing half of the land to be sold. That would make housing available sooner."

"Kern must be doing a favor for Jones to have Jones support this plan," Pat said. "Maybe he's contributing to Jones's election campaign."

"That seems too simple. Jones should be able to get that without the risk of being criticized for meddling in a government transaction," Gary said. "I don't know why Jones wants to help Kern, but we now know why Kern wants Eastman to be administrator, once he learned that Eastman is eager to help Jones simplify things."

Pat smiled. "You're pretty sharp for a retiree," he said, causing Gary to nod and smile. "So, we understand what motivates Kern and Eastman.

But we don't know why Jones wants to help Kern. And I don't know what to do about it."

"I don't know either," Gary said, his smile disappearing. "But I do know that you could be in a dangerous position. If Jones sees you as a barrier to this deal, you definitely won't be the administrator—Eastman will. And you may find yourself looking for a new job."

Pat spent the rest of the day thinking about what he had learned from Gary, while focusing on routine work at his desk. He didn't know Chairman Jones well, only interacting with him when he made county planning presentations. Still, at a recent board meeting, he had witnessed Jones give a public tongue-lashing to a human services manager. She had overestimated the social services budget the county was projected to receive from the state, resulting in a shortfall of county funds.

Jones had glared at the manager as she finished her report. In his sixties with a graying mustache and a thick torso, Jones often waved his long arms to help make his point. He was an imposing figure behind the boardroom table, looking bigger sitting than standing.

Jones asked the human services manager how she expected to make up the shortfall. Without letting her answer, he asked her what programs to cut, how much of a tax increase would be needed, and why these services were even necessary for a county where people shouldn't need public support. When she tried to answer, Jones interrupted her, flailing his arms and making the point that county commissioners would feel the consequences of her error from the voters. He stressed that he hoped this would never happen again, and dismissed her after she apologized. Pat and probably everyone in the room had been glad to see her finally escape his wrath.

Pat put himself in the human services manager's place. How would he react if he were attacked by this formidable man? He was already anxious about confronting Eastman. If he were forced to deal with them together, he would go against two powerful and shrewd people. Would he have the confidence and skill to overcome them?

———•••———

Pat picked up Billy at after-school care. Pat was always excited to reach the day of the week when June's custody of Billy ended and his began. He sensed that Billy was excited as well. The snow had melted, and they took Billy's football to the backyard after supper.

"Dad, throw me the ball!" Billy shouted, starting to run.

"Keep running, and we'll see if you can catch a touchdown pass."

Billy ran diagonally toward the backyard corner, and Pat threw a pass that Billy caught over his shoulder.

"Touchdown!" they both yelled. Billy threw the ball back and then ran to Pat, leaping to give him a high five. Pat was thrilled at Billy's athletic ability and enthusiasm, which he also had seen in Billy's soccer games. He made sure to only watch and cheer, though, holding to his goal of letting Billy explore sports without any pressure.

It was good to clear his mind, but after Billy went to bed, thoughts of the conversation with Gary and the corrupt politics in the county crept back in. He had followed Gary's footsteps in helping create a great county organization, which others, like Mary Beth, valued and held to high standards. He couldn't let the organization be tarnished by closed-door, unethical manipulations like those Jones, Eastman, and Kern seemed to be conducting.

Pat needed to take action—no action would lead to Eastman becoming administrator. Pat would lose their fight, with consequences that could hurt his career. The county would also lose, led by unethical leaders whose goals were for private gain instead of public services to improve the lives of taxpaying citizens.

When Pat woke the following morning, he was committed to doing what he needed to do—ready to go to battle and fight for himself and the county.

5

The administrator interviews were two weeks away. Pat wasn't sure how to stop Eastman from being selected, but his first step was to talk to Mary Beth. She motioned for him to come into her office while she finished a phone call. Pat noticed a family picture on her desk showing her standing beside her husband—a tall man with a friendly smile—behind their two kids.

Pat told Mary Beth the information he'd found: Kern Development had recently bought the strip mall property, and Doug Kern had lobbied for Eastman to be administrator in a meeting with Chairman Jones.

"That sounds fishy to me," Mary Beth said. "I'm curious, but I need to be careful."

"I understand; I'm not asking you to do anything. But it would help to bounce some ideas off you."

"Okay. Just remember that Jones can be vindictive. With my husband's reduced hours, I can't risk losing my job."

Pat nodded. He shared with her his thinking that Kern probably wanted to develop the property half designated for housing, and would likely prefer to do this without going through a bidding process. Pat also told her that Jones might have connected Kern to Eastman, because if appointed administrator, Eastman could help waive the bidding process.

"No wonder they don't want you to be administrator," Mary Beth said. "But why is Jones willing to help Kern? Why's he offering East-man to help Kern get what he wants?"

"That's the big question. I'm going to try to find the answer."

"Are you sure you want to do that? Jones is powerful—you could be risking your job."

"I guess so. But it's a risk I have to take. I love working for this county," Pat said, looking up again at Mary Beth's family photo. "I don't want to see jerks take it into the gutter."

"Okay. I'll keep my ear to the ground. There's not much else I can do," Mary Beth said.

"What about the other commissioners? Would any of them go against Jones if they knew what was happening?"

"Jones controls most of them, but he's often at odds with John Larsen. They're the two longest-serving commissioners. I don't know how you'd want to approach Larsen, but I have tremendous respect for him."

Pat remembered Gary calling John Larsen a stand-up guy. "I'll ask to meet with him. And I'll keep you posted."

"Good. But if Jones learned I advised you to see Larsen, it would only take him a few seconds to boot me out the door. And Larsen wouldn't be able to stop him."

Pat walked to the elevator. Mary Beth had confirmed the danger of his involvement. She was right that he was risking his job, which could also put Billy at risk if he couldn't support him at his current level. He thought about what that would look like, if he had to cut Billy's summer camps, or ask June to spot him. There was the mort-gage on the house too. He got off the elevator deep in thought, not seeing one of his planners enter until the planner said good morning. He looked up, feeling determined.

The next day, Pat scheduled a short phone call with Commissioner John Larsen. Larsen was quiet when Pat asked to meet with him about a confidential matter.

"I hope this isn't lobbying for the administrator position, as Jack Eastman has been doing," Larsen said.

"No. It's about the strip mall property. I'm concerned about the county's purchase of it and would like to meet somewhere other than your office, if possible."

After a long silence, Larsen asked Pat to meet him for breakfast at a restaurant near his home.

That afternoon, Pat looked up Larsen's bio, which was used in county publications. Larsen had received an engineering degree with support from the U.S. Navy and served his required four years of active duty on a submarine. He entered seminary school, but his active involvement as a volunteer in Big Brothers and food shelf programs influenced him to leave the seminary and take a position with the county's United Way chapter, where he rose to the executive level. He ran for county commissioner and was elected to his first term ten years ago. Pat was impressed.

The next morning, Pat arrived at the restaurant ten minutes early, thinking of what he would reveal to Larsen, and how Larsen might react.

When Larsen sat down, a waitress greeted him like a regular and brought him a caffe latte, filling their booth with a pleasant aroma. A fit man, probably in his mid-fifties, Larsen ordered granola, fruit, and yogurt. He wore his hair short combed to the side, with dark-rimmed glasses and a starched button-down shirt. "Okay. What's on your mind?" Larsen asked, sitting very still and looking calmly into Pat's eyes, while folding his hands on the table.

Pat sat up straight, feeling under Larsen's command, and took the plunge. "Commissioner, I think that Chairman Jones, Doug Kern, and Jack Eastman have plans to manipulate the county's purchase of the strip mall property for some hidden benefit."

Larsen's eyes widened. "That's a serious accusation. What evidence do you have?"

He hadn't expected such a strong first reaction from Larsen. Pat swallowed hard and concentrated on giving his answers slowly and clearly. He told Larsen that Kern Development had recently bought the property and that Chairman Jones was asking Eastman to help him simplify the county's purchase and development. He said he also had heard that Doug Kern was lobbying for Eastman to be appointed administrator.

"How did you find out about this?"

"I decided to investigate when I heard stories that Eastman was bad-mouthing me to Chairman Jones and others."

"That isn't shocking," Larsen said. "People like Jones and Eastman who want something can be jerks. But do you know for a fact that Jones asked Eastman to help Kern on the property development? What's your source for that information?"

"I'm keeping that confidential," Pat said. "I've got a lot of friends at the county."

"I know you do. Sam Harris told me you're one of our best managers, and the board respects you. So, what do you think Kern is trying to get out of this?"

Pat didn't expect this praise and stumbled for a second before answering. "I don't have proof, but my guess is that he wants to be the developer of the housing half of the property, and doesn't want to go through a bidding process."

"That makes sense, given the potential profit," Larsen said. "Again, though, this isn't shocking. His purchase of the property was shrewd. How is Jones involved?"

"Jones, with Eastman's help if he was administrator, could influence the board to reverse its vote that requires the county to buy the entire piece of property. If so, Kern would keep his half for housing and have his company develop it, avoiding the bidding process," Pat said. "But I don't know why Jones would want to do that favor for Kern. It makes me suspect that someone behind the scenes might benefit."

Larsen took a deep drink of his coffee. "If that's what Jones wants to do, it does raise ethical and legal questions. By waiving the bidding process, the county would forego the opportunity to have another developer buy and develop the land at a lower price, saving taxpayers money. If Kern's housing development results in some financial benefit to Jones or someone associated with Jones, that would be a conflict of interest. You would have a board chairman voting for a transaction that benefits him personally."

Pat nodded. "That's what I've been thinking."

Larsen was silent, looking at people being seated. He turned to Pat. "This is risky business, but you might be on to something. Why don't you continue your quiet investigation, especially on who will benefit if Kern develops the property. I'm going to have a talk with Jones. Then let's meet here again next week."

"Sounds good," Pat said, getting up and following Larsen out. He felt both energized and anxious, realizing how deeply involved he was getting in county politics.

Before Larsen got to his car, he turned to Pat abruptly and said, "So, you're eager to be administrator."

"Yes, sir. I want to help the board develop a new vision for our county." He didn't know why he added "sir" to his answer, but Larsen seemed satisfied.

"Okay, good. Let's go to work. And call me John."

After Larsen drove away, Pat sat in his car momentarily, glad to have gained a strong ally in his battle against Eastman.

Pat finished work on Friday and drove home, deciding to stay late Monday afternoon to look in the county files for answers to Larsen's questions. He was glad to be in his house after such an eventful week.

He loved his prairie-style house built in the 1920s, a small but roomy two-story home perfect for Billy and him. On Saturday, he cleaned his yard and prepared it for winter before it snowed again. He was excited to see Billy's last soccer game of the season on Sunday, which June would bring Billy to since he was with her that weekend.

When Pat arrived at the game, June greeted him, asking how he was doing. Pat tried to return her friendliness. He couldn't tell if she was still angry over him not letting Billy go to the birthday party. But Billy interrupted their conversation when he yelled, "Dad!" from his position on the field—the game was starting and he was letting Pat know that he should be watching him. Pat, June, and her husband stood on the sideline, all cheering for Billy as he ran down the field, kicking the ball ahead of him.

After the game, Pat joined the other parents in taking the boys to a restaurant for pizza, where Billy wanted his family to sit together at the same table. Pat was fortunate to be near another father he could converse with, reducing his awkwardness around June and her husband.

The first year after their divorce had been difficult, with Pat and June arguing almost every time they interacted, despite their pledge to put Billy's needs above their own. They gradually improved their interactions, but June's emotions often surprised Pat. For example, he still didn't know why she had gotten so angry at him about the neighbor's birthday party. She knew Billy was scheduled to be with him on that day.

———•••———

Pat waited until late Monday afternoon for people to leave work before beginning his search for answers to Larsen's questions. He opened the locked door to the county's file room with the master key available to directors and entered the room alone. Row after row of file cabinets stood before him in silence, containing years of information unguarded by file clerks. The light from the windows dimmed rapidly as the evening came.

Pat settled in at a table with a tablet of graph paper and a ruler to help list the details he expected to find. He felt he was at his best in what he needed to do. If there were anything to be found, he would find it.

He thought about Larsen's questions. Who would benefit if Kern developed the housing property? What interest could Jones have in Kern's development? He decided to investigate two possibilities. Maybe Jones owned a part of Kern Development or something related to the strip mall, which would increase in value if Kern were successful. Or perhaps Jones was linked to someone on Kern's team and wanted to benefit that person financially.

Pat checked ownership records to see if Jones had been an owner of a strip mall business, or if he owned a share of Kern Development. He struck out. The sale of the strip mall property to Kern was straightforward; no connected properties or items of value were owned by someone else. The ownership of Kern Development was also clear. It was a privately held company owned by the founder, Doug Kern, and two partners. There were no links to Jones that Pat could see.

He turned to the other possibility—a potential link between Kern's team and Jones. He first looked in county files for projects that Kern Development had led. He found that the firm outsourced several functions to subcontractors. Intrigued, he considered the possibility that Jones might be linked to one or more of these subcontractors.

He began by patiently searching the files to make a list of subcontractors that Kern used for county government projects and then using a matrix chart on his graph paper to assemble the information.

He focused on a small group of subcontractors that seemed to be employed on almost all of Kern's projects, particularly a plumbing company and a heating and cooling company. The ownership records for these companies didn't show evidence that Jones owned any part of them. He next thought about a potential family connection between Jones and one of the companies. Mary Beth came to mind; she most likely knew about Jones's family.

Pat called Mary Beth, surprising her at home. He explained that, at Larsen's request, he was investigating potential links of Jones to Kern Development. She said she didn't know of any family connections, but she did know that Jones had two daughters, one a single music teacher and the other a stay-at-home mom with two kids. Pat asked if she knew the last name of the married daughter. Mary Beth said the daughter was in her second marriage—she believed to an engineer with a last name similar to "Isaacs."

"Thanks. This is really helpful," Pat said.

Mary Beth was silent. Pat waited, but she didn't respond. "Are you okay?" he asked.

"Look, I believe in what you and John Larsen are doing," she said, "but it makes me very nervous."

"Mary Beth, I won't say a word to anyone about your helping me."

"I hope not."

"I won't, but you should feel good that you're helping stop corruption in the county."

Pat again checked the ownership records, this time looking for someone named Isaacs. No one with that name was listed for the plumbing company, but he found that a mechanical engineer named Jerry Isaacson was one of the heating and cooling company partners. He then searched marriage records and found that Isaacson had married the daughter of William Jones, the current county board chairman, four years ago. Pat looked up from the table and smiled to himself.

He had found what he was looking for—a conflict of interest for Chairman Jones. He now knew why Jones wanted Eastman to help simplify the purchase and development of the property. If Jones and Eastman could influence the county board to remove the requirement for a bidding process, Kern would be guaranteed to develop the housing. If Kern, as usual, contracted with his favorite heating and cooling company, then Jones's son-in-law and daughter would benefit financially. Jones, one of the board members voting to approve this project, would have an obvious conflict of interest. Pat couldn't wait to tell John Larsen.

———•••———

When Larsen and Pat sat down for breakfast two days later, Larsen quickly got down to business.

"Pat, your quiet research is no longer quiet. Eastman saw your name on the checkout list for the strip mall file, and Jones is angry that you seem to be getting involved in something that's none of your business."

"That's not nearly as damaging as what I've found," Pat said.

"I'm eager to hear it. But first, you should know that Eastman has drawn up a new org chart for Jones that merges your office with others. It eliminates your position. Jones is already selling it to me, to be implemented once Eastman becomes administrator. They want you out."

Pat was silent, staring at Larsen and remembering Mary Beth's words about his job being at risk. He didn't know what to say.

"This came up without me mentioning you," Larsen said. "I told Jones I'd heard Kern bought the property and asked him about the county's strategy. He put a full-court press on me about how we didn't need a bidding process with Kern already owning the land, and we could have housing available sooner than we thought. He plans to talk to other commissioners about it."

Pat sat stock-still, his fists balled at his side beneath the booth's table, thinking about Larsen's news about the elimination of his position.

"Jones also spoke highly of Jack Eastman, saying that Eastman had his vote for administrator," Larsen said. "He didn't think you and Eastman would work well together, especially since you seemed to be meddling in the strip mall project. That's when he showed me Eastman's revised org chart—your planning director box was gone."

Pat sat back in his chair, feeling that Eastman had hit him in the head with a roundhouse punch, striking him before he had a chance to punch first. He closed his eyes momentarily.

Larsen leaned forward. "Come on—this isn't the end of the world. What did you find?"

Pat told Larsen about his discovery that Jones's son-in-law was a partner in the heating and cooling firm used frequently by Kern Development. If Kern was selected by the county board to develop the housing—with Jones joining other board members to vote his approval—and if Kern subcontracted with Jones's son-in-law's firm, Jones would have a clear conflict of interest.

Larsen stroked his chin and looked at Pat for several seconds, his eyes narrowed, with a slight smile. "I've suspected things like this for years, but this is the first real evidence I've had. I'm inclined to go public with this. I'll be sure to keep your name out of it."

"What do you think will happen?" Pat asked.

"The press loves scandals, so I'll make sure it gets their attention. Once it's in the news, I'll bring it up in a board meeting, depending on what Jones does. I'm sure he'll try to ride it out as if nothing happened."

"Will he be able to do that?"

"Not if I can help it. I'll demand an investigation. My goal is for Jones to resign."

Pat nodded, glad to hear that resignation was Larsen's goal. If Jones resigned, Eastman would lose power and have a much lesser chance of becoming administrator. Pat knew he should control his expectations, but he had hope again. The fight with Eastman was not over.

6

Pat pictured Eastman's new organization chart as he drove to the office after breakfast with Larsen. Eliminating Pat's position was a shrewd move, demonstrating again that Pat had underestimated his adversary. But Pat had succeeded in his research into Jones's conflict of interest. He decided to conduct similar research to learn more about Eastman. He began by reviewing Eastman's position description and bio.

In charge of the county's financial operations, Eastman had a sensitive position. He was a critical resource for the county administrator and board in developing the annual county budget, using revenue forecasts and expense estimates. He helped the board answer the publicly visible question of what level of tax increase might be needed each year.

From Eastman's bio, Pat found he'd been responsible for similar functions in other local governments, most recently as a city manager in Ohio. Eastman also had experience working for consulting companies in public finance, often moving back and forth between public and private organizations.

Pat's interest grew when he found that Eastman had been active in the Ohio chapter of the city and county management association, similar to Pat's involvement in the Illinois chapter. Pat looked up the current officers of the Ohio association and found a good friend of his, Denny, listed on its executive committee.

Denny previously worked in Illinois, and he and Pat had become close through association activities, often having dinner and drinks together. They would try to outdo each other with stories about politicians and others who disrupted their work. Pat often gave up, laughing at Denny's entertaining descriptions of outrageous examples.

Pat called Denny and told him that Eastman and he were competing for the administrator position, asking what he knew about him.

"You're in for quite a ride," Denny said. "You may want to get yourself a bulletproof vest."

"So, you've seen him in action."

"I'm not a fan of Jack Eastman. I watched him climb to the presidency of our Ohio chapter. It wasn't pretty. Think of the worst politician you've dealt with—boastful, untrustworthy, and manipulative."

Pat grimaced into the phone, not liking what he was hearing, even though he knew it was true. "He's been smearing me to our county commissioners."

"Not surprising. Eastman moved up in our chapter on the coattails of the previous president, criticizing his competitors and making himself indispensable. A lot of the members thought he was an arrogant jerk. Including me."

"What about his success in his city and county jobs?" Pat asked.

"He's a local government financial genius, and elected boards depend on him. But I've heard he's secretive, with no support base among the staff, so a new election or leadership turnover often results in his job-hopping."

"I guess I have my hands full competing with him."

"Yeah, I wish you luck."

Pat was about to hang up, but Denny cleared his throat, seeming to have more to say. "You know, Eastman has another side," he said. "His son is autistic. The governor asked Eastman to chair a task force to recommend new state education policies for autistic children.

Eastman's arrogance, in that case, probably helped make a positive impact with the legislation that passed."

Pat remembered Eastman's son looking at the ground while standing behind Eastman at the county picnic. Although Denny's news of Eastman's leadership in helping autistic children helped Pat see a positive side of Eastman, it didn't soften his view of him—he was still the man trying to get him fired.

The conversation with Denny rounded out Pat's views of Eastman. Knowing the strengths of his opponent was oddly motivating.

———••———

When Pat retrieved the newspaper from his porch the following day, his eyes were immediately drawn to a short article on the front page with the headline "Chairman's Votes Benefit Son-in-Law." He brought the paper into his kitchen and sat at the small table near the window where he and Billy ate most of their meals. A cardinal in the oak tree next to the house sang its morning wake-up call as Pat opened the paper to read the full article.

The reporter described Chairman Jones's item on next Tuesday's board meeting agenda, which proposed allowing Kern Development to begin work on the housing half of the strip mall property without a request for bids. The story claimed that a board approval to waive the bidding process could benefit Chairman Jones's son-in-law, Jerry Isaacson, a Kern subcontractor. The story also included three past county projects led by Kern Development that had used the same subcontractor. The reporter closed with a quote from Commissioner Larsen, who said he'd like a full airing of this potential conflict of interest at the board meeting on Tuesday.

Pat smiled, shaking his head in admiration of Larsen. What Larsen had predicted was coming true. He hoped it led to what he and Larsen wanted—the resignation of Chairman Jones.

Pat had a voicemail message from Mary Beth when he arrived at work. She was home with a sick child but wanted Pat to call her immediately.

"This newspaper story is incredible!" Mary Beth said. "Did you leak information to the press?"

"No, but I informed John Larsen of the connection between Kern and Jones's son-in-law. Larsen seems to be moving quickly."

"Impressive. I didn't think you would find anything, although I know Larsen has been suspicious. But you can't count Jones out. He is a master of getting votes from the other commissioners to support him."

"We'll see how Larsen does. I understand why you respect him."

"I'm rooting for him," Mary Beth said. "Larsen might be able to put enough pressure on Jones for him to resign. But Jones will probably give in on the bidding process and try to have this all blow over." Pat remembered Larsen saying that Jones would probably try to act as if nothing had happened.

"I hope not, but I understand what you mean by Jones's vindictiveness," Pat said. "He showed Larsen a new org chart prepared by Eastman that eliminates my job."

Mary Beth was silent. "You're really on thin ice," she said. "I'm glad you're working with Larsen and hope the two of you have a good ending. By the way, Kathy, the chairman's secretary, wants to meet with me tomorrow morning."

"Do you know why?"

"No, but I wanted to alert you. Maybe there will be another surprise."

At this point, Pat thought nothing could surprise him. But that afternoon, two of his best employees stopped by to discuss the newspaper article. They didn't think much of Chairman Jones and hoped this news might result in a change of county leadership. They also told Pat they hoped he would be selected as county administrator.

Pat didn't expect this. He knew he was a competent leader; he needed to be to accomplish the work he cared about so much. But he was surprised to hear this praise, similar to how he felt when Larsen told him he was one of the county's best managers.

———•••———

Mary Beth came to Pat's office before lunch the following day and closed the door. "I met with Kathy this morning. She's upset, but I can't really talk about it. Bottom line, she's hoping the news in the paper about Jones might result in him leaving."

"Why can't you talk about it?"

Mary Beth frowned, looking away from Pat. "She has to be the one to tell people. I made that clear to her, and she agreed. So far, I'm the only person she trusts."

"You've said that Jones may survive. What would Kathy do in that case?"

"I'm not sure. She wants my help in finding another job in the county. But all I can really do is help her look for job postings and be a good reference. Do you have any thoughts?"

"If I weren't in such a precarious position, I might be able to help her find another job," Pat said. "I'd be glad to talk to her if that would be helpful."

"That's generous. I'll tell her. If you met with her, you wouldn't want Jones to know about it. Neither would she. I'll see what she thinks."

Pat valued county employees and their development, so it was easy for him to offer to help Kathy. But he also sensed that something significant had happened. He wondered if he might learn from Kathy what upset her.

———•••———

Pat was glad he had Billy the weekend before the Tuesday board meeting, where he imagined the clash between Jones and Larsen might determine his future. He filled the weekend with activities with his son, distancing himself from those thoughts. He took Billy to the Friday night high school football game, and they stood and cheered in the crisp air when their home team won. The next day, Pat asked Billy to help him rake leaves on their lawn. He created a high pile of leaves that he fell into, attracting the attention of the younger boy next door. The two of them ran and rolled through the leaves, then rebuilt the pile for their next turn.

On Sunday, Pat drove Billy to see the eagles at the river dam. Several eagles sat high on leafless branches in the trees along the riverbank, dark shapes silhouetted against the sky. Pat and Billy waited for one to fly down to the water to catch a fish. A soaring eagle suddenly dropped in front of them to the water below the bridge where they stood, talons extended at the last second to spear and grip a large fish. The eagle flapped its wings rapidly, straining to lift the fish into the air. It struggled, flying for several seconds just above the river's surface, until it finally ascended, taking the fish to its nest in the highest fork of a tall tree.

Billy turned to his dad, wide-eyed. "Wow!" he exclaimed. Pat smiled and leaned down to hug him, thrilled like Billy to watch this majestic bird capture fish to stay alive.

7

The seven county commissioners sat in a semicircle in the front of the room at the county board meeting, with Chairman Jones in the middle. The newspaper article had created interest in the meeting, attracting a larger crowd than usual. Unlike at most of the board meetings, a television crew was set up in the hall outside of the boardroom for interviews after the meeting. Two newspaper reporters sat in the second row with pens in their hands and clipboards perched on their knees. A steady hum of conversation filled the room.

When Pat walked down the side aisle to his chair, he noticed Eastman and his heart rate quickened. Eastman was already sitting, and he had found a seat near the center aisle, in full view of Chairman Jones. He turned his head to watch Pat sit on the side of the room, and their eyes locked momentarily. Eastman quickly looked down at his agenda while Pat, his jaw clenched, stared fiercely at him. This was his enemy, and Pat took the measure of him. He felt superior when Eastman lowered his eyes, but it was of little comfort—he knew Eastman's threat was not in a direct confrontation but in what he did behind the scenes.

Board staff introduced each item on the agenda, and Chairman Jones either asked for discussion or a motion and vote. Several routine items were approved unanimously by board members. When they got to the agenda item about waiving the need for bids for the strip mall property development, Chairman Jones moved approval. Another commissioner seconded the motion, and Jones asked if there was any discussion.

"Mr. Chairman, I believe that waiving the bidding is inappropriate in light of the recent newspaper story," Commissioner Larsen said.

"Commissioner Larsen, that story is way off base," Jones said in a deep voice. "It's ludicrous to think I'm trying to benefit my son-in-law. But we can return to the original plan of getting bids if that makes you feel better. It's just going to delay having housing available for our county."

Larsen suggested that the chairman amend his motion to direct staff to conduct a bidding process as originally planned. Jones offered the amendment, and the motion passed unanimously. Pat thought of Mary Beth's prediction that Jones would give in on the bidding process.

Larsen then made his own motion, proposing that the board ask the county auditor to investigate past county projects involving Kern Development, to determine if there were any conflicts of interest.

"That's completely unnecessary, a waste of time," Jones said, raising his right arm as if to wave Larsen's idea away. But the motion was seconded by Commissioner Sally Rogers. In the discussion, two board members who were long-time Jones allies agreed that an audit was unnecessary. But they lost. The motion passed four votes to three.

Larsen kept the floor, informing the board that the newspaper had requested all public records for county construction projects over the past five years. Jones scowled as Commissioner Rogers said, "We need to get a handle on this."

Larsen proposed one more action. He moved that the board postpone its interviews for county administrator until it heard the auditor's findings. Jones, throwing both hands into the air, stated that this wasn't necessary either, but this motion also passed four votes to three.

After addressing a few more routine actions, the board adjourned the meeting. Both Jones and Larsen were approached by reporters wanting interviews, accompanied by TV camera crews. Pat tried to stand inconspicuously near them so that he could listen. He noticed Mary Beth looking at him with interest. Pat moved closer, wanting to hear as much as possible.

Jones downplayed the board meeting, saying any issues were minor. He was okay with going back to a bidding process. He had just tried to shorten the time to build the housing. He knew young county families were waiting for the affordable housing planned to be part of the development.

Larsen reinforced the importance of the audit in determining whether there were any conflicts of interest in county-funded projects. He wanted to ensure that public funds from county taxpayers were being invested in a fair and transparent way, without having even the appearance of manipulation for someone's benefit.

The staff, community members, and others in the audience exited the room. The lines of people in the aisles converged, and Pat found himself standing next to Eastman, who stared at Pat angrily. "Bastard," he muttered. Pat stared at him with half-closed eyes and said, "That's just the beginning," surprising himself with an animosity he had never felt at work. But he did not feel triumphant. As Mary Beth said, Jones wasn't planning to go anywhere.

Pat shut the door to his office and walked to the window, thinking about Jones's performance at the board meeting. Although Larsen was effective with his motions to keep the bidding process, initiate an audit, and postpone the selection of a new administrator, Jones's bluster dominated the meeting and press interviews. Pat hoped the audits Larsen had requested would lead to Jones's resignation. But, after watching Jones's performance, Pat was afraid that he might survive, which meant that Eastman would win and Pat would lose.

He'd been naïve, believing commitment, professionalism, and hard work would lead to advancement. What would he do if he lost his job? Pat imagined how his staff, friends, and family, especially his father, might react. His insecurity reminded him again of high school, where he had succeeded with good grades, but lacked the confidence of leaders like Dave.

He turned from the window to look at his office—a generous space that included two easy chairs and a coffee table on one side and his desk and bookshelves on the other. He loved the comfort of this room in which he had spent so many hours leading efforts to improve the county. He hated the possibility of losing this home base.

Even if he found a well-paying job, possibly for a developer or consulting company, his reputation would take a hit. People close to him would conclude that he had failed at the county, the organization they knew he loved. The loss of his public sector role could also hinder his chances for future positions in serving the public, the purpose that had motivated him in his career.

Maybe more than anything, he again feared how losing his job might affect Billy. What if he couldn't afford his home because he was suddenly out of work or forced to take a new job at a lower salary? If he had to move into a small apartment, would June push to increase her time with Billy?

When Pat awoke the following morning after a restless night of sleep, his thoughts returned to the meeting. He grew angry at the possibility that Jones and Eastman might win; he'd had enough of their deception and aggression. And Jones's holier-than-thou claim that he wanted to waive the bidding so that young families could get into affordable housing earlier . . . it disgusted him. Pat clenched his jaw and rolled back his shoulders, like a Marine pictured on a recruitment poster, reminding him of Dave, a Marine professional warrior.

In his junior year of high school, Pat made the varsity wrestling team. His first match was against a wrestler from Kennedy High in the Kennedy gym. His parents were there, seated with Central High fans. He could tell his father was proud of him, although his words of praise were limited. His mother's main concern was that he not get hurt. The Kennedy fans sat across from them, including students rooting loudly for his opponent.

Pat wrestled well, taking down the other wrestler in the first period and reversing him in the second, leading 4–0. His confidence soaring, he attempted to pin the wrestler in the third period, exerting himself as he tried several holds. But Pat became winded and off-balance as he tried to cradle the wrestler and move him on his back. He was too high on the wrestler's body, losing his leverage. The wrestler countered, flipping Pat on his back. Pat squirmed while the wrestler pressed his shoulders flat. The referee slapped the mat, signaling that Pat had been pinned. The Kennedy students exploded, their cheers and taunts deafening.

Pat walked off the mat, and his coach shook his head. "I hope you learned your lesson, Stevens. Next time just ride him out." Central fans were quiet as the Kennedy students continued to cheer. Pat glanced into the stands, but his parents had left.

That night, his father said nothing about the wrestling match. Pat went to bed early. He knew he might lose some future matches, but he silently pledged to never embarrass himself again.

On his drive to work, Pat thought of his days of working for Gary, a simpler time when his goals were clear and he could proceed in a planned way to attain them. He had often thought Gary's focus on political intrigue involving county commissioners was a distraction and waste of time. Now Pat was aware of how important that had been for Gary's survival, and for keeping Pat and other staff free from barriers that would hinder their work. He called Gary that morning and described what had happened at the board meeting.

"Pat, I wish I was there to help you," Gary said. "I know I advised you to keep your powder dry. It's time now to get out your gun. You need to protect yourself and help Larsen, God bless him."

Gary's counsel was good for Pat. It framed the conflict—a fight of good versus evil, like his favorite western movies. And it calmed Pat's anger, replacing it with a cold determination. He readied himself for the next stage of the battle.

8

Kathy was already sitting in a booth when Pat arrived for breakfast. She'd chosen a pancake house restaurant, busy with truck drivers and road workers eating Denver omelets and short stacks. A young mother who sat nearby treated her two children with blueberry pancakes topped with syrup and whipped cream.

Pat looked across the table at Kathy with curiosity. She had only ordered a cup of tea. In her mid-thirties, she was a small woman with brown hair swept behind her ears, wearing a red-and-white sweater that reminded him of cheerleaders' sweaters in high school. Her attentive eyes worked to connect with him. She seemed ready to show her loyalty to him and the team, but he wasn't sure what she wanted from him.

She thanked him for meeting, looking down occasionally, with her sentences losing steam before ending. She described her interest in changing jobs, but he sensed that she had more she wanted to say.

"I'm looking for a new job because I'm uncomfortable around Chairman Jones," she said.

"Why?"

Kathy hesitated, lowering her eyes. "Mary Beth said you would understand."

"What makes you uncomfortable?"

She hesitated again. "He touches my arm and back and keeps inviting me to have a drink with him."

Pat became alert and studied her face. "That sounds like sexual harassment."

"Maybe. I just want to get away from it."

Pat's mind raced, thinking her information might give him a decisive advantage over Jones, but he knew he needed to be sensitive with her. She was the one directly experiencing this awful thing, not him.

"Have you thought of talking to human resources?" he suggested gently. "They enforce policies against this sort of thing."

Kathy's eyes widened, and her body recoiled into her seat. "No, I'm afraid Chairman Jones would find out. I couldn't be around him if he knew what I was accusing him of," she said.

Pat explained that an investigation by human resources could lead to her being relocated to a new job, which Pat might be able to help her find. She seemed intrigued, but she wanted to keep things quiet, only talking with him and Mary Beth. "I don't know which is worse—having him continue to come on to me, or having him furious because I told someone about it," she said.

Pat told her he would think about a new job and get back to her. When he walked to his car, however, he thought about the opportunity she had presented. If there was a way to use Jones's harassment of Kathy to get him to resign, Pat would win the battle against not only Eastman, but Jones as well. He thought about Kathy's request to keep things quiet, but decided to contact Sam Harris in human resources. He needed to see what was possible.

After scheduling a time to meet with Sam that afternoon, Pat sat quietly in his office, thinking. The possibility of Jones resigning because of his sexual harassment seemed more powerful than using Jones's conflicts of interest, which might take weeks to prove through the audit. His thoughts were interrupted by Mary Beth's arrival. She closed the door and sat down, her face red.

"I just got done meeting with Kathy," Mary Beth said. "She's nervous as hell after her breakfast with you this morning. Are you really going to communicate that she is being sexually harassed?"

"I don't know yet."

"I don't want her to get hurt. She told you she doesn't want it to be public. If Jones gets wind of this, he'll deny it, say it was a misunderstanding, and then get even with those trying to use it."

"I appreciate your concern, but let me figure out what to do. This guy is bad for Kathy, me, and the county."

Mary Beth stared at him for a few seconds, uncharacteristically silent. "Do you really know what you're getting yourself into?"

Pat looked at her, narrowing his eyes, and didn't reply. She got up abruptly and left. He understood her feelings, but it didn't change his view of the opportunity presented by Kathy's news. Mary Beth had been helpful, but, like others, she feared Jones. Pat was heading down a path he hoped would have a good ending. Mary Beth needed to stay out of the way.

Sam Harris welcomed Pat to his office, wearing his usual bow tie and wire-rimmed glasses. Pat was always amazed at how meticulous Sam kept his office, which featured three framed diplomas on the wall behind his desk. Pat knew that what he was going to propose might be difficult for Sam to accept.

"I'd like this discussion to be in strict confidence," Pat said. "We have an employee getting sexually harassed. It's complicated because she doesn't want to take action."

"You know we have an obligation to address those situations," Sam said. "They're unacceptable."

Pat explained that the employee was Kathy, secretary to Chairman Jones, and that Jones had touched her arm and back and invited her for drinks. Sam's face fell, and he shook his head. "What a mess that will be. Any action we take will be picked up by the press."

"Maybe we can avoid that," Pat said. "Kathy doesn't want any publicity. She just wants it to stop."

"What are you suggesting?"

"What's your process if an employee comes to you after being sexually harassed?"

"The employee needs to make a formal complaint to trigger an investigation. It would be kept quiet, but I would have to inform Chairman Jones and Commissioner Sally Rogers, the board's personnel committee chair."

Pat looked at Sam for several seconds. "You know this guy Jones isn't good for the county. I'm going to try and force him out so that you and Kathy won't have to go through that process."

"Are you crazy?" Sam said. "He'll explode! And then he'll call me, telling me to work up a justification for firing you."

"He already wants to fire me. I don't know if you've heard that he and Eastman want to eliminate my position, once Jones gets Eastman appointed administrator."

Sam's jaw dropped. "I haven't heard that."

"I'm banking on Jones not wanting to go through another investigation," Pat said. "The Kern audit is round one of this fight. An investigation of potential sexual harassment would be round two. Don't you think he might want to avoid that, especially if, by resigning, no one would even know about the harassment complaint?"

Sam looked down at his desk and twisted one of the ends of his bow tie. "What if Jones decides to stay and fight both investigations? Would Kathy be willing to file a complaint?"

"I think so. But that's related to another question I have for you. I'd like Kathy to lateral into a vacancy in my department. I'd also like to move her things so that she isn't around Jones after I confront him with her accusation. Can you help arrange for that?"

"I can make that happen, although I don't like it. Jones could complain about her job change without an application process and potentially intervene," Sam said. "But we can do it, and if need be, we can give Kathy some days off. When are you planning to see Jones?"

"I hope to do it this week," Pat said. Sam shook his head and frowned, but Pat was done talking. He thanked Sam and left.

When Pat returned to his office, he felt satisfied that he now had a plan, after struggling over how to counter Eastman and Jones. He had nothing to lose. Without this plan, Jones and Eastman had a good chance of winning, regardless of the Kern audits.

The only thing Pat had left to do was to talk to Kathy.

———•••———

Pat waited until he was home to call Kathy, where there would be no distractions or interruptions. After supper, he went upstairs and sat at his desk in the small third bedroom he'd converted into a study, with pen and paper to take notes.

Kathy picked up the phone after one ring. She was excited to hear that she would be changing jobs, and she was glad that no news would come out about the harassment if the chairman resigned.

"He's going to resign, right?" Kathy asked.

"I can't imagine he would want to go through two investigations, with the press publicizing every step," Pat said. "But we need to be ready if he doesn't resign."

"What would I have to do if he doesn't resign? All of this is giving me a stomachache."

"You'd have to file a complaint with human resources. They would conduct an investigation, and you would need to tell them what Chairman Jones did to you."

Kathy was silent. "I don't know if I could do that," she said.

Pat hesitated, not anticipating her resistance. If he didn't have Kathy prepared to file a complaint, he would lack one of his most powerful cards.

"You would be doing it for other women in the county, as well as for yourself. We can't have these situations happen. You wouldn't want Jones doing this to other women, would you?"

Pat could hear Kathy breathe deeply. "No, but I hope I don't have to file a complaint," she said.

"I think it will all work out," Pat said, ending the call.

But Pat didn't know if it would all work out. For it to stand a chance, though, he knew he needed to succeed in pressuring Jones to resign and winning his battle with Eastman. Yes, Kathy faced some minor potential risks, but without her it was possible he didn't have enough to go on. He needed to act for the good of the county.

Later that afternoon, Pat scheduled a meeting with Jones on Friday at two o'clock and asked the subject be listed as "Kern Development Options," hoping Jones would think he might be trying to help him.

Pat then called Kathy, telling her to plan on taking Friday off so that she wouldn't be present when he met with Jones—and also that Sam Harris would arrange for her to move to her new job. All she said was, "Okay," with a muted voice.

That evening, Pat walked around the block in his neighborhood, only wearing a light jacket. It was a cool November night, with a clear sky full of stars. He smelled smoke from wood burning in a neighbor's fireplace. As he replayed the conversations with Kathy and Sam in his head, the cold breeze knifed into his side, causing his nose and ears to ache. He kept walking, turning at the end of the block, and then feeling the full force of the cold wind blow directly into his face. He squinted, closed his mouth, and moved down the sidewalk, his forehead and cheekbones pushing against the bitter wind step-by-step. By the time he got home and entered his warm house, he felt calm and ready. What would be would be.

———◆◆◆———

Pat arrived at Chairman Jones's office a few minutes before two o'clock. Jones came around the corner with a look of disdain and motioned for Pat to enter his office before him. Jones sat behind a massive oak desk, a barricade against any threats, with the American flag hanging on a pole in the corner of the room.

"So, what do you want, Stevens? What do you mean by Kern Development options? This is a mess, and I think you've played a part in putting me in the crosshairs."

"I agree—it's a mess," Pat said. "And I know how you can fix it."

Jones looked at Pat with a scowl. "You're crazy, and you're wasting my time. You have no idea how this county works."

"I think I do. You need to resign before things really get messy."

"What?" Jones yelled, his face contorted. "Who do you think you are telling me to resign? You're the one who should resign—before you get fired!"

"I want you to hear me out, and then you can decide what you want to do," Pat said. "Your secretary, Kathy, is accusing you of sexual harassment."

Jones stared at Pat. "Are you kidding? If she's told you that, it's a lie."

"She did tell me, and she's ready to go to human resources to file a complaint."

"Let her do it!" Jones shouted. "Nothing ever happened."

"Sam Harris will contract with an equal employment opportunity consultant to determine that," Pat said. "Commissioner Rogers and her personnel committee will provide oversight and recommend actions based on the investigation's findings."

Jones looked down at his desk and shook his large head back and forth. "I need to talk to Kathy. She misinterpreted things, and I owe her an apology. If she files a complaint, the press will turn it into a circus for her, as well as for me."

Pat looked at him quietly. "She doesn't want to talk to you, and Sam is arranging for her to start work in a new position on Monday."

"So, what do you want, and why are you the messenger?" Jones said. "Is this retaliation for me not wanting you to be administrator? I have a family. Are you trying to ruin me?"

"You haven't heard my full message yet," Pat said.

Jones stared hard at him. "Go on."

"If you resign, Kathy won't file a claim, and she, Sam, and I won't tell a soul about your behavior with her. You could say you're resigning because of the Kern audit or whatever reason you come up with."

"This is blackmail!" Jones said. "I think I'll let them go ahead with the investigation. Kathy is probably calling an innocent conversation sexual harassment because you told her it is."

Pat kept looking at Jones, choosing not to respond. "You have the weekend to think this over. If I don't hear from you by noon Monday, Kathy will file her complaint that afternoon, and Sam will inform Commissioner Rogers before Tuesday's board meeting that she has a new agenda item for her personnel committee."

Jones, scowling, breathed deeply in and out and gave Pat a hateful look, probably thinking of ways to destroy him.

Pat stood up. "One more thing. When you resign, I suggest you take Jack Eastman with you. Otherwise, I predict he won't fare well in the Kern Development audit."

Pat felt Jones glaring at him as he left the office. Pat walked through the halls to his office, closed the door, and stood before the window. He stared outside at the traffic, feeling a tight tension in his shoulders. He had just made the most dangerous move of his career. He'd accomplished what he had planned, but he couldn't predict how Jones would react. What happened next could go in several directions, many of which might result in him losing his job. He continued to stare out the window, trying unsuccessfully to lose himself in the flow of the moving cars.

He needed to get back to work; he had a plan to carry out. He called and updated Sam, who had spoken to Kathy and arranged for her to move to a new office. He then called Kathy at home and informed her of his conversation with Jones. She was silent when he described again the two directions in which the situation could go. He assured her that she would have his and Sam's full support if Jones didn't resign and she filed a complaint.

Pat considered calling Larsen and Mary Beth, but he decided against it. He was in this fight with Jones and Eastman alone, and they would hear about it soon enough. He tried to put his anxiety and uncertainty aside and focus on moving forward, one step at a time.

———••———

Pat didn't have Billy that weekend, and he didn't know what to do with himself other than worry about what actions Jones would take. He attended June's church Sunday morning, where Billy sang in the children's choir. Being with Billy grounded him, especially when he was under stress. He didn't attend church regularly, and June was surprised to see him. She and her husband made room for Pat to sit in their pew.

When the church service was over, Billy joined June and her husband. He was surprised to see Pat. Pat hugged him and told him how great the choir sounded. They walked to the parking lot, soaking in the warmth from the bright sun on a chilly day. Pat turned to June.

"How about if I took Billy to lunch? I'll have him home by two o'clock."

The pleasant look on June's face turned into a frown. "You're the one who gets upset when I don't give you advance warning."

"It's just lunch."

"Yeah, like my request to just have him for a birthday party."

Pat turned to watch people exiting the church, listening to children's laughter and their parents' chatter. A weight descended on him.

He was stressed enough by his battles at work; he didn't need to have June's anger directed at him.

"You're impossible," Pat said.

"I'm just never ready for your double standards."

"Right, like you're perfect," Pat said, his raised voice attracting looks from people walking to their cars. "Why don't we ask Billy? Do you want to come to lunch with me, Billy?"

Billy looked at the ground; he then shut his eyes and put his hands over his ears. June's husband gently took her elbow as she stared at Pat with a horrified look. "We need to go," her husband said. He moved June and Billy into their car.

Pat stood still watching them, knowing he had violated an agreement with June to never put Billy in the middle of their arguments. His anger left him, and his eyes watered. He imagined that several church members who had just heard a sermon about peace and love had witnessed their exchange. Pat spent the rest of the day in front of his TV, mindlessly surfing through sports channels, unable to get the picture of Billy covering his ears out of his mind. What a fool he had been.

On Monday morning, Pat cleared staff meetings from his calendar and waited in his office for the call from Chairman Jones. He tried to look at his department's budget reports as he waited, but the numbers began to swim before his eyes, becoming meaningless.

At nine o'clock, Pat received a call from Sam, whose first words were, "Pat, all hell has broken loose!" He told Pat that Jones had just left his office. Earlier that morning, Jones had called Kathy at home and apologized for any misunderstanding. Jones told her it was okay if she wanted a new job, but he wanted to know who she had talked to so that he could clear the air with them. Kathy, probably browbeaten and scared, Sam guessed, had named Pat and Mary Beth.

Using that information, Jones had given Sam two orders. He directed Sam to end Mary Beth's appointment as the county's lobbyist, demoting her to her previous civil service position. He also told Sam to start the process of firing Pat for inappropriate meddling and obstruction in the strip mall project.

Pat was speechless, holding the phone to his ear for several seconds.

"Are you there?" Sam asked.

"Yeah."

"I need to do what he says," Sam said, "or he's going to fire me, too."

Pat remained silent. He finally said, "I didn't expect this. Let me get back to you." Then he hung up, staring down at his desk. He couldn't believe it.

9

Shortly after Pat ended his call with Sam, Mary Beth arrived at his office. He waved her in, and she quickly closed the door behind her, her face flushed and eyes wide. Instead of saying hello, she shook her head with her lips pressed together.

"What the hell is going on? I've gotten two calls—one from Kathy, who could barely talk about a call she had from Jones this morning, and one from Jones, who told me that he's ending my appointment as lobbyist and I should see Sam Harris on a reassignment. Are you aware of this?"

"Yes." Pat tried to stay calm.

"Well, what are you doing about it? You've thrown Kathy to the wolves, and you've jeopardized my career as a lobbyist—and probably my income, which pretty much supports my family right now."

"I'm sorry it took this turn," Pat said. He motioned for her to sit, but she shook her head again. "I feel terrible. But you should know, Jones has also told Sam to start the process of firing me."

"That's unsurprising—I've told you that that could happen when you mess with Jones. Is there anything you're going to do, or will we all just die? I thought you had a plan."

"I do. This isn't over yet."

"I'm not going to hold my breath," Mary Beth said, leaving his office as abruptly as she'd entered it.

Pat sat staring at the door Mary Beth had exited, wondering why he had not anticipated this. He'd thought that the worst case would be Jones letting Kathy go ahead with her complaint and then fighting it instead of resigning. But Jones had now gone on offense, using all the blustery power he still had. Kathy would likely be so shell-shocked that she wouldn't even consider filing a sexual harassment complaint.

He stood up and paced back and forth, his mind racing. He stopped at the window, feeling like he had been hit in the stomach, knocking the wind out of him. All he had worked for was lost, it seemed. He knew he needed to take action, but he was stunned and temporarily paralyzed. He didn't know where to start.

His thoughts finally returned to Kathy and her importance in his potential next steps. He needed to call her.

He was able to reach her at home and told her he had heard about Jones's phone call.

"I'm sorry—I didn't expect this," he said.

Kathy was silent. Pat heard a dog barking in the background.

"We still have a good case," he said. "I'd like to go ahead with what we talked about."

"Are you kidding me? The chairman said you won't even have a job with the county."

Pat looked at the ceiling, wondering how he could persuade Kathy to stay open to filing a complaint.

"I still think Jones will resign, especially if you're ready to file a complaint if he doesn't."

Kathy stayed silent, and Pat decided to be direct. "Are you willing to file the complaint if necessary?"

"That sounds like suicide," she said.

Pat closed his eyes and shrunk into his chair, holding the phone to his ear while his chin dropped to his chest.

He played the only card he had left. He told Kathy he had a lot of respect for Commissioner John Larsen after discussing the strip mall audit.

"You know that Jones and Larsen often disagree," he said.

"Yeah, they don't like each other."

Pat sensed an opening. "I'm sure Larsen would support you if he knew about Jones's sexual harassment."

"How?" she said.

"By helping us confront him. Would you feel more comfortable filing a complaint if Larsen thought you should?"

Kathy hesitated. "Maybe."

Pat sat up in his chair, his eyes open. He suggested that he alert Commissioner Larsen about Jones's sexual harassment of her and ask him to keep it confidential. Then either Larsen or he would get back to her. "Do I have your permission to inform Larsen?" he asked.

"Yeah, but I'd like him to call me."

"Okay. I really appreciate this, Kathy. You're in an awkward position, and you're being very brave."

Pat exhaled after hanging up, feeling he had just dodged a fatal bullet. Kathy could have deserted him in the face of the chairman's power. But she'd given him life.

———•••———

Pat thought about how he'd approach Larsen. Larsen might feel blindsided by the sexual harassment news. He might be upset by not knowing about Pat's attempt to force Jones's resignation. Pat slowed down as he walked to Larsen's office after realizing how fast he was going.

Larsen invited Pat to enter after he ended a phone call, and Pat closed the door. Unlike Jones's office with its massive desk, Larsen's office was open; visitors could sit at a narrow credenza across from him or at a round table. Larsen motioned for Pat to sit at the table and joined him.

Larsen smiled and said he hoped Pat's news wasn't as bad as Pat looked. Pat tried to smile, but he couldn't. Instead, he informed Larsen about Jones's sexual harassment of Kathy. Pat told him he had suggested to Jones that he resign—and that if he did, Kathy wouldn't file a complaint. Pat also told Larsen about Jones's orders to Sam Harris to start the process of firing him and reassigning Mary Beth.

Larsen looked at Pat in silence. Pat couldn't tell what he was thinking. He worried that Larsen might be feeling that he had gone too far.

Finally, Larsen said softly, "This is an incredible development. I knew you were good, Pat, but I underestimated you. Your plan is sound, and I agree with you on getting Jones to resign. His treatment of Kathy is terrible. Now I know why she hasn't been herself lately."

Pat breathed deeply and closed his eyes momentarily, almost tearing up in gratitude for Larsen's affirmation. But he quickly recovered, alert to what Larsen would say next.

"But tell me," Larsen said. "How can I help, given what's happened this morning? What are your thoughts? I have no problem confronting Jones, if that's what's needed."

These words increased Pat's sense of relief, and he switched into his action-plan mode. He had carefully thought through the next steps.

"First, I think Kathy would value your call," Pat said. "We need to make sure she's willing to file a complaint if Jones doesn't resign. And if it comes to that, she needs to know that she would have full support from county leadership."

"I'd be glad to call Kathy," Larsen said. "I've always thought highly of her."

"I think your willingness to confront Jones is also important. He needs to know that you know about Kathy's accusation of sexual harassment, even though he'll strongly deny it. He also needs to know that you're aware of my offer to not have Kathy file a complaint if he resigns, and that you support this plan."

"Confronting Jones would be my pleasure."

Pat was silent for a moment, satisfied. He had accomplished what he wanted. But he told Larsen that he had one more suggestion.

"You might want to remind Jones that Sally Rogers chairs the board's personnel committee and that she has been a leader in empowering women staff at the county."

Larsen nodded. "Good idea. Sally would be furious if she knew that Kathy was harassed. I'll tell Jones he'll have an uphill battle if he fights the complaint."

Pat nodded. He couldn't think of anything else to suggest.

"Great work, Pat. I'll follow your marching orders and let you know what happens."

——•••——

Pat returned to his office and closed the door, feeling more and more relieved—his face, neck, and shoulders began to loosen. He sat down, shut his eyes, and tried to breathe deeply.

Ever since the call from Sam that morning, he'd been assuming the worst—that he would be out on the street with no job in a matter of days, saddled with guilt over jeopardizing other people's careers, as well as his own, and fearing the impacts on Billy. His confidence plummeted when he learned that Jones had decided to go on the attack. But things were turning for the better. His admiration of John Larsen continued to grow. He couldn't believe that Larsen viewed Pat's plan as "marching orders," recommendations that Larsen would carry out without questions or debate.

Pat made a short call to Sam and told him he was working with John Larsen.

"I hope to have things resolved by noon."

"What's your resolution?" Sam asked. "I've been worried ever since we talked."

"I'll tell you later. Why don't you also update Mary Beth that I'm working with Larsen." He hung up before Sam could ask more questions.

Pat got up and stood by his office window. He watched people strolling by on the sidewalks and cars driving through the intersection. A bus unloaded several riders at the stop below his window. It was midmorning, and life was going on—ninety minutes before the deadline for Jones to call. He dug out a professional journal from his reading pile and selected an article on land-use trends. He sat back in his chair and tried to read it while waiting.

Shortly after eleven, Pat received a call from John Larsen.

"Pat, my talk with Kathy went very well. She started to cry, thanking me for our support. She's been afraid of Jones for a long time."

"That's great," Pat said. "Were you able to talk to Jones?"

"Did I ever. I walked into his office and told him I knew about his harassment of Kathy. He yelled at me—said it was a lie. I told him I also knew about your plan and that he should take advantage of it. Otherwise, it will be a mess, with sexual harassment accusations mixing with conflict-of-interest audits. Jones told me to leave before I was done talking. He didn't give an indication of what he was going to do."

"Thanks," Pat said. "We'll see if I hear from him before noon." Larsen hung up after asking Pat to keep him informed.

Pat went back to leafing through the journal. Things were moving in the right direction, but he was still anxious. Jones was unpredictable.

Fifteen minutes before noon, Pat got the call he had been waiting for. Jones told him he would announce his resignation at Tuesday's board meeting. Pat immediately informed Kathy and Sam. Sam congratulated him, and Kathy thanked him three times.

Pat knew he had to wait for the board meeting to see if Jones would resign. But after he hung up, he stood motionless for several seconds until he finally pumped his right fist twice in the air.

10

Chairman Jones opened the county board meeting with a long speech about his memories and accomplishments as a commissioner for the county. Pat watched from the staff seats on the side as usual. He didn't see Eastman in the room. Jones closed by announcing he was resigning to spend more time with his grandchildren.

Each commissioner thanked Jones for his service—several telling stories about working with him on projects to benefit the county. When they were done, Jones said some final words of gratitude and left the room. People applauded as he walked out, many probably beneficiaries of Jones's favors, through both ethical and unethical uses of his power.

Before moving to board business, Commissioner Rogers proposed that they take action to select their new leader. She moved that John Larsen be approved as the new board chairman. Her motion was seconded and, without discussion, passed unanimously.

Larsen invited Pat to his office after the meeting ended and reporters finished their interviews. When Pat began walking down the hallway, Doug Kern grabbed his sleeve and asked for a minute of his time. He was flamboyant as usual, with a purple-striped shirt open at the neck to display a gold chain. He moved closer to Pat to look at him face-to-face.

"I wanted to make sure there's no misunderstanding of my role in this drama," Kern said. "To do business in this county, you quickly learned not to get crossways with Chairman Jones."

Pat looked at him quietly. "I imagine."

"Jones pressured me to contract with his son-in-law's company on county projects, and he pushed me to work with Eastman, who he said would be the new administrator. I had to play his game. There was nothing personal against you—we've always been good friends."

"I understand how Jones would have done that," Pat said, not smiling as he might have previously.

"Well, look, my man, we have a new heating and cooling contractor, and we're ready to give you the best bid to develop the strip mall property," Kern said with a grin as he left. "And next year, you can count on the Cubs being better than the White Sox!" Pat nodded with a slight smile—Kern would always be the same, no matter what happened.

Larsen welcomed Pat as Pat came into his office and sat down. "You've done great work," Larsen said. "I'm going to talk to Sam about having the board approve you as acting administrator next week. Once he gets through all the interviews, I'm sure you'll be named as our new administrator. Sound good to you?"

"Yes, it does. I appreciate your confidence and am excited to work for you and the board."

Pat left Larsen's office and decided to take the afternoon off. He would be alone the rest of the day and evening since Billy was with June. He walked slowly to his car, his feet almost dragging. All he could think of was retreating to the sanctuary of his house.

After closing his front door and hanging up his coat, he looked at himself in the dining room mirror. Suddenly his face broke into a grin. He had beaten Jones and Eastman!

They'd made two power plays against him, first attacking his reputation and then trying to eliminate his job. He had gone from defense to offense, as he had rarely done in his life, and Jones and Eastman had paid dearly. His moves were not instinctual reactions, like punching Miller's friend in high school. He had made plans and then adapted to developments he could not predict.

Larsen had played a critical but unexpected role—he was a mature leader Pat had looked to for direction. But at the peak of the battle, Larsen had looked to Pat and followed his recommendations. The supporting words from Pat's staff were also unexpected, and his sense of being a trusted leader had never before reached this level. He would be starting his new job as county administrator with precisely the kind of leadership that he had lacked ever since high school. He thought of those days, understanding better the confidence exuded by fighters like Dave and Beck, fearless in confronting rivals who challenged them.

He'd been naïve about how the world worked, on so many levels, but no more of that now. He knew there would be fights in the future, but he was ready to battle any new enemies he might face.

Pat's power felt physical, his chest expanding with his breaths. He thought of getting into better shape, approaching work like a trained athlete approached competition, striving to win and learning from losses. He pictured himself standing tall, confident and powerful.

———•••———

The following morning, Pat read the newspaper as he ate breakfast, focusing on the story with the headline "County Chairman in Property Audit Resigns." He started thinking of the first steps he would take as the county administrator. He also thought again of the need to guard against anyone who might threaten him.

One of Pat's priorities was to connect with Mary Beth. He wanted to clear the air with her after their tense interaction. He called her, and they scheduled a time for her to come to his office. When she arrived the next day, Pat could sense that she was cautious. She congratulated him on becoming administrator, having run into Chairman Larsen that morning and learning his plans to appoint Pat.

"Quite a victory," she said. "Your enemies are out the door, you're getting promoted, and you have a new ally in Kathy."

Pat nodded and thanked her. He was quiet, thinking she didn't fully understand what he'd been through.

She filled the silence. "I feel for Jones. You probably saw the newspaper this morning. I'm sure this is not how he wants to be remembered after many years of public service."

Pat looked intently at her. "How can you feel that way about him? He deserved what he got."

Mary Beth leaned back and seemed to put up a shield. Her tone became measured. "Human beings make mistakes. I know his wife and daughters; they're good people. I'm sure that whole family is hurting this morning."

Pat turned away and looked at his watch. He kept his expression neutral. "Jones made mistakes that I'm not going to tolerate. I wanted to meet with you this morning to discuss how we can work together. But if you're going to side with people like Jones, we'll have challenges."

Mary Beth stiffened, sitting up straight and enlarging her presence. Her dark eyes stared intensely at Pat, her face reddening. "I don't appreciate being talked to like that. You've had a great win, which will benefit the county. But what has it done to you? I helped you, Larsen supported you, and Kathy trusted you—because you were a genuine person who cared about the county. What are you now? Is it you against the world?"

"I thought you'd appreciate the outcome, given the potential risk to your job."

"Sure, the outcomes are positive. But not how you did it. You violated Kathy's trust in you by telling Sam that she had been sexually harassed. You manipulated her into agreeing to file a complaint if Jones didn't resign. If Jones had let the complaint be filed and fought it, the entire organization would have known that Kathy was the accuser, which could have put her in a bad spot. If Jones had won—which he could have—Kathy's reputation and future job possibilities in the county would have been close to zero. You're lucky things turned out the way they did, but that doesn't justify using Kathy to get what you wanted."

Pat didn't know what to say. He knew there was some truth in Mary Beth's words, but he thought he had dealt with those risks and it was time to move on. He looked at his watch again. "I need to get back to work."

Mary Beth stood up. "I understand your feelings because I know what you've been through—and don't think that I don't know—but I hope you'll get off your pedestal and rejoin the human race the next time I see you." She turned and left his office.

Pat stared at the door that she had brusquely shut on her way out, despite the fact that it had been open on her arrival. What had just happened? This was a side of Mary Beth he hadn't seen before, and he certainly hadn't expected this assault.

Pat was disturbed by her words, but he tried to put them out of his mind. He wanted to be the person he had identified with the day before, mature and confident. He spent the rest of the afternoon reviewing his staff's proposed county planning process and budget, successfully putting what she said behind him. But on his way out of his office, he noticed the picture of Billy on his desk—especially his happy, radiant smile—and heard Mary Beth's words about rejoining the human race.

11

On Friday afternoon, Pat arrived at the after-school center to pick up Billy, looking forward to having him for the next week. He was relieved, no longer worrying about getting fired or having to change his support of Billy. Although the fall temperature was cool, the kids were playing a pickup soccer game outside. He got out of his car to watch. The game ended, and Billy ran to him, hugging him and shouting, "Daddy!"

During the car ride home, Billy chattered about his day.

"Michael and I played four square at recess and beat almost everyone!" Billy said. "We also raced the older kids and almost won."

"So, you're enjoying school?"

"Yeah, Miss Colbert likes my writing. But the best is being with Michael on the playground."

Pat's eyes moistened as he listened to Billy continue to talk about his day, not wanting to disturb their warm bond with words.

"What's for supper?" Billy asked after he finished talking about school.

"How about if we eat at the deli? You can help me celebrate."

"Celebrate what?"

"I think I'm getting a new job at work."

"Okay. I want a ham and cheese sandwich!"

After they were seated, their waitress came to take their order. She was a college student who had served them before and enjoyed talking with Billy.

"How's school?" she asked Billy.

"Great!"

"Do you have a best friend?"

"Michael!" Billy said, glowing in response to her interest in him.

As they bantered, Pat realized she reminded him of Kathy at work—petite, cheerful, and innocent. He thought of Mary Beth's words about how he had used Kathy, and he winced, uncomfortable with the possibility that she might be right.

When Pat tucked Billy into bed that night, Billy asked, "Can I play with Michael this weekend? His mom is going to ask Mommy."

"I'll talk to your mom," Pat said. June had not told him about these plans. Probably sensing Pat's hesitancy, Billy pleaded with him, and his charms were effective as usual.

"Michael wants me to come to his house. Can I? Can I?"

"Yes, you can. Don't worry."

Billy said, "Yes!" and Pat knew that Billy wanted the tension between June and him to go away, just like he wanted them all to sit together in the restaurant after his soccer game.

After leaving Billy's room, Pat sat in the recliner in his study. He thought of his argument with June in the church parking lot. Pat knew he owed June an apology for trying to get Billy to choose him over her. He had put his needs ahead of Billy's.

It wasn't too late to call June, so that was what he did.

"Billy told me his friend Michael wants Billy to come to his house this weekend."

"His mother just called me tonight, and I was going to tell you tomorrow," June said. "I'm not trying to disrupt your and Billy's schedule."

Pat could feel June becoming defensive, probably thinking he would criticize her for failing to tell him beforehand. "I just wanted to tell you it's okay with me," he said. "What time does his mother want Billy to come over?"

"Saturday afternoon. She offered to pick Billy up at my house."

"Okay, I'll bring him over after lunch."

Pat waited for an acknowledgment from her, but she was silent.

"I'm also calling to apologize for my behavior at church," he said.

"You owe me an apology. You violated what we agreed to in our divorce, never involving Billy in our stupid quarrels. You hurt him, and you hurt me."

Pat tensed up, and his breathing quickened. He could have lashed back at her about how ridiculous it was to prevent Billy from having lunch with his father. But he didn't because he knew she was right. "I know, and I'm sorry. I'll never do that again. I also should have let Billy go to your neighbor's birthday party."

"Yes, you should have. You always need to get what you want."

Pat steeled himself again, bothered by her criticism and use of "always." But he kept going. "I know I've been a jerk at times, probably influenced by stress at work. I'm going to try to change that."

"I'll believe that when I see it."

"Fair enough." Pat was quiet. He couldn't go much further.

June finally spoke after several seconds of silence. "I appreciate your apologies and your pledge to do better."

They hung up, and Pat took a deep breath, releasing the tension in his shoulders. He could have let himself get irritated, since June had not owned her part in their conflicts. But he knew he was the bigger problem.

He sat back in his recliner and picked up a novel, but he stopped and put it down. He couldn't stop thinking about the events of the past few weeks. The confident power he had felt the other day was shifting. Mary Beth's words came back to him again. He realized that not only was she right about Kathy deserving better treatment from him, but Mary Beth herself deserved better treatment as well. She had found information about Eastman's meetings with Jones, advised him to talk to John Larsen, and alerted him about Kathy, without violating Kathy's need for confidentiality. In return, he had almost caused her to lose her job, and he had gotten angry and cold when she became upset. How could he be so stupid?

He thought again of the conversation he just had with June, the person who probably knew him better than anyone. He had often gotten defensive when she criticized him, convinced he was right. But he believed her tonight. He had been a jerk. He had failed to think about the impacts of his behavior on her and Billy. He had always blamed her for the breakup, but he could now see more clearly how his faults contributed to their divorce. This same pattern of righteous behavior was pushing Mary Beth away from him at work, after she had helped him so much.

It was dark outside, the house quiet. Pat sat in his recliner with only his reading light turned on, and pushed the recliner all the way back. He began turning over all he'd experienced in the last few days. He tried to reconcile his realization that he needed to be a better person with the fight he had just gone through with Eastman and Jones.

The fight had been a war. He couldn't think of an alternative way of dealing with the severe threats he had faced. As Gary had advised, going to battle had been necessary and unavoidable. He had won and felt triumphant about it. But this wasn't an athletic competition, in which winners and losers shake hands and live to play another day. That type of competition was constrained by rules and standards of behavior.

The costs of a battle with no rules—whether a war for military superiority or a battle for organizational leadership—were to people's lives. Losers like Jones and Eastman—or victims like Kathy—had parts of their lives destroyed. Mary Beth was right about the impact on Jones's family. It wasn't hard to sympathize with them once he thought of her perspective. He also thought of Eastman, his beautiful wife, and his autistic son. His victory over Eastman had hurt that family as well.

Pat closed his eyes as the painful realization came to him. The costs of conflict on human lives also included costs to the winners. Even though he was victorious over Jones and Eastman, there was a cost to himself. He was so obsessed with winning that he had left the human race, as Mary Beth said.

His behavior contradicted his career decision, the one he had made many years ago as he sat by the campus pond. He had chosen to work as a public servant to help society, to help improve the lives of its citizens. In his battle with Eastman, he had cast aside these ideals as he moved from defense to offense. He had not cared about collateral damage to those innocently swept into the conflict, including the impacts on Billy and June.

His thoughts were interrupted when the phone rang. It was John Larsen.

"Sorry to be calling you late on a Friday night," Larsen said. "But Sam asked me on the way out today what we should do about Jack Eastman. Do you have any thoughts?"

Pat remembered that he had told Jones to take Eastman with him, since Eastman most likely would be fired for helping manipulate the sale of county land. But Pat's thoughts now were about Eastman's family.

"There are grounds for firing him," Pat said. "But how about asking Doug Kern to give him a job, with the pledge that Eastman never work on projects in our county?"

"Brilliant," Larsen said. They hung up and Pat sat quietly, nodding to himself.

Pat turned to pick up his novel again, planning to lose himself in a good story. As a boy, he had enjoyed stories of good versus evil. He loved to watch movies where the conflicts were often resolved by a gun battle. One western he had watched several times was *Shane*. When Shane rode to town, his horse trotting to thunderous music, Pat's anticipation of the impending fight was intense. Shane, the protector of the farmers, was riding to confront the cattleman's cowboy killers. Pat participated vicariously in the violent shootout that Shane ultimately won.

Pat's feelings of triumph after beating Jones and Eastman reminded him of his satisfaction in Shane's victory. This was the culture in which Pat and other American boys grew up, where righteous male authority confronted evil. But Pat now knew that these battles hurt the lives of both the winners and losers. The movie ended with Shane riding off alone, leaving the family that had taken him in, unable to join the human race.

This culture led Pat to break Miller's friend's nose in high school, even though he knew it was stupid for him to punch him so hard. It led to Dave being celebrated as the most powerful fighter at Central High and Beck at Kennedy High. It also prompted Dave—more rewarded for his fighting skills than anything else—to join the Marines to become a professional warrior.

Pat didn't see much of Dave after the fight with Miller in 1967. He heard that Dave had applied to join the Marines that summer. In August, Pat had traveled to the East Coast to begin college. He soon made new friends and enjoyed liberal arts courses. He'd all but forgotten his time at Central High, until he received a call from a high school friend in the spring semester of Pat's first year of college.

Pat's friend told him that Dave had been killed soon after arriving in Vietnam. A North Vietnamese battalion had overrun his platoon. This news shocked Pat; Dave had seemed invincible.

Dave's death was influenced by the same male culture that influenced Pat's battle with Eastman, a culture that simplified conflicts as good versus evil. Eastman represented evil to Pat as a North Vietnamese soldier was evil to Dave. Pat knew now that these conflicts were much more complex. Dave had been sent to Vietnam to fight in a war started by American politicians, confident of their power and assured of their victory over evil communists. But Dave had been killed in a war that had no resolution. He was nineteen, confident and so young. He had lost his life, one of over 50,000 Americans, in a war where there was still no consensus about what was good and evil.

The conflict with Eastman was also complicated. Pat saw him as an evil adversary who needed to be defeated. But Eastman was also a husband and a father of an autistic child, and had worked to improve the education of autistic children. To just think of him as evil was an oversimplification.

Pat got out of his chair and left his dimly lit study for the kitchen. After turning on the lights, he dialed Mary Beth's work number. He apologized in his voicemail, saying he hoped she would forgive him. He told her he would like to get together with her on Monday—he wanted to apologize to her in person and hear her feedback on how he could be a better leader. He also wanted to discuss her ideas on improving the county.

Pat checked on Billy on the way to his bedroom and found him sleeping soundly. He straightened Billy's blankets and kissed him on his forehead. He lingered, looking at him with affection. He was lucky to have this wonderful son. He left Billy's room, turned off the lights, and went to bed earlier than usual. He felt exhausted, ready to restore himself for a new day.

A Father's
Heir

1

Returning to his office from a client meeting, Dana noticed the pulsating red light on his phone, signaling he had a voicemail message. He listened to it and frowned. His younger sister, Frida, wanted him to call her immediately. He dialed her number, guessing her call was about their father's lung cancer. Usually, his mother would call to update him. That Frida was calling seemed ominous.

"We brought Papa to the hospital again this morning," Frida said quietly. Her voice caught. She didn't seem to want to say the words she needed to say. "They'll be keeping him here. He's not doing well."

Dana steeled himself. "I was afraid of that."

"His cancer has spread, and he doesn't have much time left," she said. "That's what the doctor says."

Dana closed his eyes. The news didn't surprise him, but it was a blow to his chest. "How's Maman doing?" he asked. His first concern was for his mother.

"She's crying a lot—she can't talk to people without breaking into tears. She asked me to call you."

Dana's breaths grew shallow as he imagined his mother's suffering.

"Papa wants to see you," Frida said.

"Why?" He could hear the irritation in his voice. His father rarely talked to him, and usually just in grunts and nods, especially since Dana had graduated. To celebrate his master's degree, his mother had served one of her wonderful Persian meals, but his father had barely looked at him the entire evening.

"I think he wants to talk to you about the company," Frida said.

"He should be talking to Mehdi about that."

Dana had always assumed his older brother, Mehdi, would take over the company's leadership when their father was gone. So, why did his father want to talk to him?

"Papa and Maman would like to see you tonight," Frida said. "And they only want you there, not Mehdi and me."

Dana grimaced and shook his head. "What's this about, Frida?" She seemed ready to cry at any moment, which Dana understood, given her closeness to their father.

"I don't know—maybe Papa feels the end is near and wants to talk to each of us separately."

"All right. Tell them I'll be there."

At a little after five o'clock, Dana put some reading material into his leather briefcase and stacked his communications work for the next day into neat piles on his desk. His private office, a reward that came with his promotion, was small but more than adequate for him after seven years in a cubicle. He shut the glass door, glancing at the modern art paintings he had hung on the walls. He was drawn especially to the still-life painting of brilliantly colored flowers.

He drove his white Mazda out of the underground parking garage and headed toward the hospital. It was a chilly Wednesday evening in Los Angeles, with more clouds and a stronger breeze than usual for March. He remembered spring break in high school when he had worked on one of his father's construction crews and nearly froze in the cold rain, trying not to show his discomfort to Mehdi and the other crew members who looked comfortable working outside no matter the weather.

Dana's father and Mehdi had always been close, but especially once Mehdi had found soccer in grade school as an outlet for his nonstop energy. In the beginning, he was one of the youngest players in the park and was run off the ball by the bigger boys. But their father, who had played soccer in Iran, would yell at him to get up, go get the ball. Mehdi became a fierce player as he grew older, stocky and compact, a natural midfielder who was good at taking the ball away from opposing players and making pinpoint passes to his wings running toward the goal.

Their father had encouraged Dana to also play. Dana tried, but his slight build and lack of interest made him one of the least-skilled players on the field. He would rather be practicing the piano—the full-sized one that his mother had convinced his father to buy for her so she could play as she had in Iran. Her welcoming encouragement of Dana to join her, combined with his father's disappointment in his attempts at soccer, confirmed for Dana that he would always favor music over sports, and his mother over his father.

Dana pressed the accelerator. He thought about the meeting with his father at the hospital, the inevitably uncomfortable conversation that awaited him.

He entered his father's room and smelled a combination of medicine and disinfectant cleanser. His mother stood to hug him. Like him, she was tall and slender, with a light complexion. Her white-streaked gray hair was fashionably styled as usual, cut just below her ears. But she was not holding together well—her eyes and nose were red from crying, with tears beginning again as she hugged him. His eyes watered—he wanted to protect his mother from her pain. She turned him to his father, sitting up against the reclined back of the hospital bed, with various tubes and sensors attached to his body. He looked ashy gray against the pale blue wall behind him.

Dana walked to the bedside, with his mother staying close, keeping one hand on his shoulder. His father's eyes were tired, but he held his jaw up—a familiar jutting, always prepared, it seemed, to thrust in front of anyone who stood in his way.

"Hi, Papa," Dana said faintly. His father raised his arm and beckoned him to come closer. He reached out to shake Dana's hand, something that Dana couldn't remember ever happening before. It was a firm grip, pulling Dana toward the bed. He stood awkwardly beside the bed, leaning back slightly, not knowing what to say or do.

"The doctors say I have very little time left," his father said. His voice was weak, but he spoke confidently, aiming his dark eyes directly into Dana's with the superiority he usually projected. That ended, however, with a series of deep coughs that appeared to shrink him as he sank into his bed. But he gathered himself after the coughing stopped, ready to talk.

"I'd like you to join Mehdi in running the company."

Dana sat down in a chair and remained silent. This was the last thing he thought his father would say, even though Frida had alerted him that he might want to talk about the company. Five years earlier, his father had named Mehdi vice president of his company, Armand Concrete, and there had been no discussion on the topic since. He squinted his eyes, examining his father's face.

"I've always wanted to leave my business to my children. I hoped you would follow Mehdi to work with me, but you chose a different path. I want you to reconsider."

Dana was silent, continuing to look at his father. His father's matter-of-fact acknowledgment that he would soon die didn't allow any room for Dana to express sympathy or concern, especially for his mother's sake. And now this unexpected request for him to join Mehdi in running the company . . . it threw him off-balance. He gripped the plastic armrests of the seat. "Mehdi will do a good job," Dana finally said.

His father shook his head. "Mehdi is great at running the crews, but he lacks the marketing talents. You've obviously done well at BG Hill."

He'd never heard praise from his father like this. He waited for the inevitable "but" that always came after his father acknowledged something he had done; however, his father had stopped talking.

"How does Mehdi feel?" Dana asked.

"Mehdi wants your help. We would make you equal partners."

"Really? After all the years that he has put into the company?"

His father explained to Dana that Mehdi wished he was born in the U.S. like Dana and Frida were, instead of in Iran. Mehdi lacked confidence in dealing with American business leaders. "Mehdi's temper sometimes gets us into trouble with our partners," his father said. "I've told him all of this, and he admits I'm right. He believes you would be a valuable partner."

A nurse entered the room and checked the monitors connected to the sensors attached to his father's body. She then adjusted the tubes that went from the IV drip into his father's arm. She was a small, expressionless woman who looked down, seeming to sense the gravity of the conversation. Dana watched her quietly fill his father's glass with water. He had never heard any of these concerns about Mehdi. He had always looked up to his older brother. Once, Mehdi had protected him from bullies, chasing them off with a big stick and shouting at them in Farsi, even though they were American boys.

After the nurse left, Dana looked at his father. "I'll have to think about this," he said. "My goal all along has been to establish my own consulting firm."

His father looked toward the window and seemed to struggle over what to say next. "I love my family," he said, his eyes shifting between Dana and his mother. Dana listened closely. Was his father preparing to apologize for the pain he had caused? No, that would be too much. Instead, he swallowed and looked at Dana directly. "I've dreamed of us being closer."

His mother took a deep breath and dabbed her eyes with her handkerchief. Dana's eyes watered again. He knew how much it would mean to his mother to have a reconciliation between him and his father before his father died. He looked at his father and, not knowing what to say, gave a slight nod, indicating he had heard him.

But his mind raced. He didn't know what he was feeling. On the one hand, he was grateful for his father's offer and wanted to make his mother happy. But on the other hand, he didn't trust his father. He hadn't felt his father's love in any of his thirty years. How could his father change so quickly, and why? Feeling his face flush and his upper body grow warm, he took off the sport coat he had worn to work that day.

Many times as a child, he had listened to his father boast to his friends about Mehdi's soccer skills. He'd watched his father show off two-year-old Frida to his friends at the ice cream shop, setting her up on the counter like a little ballerina. With Dana, it was always something like "Why don't you go outside and play with other boys instead of reading books all the time?" or "If you practiced more at soccer, you might find you like it." His mother redoubled her efforts to encourage Dana in music, literature, and drama. She attended each of Dana's music and drama events, often bringing Frida with her, and they cheered and applauded him. She failed to convince Dana's father to attend any of them, with one exception: the performance of Thornton Wilder's play *Our Town*. "They've picked Dana to be the lead actor," Dana remembered her saying. "It's a great honor. You should be proud that your son has been chosen."

His father seemed curious, but that ended once he watched the play. He complained on the drive home: "How can a woman who dies in childbirth come back to life as a twelve-year-old girl? You know, I missed Mehdi's soccer game to come." Dana had learned to steel himself against his father's criticism, going silent and focusing on something else. But his father's mockery of this accomplishment infuriated his mother. She stopped talking to him for a week, going about her daily housekeeping duties without looking at him. He finally gave in and told Dana after dinner that he was sorry he had made fun of his play.

His father tried to sit up in the hospital bed, struggling to say something important. "I'd like you to talk to Yazdan Rahbar," his father said. "He'll continue to be an important business partner for our company. I know you have done some work for him."

Dana nodded—he'd led a small communications project for Yazdan's construction company. Yazdan was one of his father's small group of Iranian friends, who all had immigrated from Iran to Los Angeles in the 1960s. Dana recalled Yazdan's piercing look that intimidated Dana and his friends when they cut in line to get food at an Iranian picnic. "Yes—I will talk with Yazdan," Dana said, seeing it as a reason not only to learn more about the partnership but also to postpone giving his father an answer. He stood up, overwhelmed by the unexpected direction of the conversation and ready to leave. He hugged his mother, pulling her close, and hugged his father gently, saying, "Thanks, Papa. I'll think about what you're proposing."

He left before his father could respond and strode down the hall, trying to understand what had just happened. He had come to the hospital to show sympathy for his grieving mother. He had begun to feel something like sadness himself, even though he and his father were not close. But his father didn't allow time for those feelings or words. Instead, he gave Dana things he had never experienced: He shook his hand, offered him part ownership of the company, praised him for his success, and said he wanted to be closer. This was a man Dana had never known.

Dana parked at his apartment building and entered his living room. He was tempted to sit down and play his piano, which he had treated himself to on his thirtieth birthday—a small, used piano that produced a rich sound after he had it tuned. He struck a piano chord at that moment, pushing the emotions surrounding his dying father away and replacing them with the beautiful sound of music.

His mother had surprised him when he was five by bringing home a toy piano a week after a neighbor taught him how to play chopstick on her piano. One evening after supper, his mother announced to the family that Dana was going to play the piano for them. He played two rounds of chopsticks, and his mother led the applause. Frida, three years old at the time, slapped her hands together. Mehdi clapped faintly and asked if he could play outside. Dana's father did not clap. He told Dana to go with Mehdi and find a soccer game. As Dana followed Mehdi out the front door, he had heard his father say, "Leila, don't buy him girls' toys. He'll turn into a sissy."

Dana turned his thoughts to his father's business proposal, which was easier than thinking about the memories and emotions his visit to the hospital stimulated. He was curious about Yazdan. His father's company did most of the concrete work on the projects led by Yazdan's construction company, similar to other Iranian partnerships in Los Angeles. Dana viewed the business dealings of these Iranian networks as complex tangles of relationships, favors, and conflict, unlike the professionalism he had experienced at BG Hill. Even if he rejected his father's offer, more knowledge about Yazdan and his father's other Iranian partnerships might help him advise Mehdi and his mother when his father was gone.

He put his briefcase on the table he used for a desk in his apartment and took ingredients out of the refrigerator for a salad—couscous, avocado, kale, and cherry tomatoes, topped by leftover strips of roasted chicken. As he ate, Dana recalled his father's stories about the rise of Ayatollah Khomeini and the dangerous Islamic gangs who persecuted Christians like themselves. "When my friends and I arrived in America," he had said, "we were amazed by all the opportunities to get ahead. Yes, there was racism, but we already knew how it felt to live as a minority—as Christians in an Islamic culture."

Dana remembered one of the scariest moments of his childhood— the bombing of the garage attached to their house. Was that an attack by racists who resented the success of his father's company, or was it a consequence of his father's participation in Iranian networks, where rivalries and conflict could be intense? He guessed it was the latter.

2

Dana picked up his girlfriend, Sarah, on Wednesday, and they drove to one of their favorite restaurants. It was a pleasant evening; the hostess seated them on the outdoor patio as the sun set. Sarah shared Dana's love of music, poetry, and art—a world he kept removed from his business challenges. He was eager to hear her views of his conversation with his father. Her perspective would be independent from the emotions of his family.

He had met Sarah while in graduate school at UC Irvine for his MBA. He occasionally attended events sponsored by the English and art departments between classes. When he walked into the art gallery one afternoon, Sarah was the only other person present. Wearing a nametag indicating she was staff, she approached him with a smile, and he was struck by her reddish-brown hair and freckles as she looked up at him. She led him through the exhibit, becoming animated as she discussed her favorite paintings. She was in her first year of employment in Continuing Education and had organized this showing with the art department. She had arrived early before hosting a Continuing Education seminar. As the time neared for his second class, he asked her if she would like to meet up after her seminar and his class. She agreed, and they ate dinner at a nearby bistro.

Before long, they were seeing each other two or three times a week, and she often slept at his apartment on Saturday nights. She proposed moving in with him, but he wasn't ready to give up his alone time.

The hostess seated more couples and small groups, and a low murmur of conversation spread throughout the patio by people ending their workweek. Glasses and plates clinked together like wind chimes as waiters served drinks and dishes of food. After they sipped their wine and ordered, Dana told Sarah about his evening at the hospital with his parents.

"The doctor told us that my father doesn't have much time left—the cancer has worsened."

"That's too bad. How's your mother doing?"

"She's taking it very hard." Dana's eyes watered.

"I'm sorry for her," Sarah said, patting Dana's hand. "I know you're closer to her than you are with your father."

It had been almost two years since Sarah had looked up at him enthusiastically in the gallery, sweeping away his natural shyness. His forehead had relaxed, and he smiled at her while she talked, feeling both pleasure and attraction.

As Dana talked about his family's situation, he moved his hands and was conscious of her watching them. He stopped and smiled.

"I love your hands," she said, changing the topic. "Promise you'll play the piano for me this weekend."

"I promise," he said.

Starting at the age of five, Dana had learned everything his mother knew about playing the piano, and he soon played her most difficult pieces. His father resisted paying for piano lessons, but he finally gave in to stop his wife's persistent demand. The piano teacher was a gentle, middle-aged woman. "How much you already know!" she had told him during their first lesson. With her guidance, Dana participated in monthly concerts with her other students and students of other teachers. His teacher entered him in piano contests, and he built a collection of ribbons, medals, and plaques. His high school music teacher encouraged him to apply to a school of performing arts to pursue a fine arts degree. But the Armand family didn't have money for that kind of education, and his father most likely would not support it even if they did.

"Can we get back to talking about my father?" Dana asked.

She sat up straig hter and looked into his eyes. "Okay. What do you want to talk about?"

"My father wants me to join Mehdi to help lead our company. I don't know if I should even consider it."

The hostess seated another couple on the patio near them, the wooden chairs scraping the patio tiles as they sat down. Water bubbled in a small fountain at the center of the patio.

"When I've been at your house, your father doesn't acknowledge you or me," Sarah said. "He doesn't seem to care about you. Why does he want you to help run the company?"

"I don't know, but he praised me with words I've never heard before, and I know my mother wants my father and me to reconcile."

"Your mother is wonderful—that first time at your house . . . she made me feel so welcome when you brought me over to meet them. Your father didn't get up to say hello—he was yelling from his recliner for her to get the TV remote from him and replace the battery. He's not sensitive to you or her. Can he really be trusted?" she asked, spearing a stalk of asparagus with her fork.

"I don't know, but I'll at least talk to my brother and sister about his proposal. My father also suggested I talk to his business partner."

The corners of Sarah's mouth turned down slightly. "You're making me nervous that you're actually considering this," she said. "You already spend too much time on business. I'm afraid you'll have even less time to play the piano or go to concerts and art shows with me."

Dana looked at her with a smile. She was too young to have the experience needed to understand the challenge of making a living, which allowed enjoyment of the arts. "I think I could maintain a balance," he said. "I'm doing that now, aren't I?"

"Consulting is one thing," she said. "But I can't see you leading a concrete company and dealing with the Iranian construction business." She paused before blurting with feeling, "Mehdi is perfect for that role—he's so Middle Eastern."

Dana knew she was referring to the color of Mehdi's skin, but it didn't bother him. Having his mother's lighter complexion, he felt comfortable moving between the white and Iranian cultures and was patient with Sarah's discomfort.

Sarah switched topics, telling Dana about an upcoming art seminar. But when he stood for them to leave, she gave him a questioning look. He imagined she was still uncomfortable with the idea of him joining Mehdi.

Leaving the restaurant, Dana guided her across the street to his car, the palm of his hand on the small of her back. He dropped her off at her apartment.

"I'll pick you up on Saturday for the concert," he told her as she got out of the car.

"The concert?" She stooped to look at him through the car window.

"The string quartet?" he said. "At the university?"

"Oh, yes!" she said. "I'm sorry. Our talk . . . I'm feeling a little distracted."

On his drive home, Dana thought about how he appreciated hearing Sarah's side, arguing for him to reject his father's proposal. It helped him better see the opposing view—the argument for him to consider it.

3

Dana met Mehdi at Babani's, a Middle Eastern café with walls the color of terracotta pots and aluminum chairs and tables. He ordered a falafel sandwich and a salad, and Mehdi ordered a large kebab of minced lamb blended with herbs and spices, saying to Dana, "No wonder you're so skinny." Dana was taller than Mehdi, but Mehdi was stocky, with powerful shoulders developed from high school wrestling. He wore a three-day beard that matched his short black hair, and his dark complexion was made even darker by spending years in the sun working on concrete projects.

Dana remembered the tensions they had had growing up—pressures that most brothers faced as they competed with each other. But their difference in age—six years—and, even more so, their differences in bodies, personalities, and interests led them to an early truce. Each went his own way, choosing a direction the other could not relate to but could support because they were not competing within the same arena. This separation, though, would not be the case if they were partners in leading Armand Concrete.

"Papa has plans for us at Armand," Dana said.

Mehdi was silent while chewing a piece of his lamb kebab. "I'm fine with them. I like splitting up our roles. You could focus on marketing and developing business, and I could run the projects."

"You don't think we'd step on each other's toes?"

"No. You have skills that I don't. I don't know much about your consulting, but I know you've been successful." Mehdi turned back to his kebab. If Mehdi did have reservations, he seemed to have them resolved, with answers he might have rehearsed.

Dana was quiet. He had no idea that Mehdi thought he was skillful or successful. Even if his reply was rehearsed, this made an impact. He exhaled—there was no sign of potential conflict with Mehdi so far.

"I've watched Papa get on your case for years," Mehdi said. "You don't have to worry about me acting like him." This also seemed rehearsed to Dana. Mehdi appeared to have anticipated Dana's concerns. How much did Papa influence that?

"That's good to hear," Dana said.

"Tara thinks Papa's jealous of how close you are to Maman. She believes every time you won a music award, Papa envied you because Maman was happier for you than she was for him."

Dana had forgotten to ask about Mehdi's wife, Tara, and her pregnancy. But he kept thinking of Mehdi's words. For Mehdi to judge his father's behavior as criticism meant a great deal to Dana—again, even if it was rehearsed. Dana's forehead and eyes relaxed.

"Tara is smart. How's she doing?" Dana asked.

"She's great—she's such a rock. I know she's uncomfortable, but she never complains. Only a few more months."

Dana thought highly of Tara. She was perfect for Mehdi, a stocky daughter of Iranian immigrants, respectful to Iranian men but astute in understanding relationships and influencing decisions that were best for her family.

"I'm excited to be an uncle," Dana said. He sometimes pictured being married to Sarah, but it would be much different than Mehdi and Tara's marriage. He didn't know if he could give up his solitude to build a family like Mehdi was doing.

On their way out of the restaurant, Mehdi turned to Dana, squinting. "One thing: If we become partners, I don't want to have anything to do with Yazdan Rahbar."

Dana was surprised by the intensity in Mehdi's voice. "Papa wants me to meet with him," he said.

"I don't know why Papa stays so close to him. Those old men, constantly talking about Iran. Their scheming disgusts me, and I have no trust in Yazdan."

Dana looked intently at Mehdi.

"He threatened to kill me," Mehdi said, a hint of fear in his eyes. "Papa said it was nothing and fixed things, but I am through dealing with him."

"Do you think he was serious?"

"Who knows? I need to go." He clapped Dana on the back and hugged him quickly before leaving.

Dana stood in the parking lot watching his brother drive away in his dinged-up white pickup. He suddenly felt tense in his shoulders. Was Yazdan's threat to kill Mehdi real or just an expression of Yazdan's anger? Mehdi had to be exaggerating.

Dana had already turned down a chance to work for Armand. When he was in high school, his father rose to vice president. He bought out the owners' shares when they retired and took over the company. Dana remembered the celebration his father's friends organized for him, where the new name of the company was unveiled: Armand Concrete. His mother had baked a large cake and iced it in gray, creating a delicate border of cinder blocks to finish it. Dana was happy for Mehdi, who had been working for the company for five years, starting while attending technical college. He was now poised to grow into a leadership role.

Dana, on the other hand, was applying to colleges—and he thought it was best to keep his parents out of the loop on that. He'd been working as a waiter in an expensive restaurant, where he felt his competence and sensitivity to people were valued—his tips, which he saved for college, seemed to reflect that. He was accepted at UC Irvine, not far from their house. Before he could fill his parents in on his plans, his father brought up his future one night after dinner. He invited Dana to work for Armand after graduating high school. "Maybe part-time at first, while you go to technical school, like Mehdi did?" he suggested. "Both my sons should be helping me run Armand," he had added matter-of-factly, but not without some warmth.

Dana surprised everyone by informing them he had been accepted by UC Irvine. His father's face fell. "What will you study?" he asked Dana.

"I'm not sure yet," Dana answered. "Music or literature."

"I won't support more than two years of college," his father said sternly. "Same as I did for Mehdi. And music and literature are not skills you need for working in the company."

Dana put up the shield he had used all his life to withstand his father's criticism. He looked at his father and mother and said, "I don't plan to work for the company."

His father stood up abruptly. "So, what? You think you're better than me? You're too good to work with Mehdi and me?" He stormed out of the kitchen, heading toward his shop in the garage. Dana's mother stood and walked over to Dana. She bent down and hugged him, her eyes brimming with tears. Dana's feelings were familiar: shell-shocked by his father's criticism and comforted by his mother's love.

After Mehdi had driven off, Dana walked to his car, curious about many things from their conversation. His main conclusion was straightforward: Mehdi was not an obstacle if Dana wanted to join the company—Mehdi would welcome him. Dana felt comforted by that. But how much would he let this influence his decision? He had checked off a box, but leaving BG Hill and running Armand Concrete with Mehdi was a giant leap.

Two days later, Yazdan welcomed Dana to his office. It was cluttered, with construction plans spread out on his desk and numerous hangings on the walls. On one wall was a large map of Iran. On another were several pictures and plaques. Dana recognized the Shah of Iran in the largest picture, shown shaking Yazdan's hand. In the photo, Yazdan wore a military uniform and was thin and upright, with a full head of black hair—unlike the aged man in front of Dana, now bald and overweight with hunched shoulders. Yazdan's expensive sport coat and large gold rings on his fingers didn't disguise his decline. His eyes, however, were alive. Yazdan was alert to Dana's every move, closely watching as he looked at the pictures and plaques.

"Those are from a time when the world respected Iran. Come, I'll show them to you," Yazdan said.

They walked to the wall, and Yazdan explained each picture and plaque. Several included the Shah and his ministers with Yazdan. "I was a commander in the Shah's police force," Yazdan said, and Dana could sense his pride in his past life in Iran. "See, here," he added, pointing. "Outstanding service award." Yazdan pointed at some newer plaques. "These are from the Iranian Business Association in Los Angeles."

"Iranian Executive of the Year. Impressive," Dana said. But his focus was not on Yazdan. The pictures on the wall stimulated Dana's curiosity about his father. Whose side was his father on in Iran during the time of the Shah? He knew about the Islamic gangs chasing his father when he was young and was aware his father worked construction. But what about the politics? What would pictures of his father have shown? There were none that Dana knew of—it would be a blank wall.

Yazdan smiled at Dana's praise. "Shah Pahlavi was making great progress in modernizing Iran until Khomeini and his Islamic fanatics revolted," he said. His voice grew more serious. "We arrested Khomeini in 1963 but didn't go far enough in controlling his followers. The riots after the arrest were terrible for my family. My father was killed."

Dana wondered again about his parents' lives in Iran. His mother had shared some experiences, such as cooking with her mother, but his father avoided talking about his. Was Dana's grandfather in danger of being killed like Yazdan's father had been?

"I'm sorry to hear that. So, then you came to America," Dana said.

Yazdan nodded. "I was twenty-nine, just like your father, although I didn't know Caveh then. We both settled in L.A., following our relatives, and first met at the Persian Grill—Caveh and I had lunch there a couple of months ago, in fact."

Dana's first memory of the Persian Grill was when he was in kindergarten. He woke up to the sound of his mother yelling at his father, who had come home drunk and fallen on their front steps. "You can sleep at the Persian Grill next time you get this drunk," she told him. After that incident, Dana's image of the Persian Grill made him insecure and afraid. He was wary of getting too close to that part of his father's life, influenced by his mother's disgust. But now, he wanted to know more about those early days.

Yazdan described the restaurant as the central gathering place for men who had immigrated from Iran. They had a back room to themselves, where they ate, drank, made deals, gambled, and sometimes fought with each other. "Your father and I would never have become owners of our own companies without the help of our friends at the Persian Grill," Yazdan said. "We all had big dreams and couldn't believe the freedom in America that allowed us to pursue them."

Dana sensed Yazdan could talk for hours about his move to America. "You probably know that my father wants me to go into partnership with Mehdi."

Yazdan nodded, motioning for them to sit on Yazdan's leather couch and easy chair. "Caveh's plan is sound," Yazdan said. "About half of Armand's business is from working with my company. I would like to continue the relationship, although I'm sorry this change is necessary because of your father's cancer."

"Why can't you just work with Mehdi?" Dana asked. Did Yazdan value Dana the way his father had said he did?

"I think Caveh probably told you," Yazdan said. "Mehdi is a good worker and supervisor, but he doesn't understand the people side of the business. Some of our clients go back to those early days at the Persian Grill. These relationships need finesse, and Mehdi often doesn't see the need."

Yazdan got up and walked to a coffee maker, asking if Dana wanted a cup. Dana declined, and Yazdan poured one for himself and returned to his easy chair.

"I've seen you in action," Yazdan said. "You and your people at BG Hill were skilled in helping my company's communications with neighborhoods and politicians. Your people skills can help Armand's image and attract new clients."

This was the third time Dana had been praised for his skills—by his father, Mehdi, and now Yazdan. It was nice to hear, but was he being manipulated?

"I'm going to have to think about it," Dana said.

"I understand. I know you've had challenges with Caveh. He is a hard-driving man and blames himself for your troubles with him. I know he wants you to help carry on his business with Mehdi."

Dana was silent. Yazdan sounded much like his father, but Yazdan went further, saying his father blamed himself for his trouble with Dana. He wasn't sure he believed those words. Did his father rehearse them with Yazdan? On the other hand, Yazdan's description of the potential for Armand Concrete made sense. Mehdi and Yazdan believed Dana would bring a new perspective, and he agreed.

That evening, Dana thought more about applying his skills and energy to strengthen Armand Concrete. Maybe accepting his father's offer could satisfy his need to run his own business. He closed his eyes, still having doubts. The hard-driving man Yazdan described never had time for his youngest son until now. Dana's lack of trust could not be changed overnight.

••

Dana and Frida visited their father the day after he met with Yazdan. He was in the same pale blue room, but the blinds were drawn this time. Their mother sat quietly in the armchair in the corner, and their father was in a deep sleep and did not wake up while they were there. After they consoled their mother, who looked at them with red-rimmed eyes, Dana drove Frida to her apartment.

When they pulled up, Dana said, "I'd like to hear your views about Papa's proposal."

"Of course, Dana," she replied. "I'll make tea."

Once they were inside her apartment and she had put on the electric kettle, she motioned for him to join her on her couch. When he saw the large vase of cut wildflowers on the coffee table, he immediately relaxed; their beauty and fragrance filled the room.

Frida had always been a sounding board for him. She was able to navigate and interpret their family relationships and behaviors and frequently saw things he missed. He marveled that she was so skilled but still so dependent on their father for direction.

"I can understand how you're surprised by Papa's offer, given how he has treated you," Frida said. "He's so good to me that it's embarrassing."

"I think you're the only person he truly loves," Dana said with a laugh. "You'll always be his little girl." He remembered how their father had helped Frida get a job at a nursing home after she had graduated from nursing school. Their father and Yazdan had built the home on land owned by an Iranian. The owner was more than glad to offer Frida a job, which she accepted and still held.

"I may be Papa's favorite," she said, "but that doesn't give me any real influence over him."

"Well, sure," he couldn't help but scoff, "it's hard for you to influence him when you do whatever he wants, like take the job he set up for you."

"I didn't just take it because of Papa—I love my job!"

"Okay," Dana said. He wondered what kind of incentive his father had given the owner to hire Frida—maybe a deal on a nursing home addition or on plans for another nursing home.

"You don't know how it feels," Frida said. "Papa is obsessed with making sure I do what he thinks is best for me, whether it's getting me a car, apartment, or boyfriend." She let out a small sigh as she stood. "I'm glad I finally have a boyfriend that Papa approves of." She went into the kitchen.

Dana smiled when she returned and filled his teacup with hot water, not wanting her to feel he was criticizing her. "I can only imagine the pressures you've felt from Papa. It's great you have a steady boyfriend—I like Babak."

"You remember Papa grilling that poor blue-eyed boy when he picked me up to go to the high school prom, almost threatening him?" she asked. "It was embarrassing. That boy never called me again."

"I do remember that. Papa has this need to control everything, and we've both felt it, although in different ways," Dana said. "I'm feeling it right now with his idea for me to help run the company. I don't know if I believe his reasons, although I agree with both Mehdi and Yazdan that it makes sense."

Frida nodded. "I think Papa genuinely wants you to lead the company with Mehdi, but of course I'll support you in whatever you decide. You and Maman are the ones who keep me sane," she said.

"You underestimate yourself. You know things about our family and the Iranian community that I'm not even aware of. You keep us together."

Frida's eyes watered as she looked at him intently. "What are you going to do?"

"I'm warming up to the possibility of accepting Papa's offer."

"How pleased that will make Maman."

"I have doubts, though. I don't know if I can work with Papa's Persian Grill friends."

"I know you would succeed."

Dana stood. "I appreciate that," he told her. "You're always there for me. Thank you."

They hugged and he left, exiting her apartment building through the gate to the street where he had parked. As he drove home, he thought it had been a good week. He had Frida's and Mehdi's support for him accepting his father's offer, and Yazdan had seemed reasonable. It would be nice to have Sarah's support, but he didn't know if that was possible.

4

Dana and Sarah finished dinner and walked to the bookstore near campus. It was a warm Friday night with a slight breeze, signaling that spring was near. He took Sarah's hand, and she looked up at him and smiled. When they reached the bookstore, a line of people moved slowly into the building. By the time they entered, the chairs were all taken, and they joined people sitting on the carpeted floor. The crowd murmured until the moderator introduced the program. It included readings by two young poets and a senior professor Dana knew from his English courses at UC; he remembered her lectures on Shakespeare.

The first two readings by the younger poets settled the crowd into a respectful silence. After they finished, the English professor walked slowly to the podium, tall and thin, with her gray hair pulled back. She introduced her selection of poems with a Shakespeare quote from *Julius Caesar*: "Death, a necessary end, will come when it will come." She began reading her poems on death and grief, absorbing language that was both striking and moving. Dana closed his eyes and saw his dying father in a hospital bed, still defiant but accepting what would come.

Sarah took his arm into both her hands and drew him close. Their eyes met, and he could feel tears forming as he listened to the poet's voice while being held by Sarah. He imagined he was in a peaceful temple listening to rhythmic incantations celebrating the life of a dying man. The professor ended her reading, and people applauded enthusiastically.

They walked to his car, and Sarah, still holding his arm, looked up at him with bright eyes and said, "Wasn't that wonderful?"

Dana nodded without speaking, still under the spell of the poet's words.

He had loved poetry ever since grade school. Each week, his mother had taken her children to the local library, where he spent hours browsing the shelves, sitting and reading in the easy chairs, and checking out books he wanted to take home. He excelled in his creative writing assignments. In high school, he was editor of the student paper, which published several of his poems.

When Dana and Sarah got inside his apartment, they turned to each other, and he kissed her, feeling his pulse quicken. They undressed and embraced each other in bed, giving each other pleasure, drawing it out until they drove themselves to finish. Sarah fell asleep with her head on Dana's shoulder and his arm gently pulling her to him. He lay still, thinking how lucky he was to have a woman who loved him so much.

They got dressed in the morning and sat at Dana's small kitchen table. He pulled out some muffins and grabbed from the fridge the orange juice he'd made the day before. Sarah helped herself to a muffin and then turned to Dana with inquisitive eyes.

"How were your meetings about your father's proposal?" she asked.

Dana was surprised Sarah hadn't asked this question earlier. Maybe they each were wary after the awkwardness of their previous conversation. He looked at her. It was important for him to be factual and stay calm. "Good," he said. "Mehdi wants my help, and Yazdan thinks I would bring new skills. Frida will support whatever I decide."

Sarah's eyes changed from inquisitive to penetrating. She set her juice glass down and looked at Dana. "It sounds like you're considering it?"

"I feel better about it than I did," he said matter-of-factly, wanting to be honest with her even though he could sense her disapproval. He wished she would listen to his words before judging them.

"What about your father and his friends?" she asked with furrowed eyebrows. "You're not comfortable with them. That's not your world."

Dana stood up and carried their plates to the sink, his neck warming. She was crossing a line. "What do you know about my world?" he said.

"Well, for one thing, I've only heard you complain about your father since we first met!"

He calmed himself, regretting that he had gotten emotional. "I'm sorry—I didn't mean to question you." He sat back down. "I just don't feel as negative about it as I did before."

She took a sip of juice and stared at him.

"Helping run Armand could be a way for me to lead my own company while making my family happy," he said.

Sarah shifted her eyes downward, covering her mouth with her hand. Dana sipped his juice. "What are you thinking?" he finally asked.

She quickly lifted her head, her eyes open wide. "What about my happiness?" she blurted loudly. She inhaled deeply, almost crying.

He didn't know what to say, surprised at her strong reactions. He stood up again, took his empty juice glass and her half-filled one to the kitchen sink, and returned to sit on the edge of his chair, preparing to be attacked.

"I don't know what I'm going to do," he said, looking down at the table. "I'm just trying to answer your questions honestly. Maybe we should talk about this later when we're both calmer?"

Sarah looked out the kitchen window, turning silent as she often did when angry. He noticed he was gripping the edge of his chair and tried to relax. "I want to be with the man who cries at poetry readings," she finally said, "not with someone consumed by Iranian business deals!"

Dana straightened his posture and looked at her through narrowed eyes. She had crossed the line again, and he took a deep breath before speaking. "It seems you're having as much trouble with my Iranian background as you are with my decision," he said, his jaw clenched.

"You don't understand. I don't want to live a life with someone like your father!"

Dana smacked the table with his palm, and his words rushed out. "No one is asking you to!" His voice echoed off the walls of the small kitchen. Crossing his arms tightly, he stared out the window, irritated by his emotional outburst.

Sarah's face hardened. She quickly stood and walked to the front door, mumbling with her back turned that she was taking the bus— and then she slammed the door behind her.

Dana's heart raced. He stood, debating whether to run after her. He looked out his second-floor window at the sidewalk and did not see her. He assumed she had already turned the corner to the bus stop. He wasn't going to go search for her. Instead, he sat on his couch, his anger growing.

He kept hearing her attack. She had criticized him, his family, and his culture. They had spent a fantastic night together, and their intimacy had fallen apart in fifteen minutes. They could've had a reasonable discussion—he hadn't decided about his father's offer yet. He knew he had let her intensity provoke him into yelling at her. But she should have known better, saying he would turn into his father if he helped lead Armand. What an insult! She knew how he felt about his father.

He lay down on the couch and didn't move for over an hour, his arms crossed. He didn't know what would happen next. He imagined his phone ringing and picking it up to hear Sarah's apology, but there was nothing but silence. As he heard her words again and again, his anger turned to pain. His heart ached.

He finally felt the need to move. He stood and looked out the window again. It was overcast, and people were walking on the sidewalk below. He saw couples arm in arm and wondered how often they fought. One woman looked up at him standing in the window, and he quickly stepped back. He needed to do something.

He decided to join the people on the sidewalk, with a vague goal of heading toward Newport Beach, about five miles away. He spent the afternoon walking there, through suburban neighborhoods and on busy roads with no sidewalks. After reaching the beach, he sat on a chair on the boardwalk, looking out at the blue ocean. He watched large sailboats with white sails crossing by each other, smoothly cutting through the rolling swells. It reminded him of a poem he had written, *The Sea*, which Sarah loved. He finally stood and turned to walk back to Irvine. He concentrated on the rhythm of moving his legs, feet, and arms, trying to push Sarah's harsh words out of his mind.

When Dana got home, he saw no messages on his answering machine. He felt better than he did that morning, but an aching heaviness settled over him. He wasn't ready to take the first step of calling Sarah. Instead, he called his mother.

"Maman, what time are you going to the hospital tomorrow? I would like to go with you."

"That would be great, Dana." Her words comforted him, as they had his whole life. "Come first for lunch," she said. "I'll invite Mehdi and Frida too."

Dana spent a lonely Saturday evening at his apartment. He played the piano and tried watching TV, but he was distracted, hoping Sarah would call. He finally found that the best way to not think about her was to look forward to seeing his mother.

He arrived at his parents' house midmorning—he wanted to see his mother alone before the others got there. She welcomed him, happy that he had come early. She gave him a cutting board and a sharp knife and asked him to chop lamb, onions, and other ingredients for their Iranian lunch.

"Remember when we went to the park when I was little?" Dana asked. "You used to practice speaking English with the other mothers while we played."

"Yes, I was always encouraging you to play with the boys like Mehdi, but you'd rather sit with me and Frida."

"I remember you saying you were proud of me," Dana said.

"I've always been proud of you, but why did I say that at the park?"

"Because I corrected you and the other mothers trying to speak English. They told you your five-year-old was smarter than they were."

His mother laughed. "I do remember now—you had learned English faster from your American playmates than we had. I remember the other mothers laughing—they told their friends about it."

Dana loved watching his mother smile at these memories, and he was able to put aside his struggles. His mother's face fell, however, when he asked her how his father was doing. "He's declining," she said. "The cancer is spreading. And the doctors are giving him morphine for the pain, which makes him groggy and sleepy."

He wanted to take her mind off his father, as she had helped take his mind off Sarah, so he asked about Mehdi and Tara.

"The baby is due in three months," his mother said.

"That's exciting for our family," Dana said.

His mother's smile was only fleeting. "Caveh wanted so much to see his first grandchild, but I'm afraid he won't," she said, looking out the window. Dana tried to show her his sympathy, in part hoping that by focusing on his mother's pain, he could escape his own.

When Mehdi, Tara, and Frida arrived, the house came alive with conversation. Tara went to the kitchen to help, and Frida set the table. She chose her mother's best dishes and silverware, which her parents had brought from Iran.

"I met with Yazdan," Dana told Mehdi.

"Good."

"It seemed to go well."

"Great. That's all I need to know about him."

The women brought dishes of food to the table, and Dana breathed in the mouthwatering scents of a homemade Iranian meal. His mother served tabouli and dolmeh, one of Dana's favorites:

stuffed grape leaves full of chopped meat, rice, split peas, and green onions. They all began eating, exclaiming about the delicious food. His mother stood more than she sat, offering second helpings or getting more bread. She was happy briefly, having created a meal to feed her family.

"It's too bad Papa couldn't be here," Mehdi said when they finished eating. "This is one of his favorite meals."

Their mother quickly began cleaning the table, taking dishes into the kitchen. The melancholy look on her face returned.

They took two cars to the hospital. Frida rode with Dana. When they were alone, she asked him whether he was all right. He nodded, saying it was hard to watch their mother suffer. She said she understood that, but it seemed that something else might be bothering him. "How are things with Sarah?" she asked.

"We've got a lot going on—let's talk later about that, if that's okay?" He had worked to disguise his feelings about his fight with Sarah, but he wasn't surprised that Frida could see through him. Frida had met Sarah several times, and they were both polite to each other, but Frida had never offered any opinions of Sarah to him.

They all arrived in their father's room at about the same time. Dana was shocked at how much his father had declined since he had seen him the previous week. His father looked at them as they greeted him, but he was distant, seeming lost in his thoughts. He breathed rapidly and had difficulty talking because of a persistent cough. His mother bent down to kiss his face and began to cry. Mehdi, Tara, and Frida each gave him a hug.

Dana stepped to the bed last and hugged his father. "Papa, I've decided to accept your offer," he said. "I'll help Mehdi lead the company." He said this without thinking, forgetting Sarah's and his own misgivings. He vaguely thought about pleasing his father on his deathbed and not caring about Sarah's concerns after she had insulted him.

His father nodded slowly, overcoming his fatigue for a moment. Everyone was glad to hear this news, his mother hugging and thanking

Dana. They all stayed for a while, making small talk, until Dana felt his throat tighten—he needed to leave. He walked out, unsure about what he had done. His sadness about Sarah weighed heavily on him.

When he got home, a message from Sarah on his answering machine asked him to call her. He dialed her right away. "I think we should talk," she said. He could not tell from her tone whether she was still angry at him or whether she missed him and was ready to make up. She suggested they meet at the bistro on Wednesday after work.

He hung up, not knowing what to feel. He was glad that their silence had ended and they were going to talk. But he didn't know what she would say, or why she chose a public setting. And why they couldn't speak sooner. He feared she might leave him. The thought of it paralyzed him.

Dana watched mindless television shows for the rest of the weekend, often old movies that he had seen before such as *Spartacus*. He felt better when he returned to work on Monday and Tuesday, but he couldn't stop thinking about what Sarah might say or do. He visited the hospital briefly Tuesday night, and his mother hugged him tightly after he said goodbye to his father.

Wednesday came. Dana tried to prepare himself for seeing Sarah that evening. His heart raced as he imagined the different directions their conversation might take.

He was in his office that afternoon when his phone rang. It was Frida—she struggled to greet him. He could hear his mother crying in the background.

Frida was silent momentarily. "Papa just died," she finally said, bursting into sobs.

Dana said he would come immediately. As he drove to the hospital, he found it difficult to believe that at sixty years old, Caveh Armand, the hard-driving man with a jutting jaw—his father and his worst critic—was no longer with them.

5

ana looked briefly at his father's body as he approached the hospital bed—all life had left his father's face. He looked ashy, his jaw slack. His mother threw her arms around Dana's neck and sobbed, and he drew her close to him, tears filling his eyes. He had little sense of grief, feeling more numb than sad. But his mother's suffering was hard to stomach. He turned and hugged Frida, Mehdi, and Tara, who had arrived before him. They were all silent except for their mother. Frida dabbed her eyes with her handkerchief.

The Iranian mortician arrived, hesitating at the door before bowing slightly and saying he was sorry for their loss. He covered their father with a Persian blanket that had a colorful, intricate design. Two nurses helped the mortician move the body to a stretcher, respectfully nodding when they arrived, and the mortician wheeled the body out. He was taking their father to the Iranian Christian funeral home.

They spent the evening together at their mother's house, attentive in every way to her; she was overcome with sadness. Dana felt close to his siblings as they tried to comfort her. Frida was the most effusive in mourning their father's death, saying, "He was so good to me." The next day, Mehdi worked with their church and the funeral director to plan the funeral, frequently updating Dana, Frida, and their mother. They scheduled the funeral for Monday of the following week.

Mehdi asked Dana to write the obituary. It made sense that Mehdi would give him this task because of his writing skills, but he felt challenged. How could he write a piece that celebrated the life of a man who had often been critical of him, a father who had never been close to him? He had tried to understand him for years, never fully knowing who his father was and why he behaved the way he did.

As a child, he quickly learned that his father's strong feelings were often accompanied by an aggressive edge. He became aware that Caveh Armand was known as a tough guy who spoke his mind, often daring people who crossed him.

When their family had visited the home of his father's cousin, Hassan, a cheerful man with sparkling eyes, Dana eagerly listened to stories Hassan told about Caveh in Iran, where he was always getting into fights, often between groups of Muslim and Christian boys. Once, Caveh was caught alone and was chased by three older Muslim boys. He escaped them by jumping into the river, almost drowning, before finally crawling onto the grass and coughing up water. When he got home, his mother yelled at him for losing his boots and told him he couldn't play with his friends for three days. Dana remembered Hassan saying, "You think your father is tough? You should have seen your grandmother."

As Dana grew older, his father told stories about what it was like coming to America in his late twenties with a wife and child, barely able to speak English. "I worked for a concrete firm owned by two Iranians," he'd told Dana and Mehdi. "They knew how much I needed the job and worked me long hours, six days a week. Lots of men quit, but I focused on learning the work, tackled everything they gave me."

"Tell us the story again about your fight," Mehdi had asked.

"The owners began to favor me," his father said. "Some Muslim workers insulted me, saying I was getting ahead only because the owners liked Christians. I finally challenged the leader, meeting him in the company's parking lot after work."

"What happened?" Dana asked.

"The man was bigger than me, but I knocked him out with one punch. Soon after, the owners made me the lead foreman."

Dana knew the obituary was not the place for him to write about vivid memories of his father's conflicts. He asked Frida and Mehdi for memories they thought should be noted, and then he asked his mother to read a draft. He became more comfortable when he saw himself writing it on behalf of his mother, portraying his father in a way that she wanted.

Still, he remembered witnessing his father's explosive anger. Once, when his father was driving Mehdi and Dana home from Mehdi's soccer game, he stopped at a bowling alley, saying he needed to do some business. Waiting in the car, they watched a man run out of the bowling alley holding his jaw, with their father chasing him. When his father got back in the car, all he said was, "He won't cheat me again." Later, Mehdi told Dana that the fight was probably over a gambling debt. That night, Dana couldn't sleep because of his fear— what if his father got that mad at him?

Once, after Mehdi teased Dana about his piano playing, they'd kept pushing each other as they walked toward the dinner table, where their father already sat. He told them to quiet down. Dana pushed Mehdi one more time, and Mehdi yelled. Suddenly, their father grabbed the chair next to him and threw it against the wall, knocking out a large piece of plaster that fell to the floor. "If you don't stop, I'm going to throw you next!" he shouted. Frida, who was three, began crying, and Dana's mother shooed all three kids into the kitchen.

But Dana didn't write about that in the obituary. He emphasized his father's immigration from Iran and his success as an American citizen, working his way up in the concrete industry and ultimately owning his own company. He was a man who was survived by a wonderful family that meant everything to him. Dana struggled with this last theme, but he justified it for himself by remembering his father's words about loving his family on his deathbed, despite his doubts about their sincerity. Everyone was happy with the obituary. The funeral director said it was one of the best he had ever seen, and his mother had tears in her eyes after reading his last draft. The funeral director submitted it for placement in the Sunday newspaper.

——•••——

Dana had informed Sarah the afternoon of his father's death that he wouldn't be able to see her that night. "I can't handle both the emotions from my father's death and my feelings about us." She had started to reply, but he cut the call short because he needed to get to the hospital.

Sarah surprised him with a call Saturday, saying she wanted to go to the funeral. When he stopped by her place to pick her up on Monday, she greeted him with a warm kiss. "I'm so sorry for your family," she said, holding him close. She stood next to him as he helped greet people arriving for the visitation at the funeral home, many from the Iranian community, a larger group than he expected. She continued to show the sympathy she had expressed in the car, making him feel their conflict was over, although he was wary, remembering her anger.

Dana's mother, Frida, Tara, and Hassan's wife sat in the row of chairs in front of his father's casket, reserved for women of the family. Several flower arrangements surrounded the coffin, the largest from his father's friend Ali, who couldn't attend because he was in prison. Another extravagant one came from Yazdan. Iranian women, many close to his mother's age, walked to the front row one by one and bent down to kiss her and the other women in the family. The intense grieving by the women surprised Dana, who stood watching with Sarah. He'd never been to an Iranian funeral—the elderly relatives who died during his lifetime had all passed away in Iran. His mother couldn't stop crying during the women's emotional display of sympathy, and tears welled in his own eyes.

The funeral director quieted the room with a short prayer in preparation for their departure to the church. He closed the casket, and his assistant helped him drape it with intricately designed Persian blankets. Before they wheeled it to the exit, where Dana and the other pallbearers were to lift it into the hearse, the director invited Dana's family into a small room off the hallway and closed the door. Hassan and his family joined them, and everyone hugged each other during this private moment of grief, with the women openly crying and the men, including Dana, wiping tears from their cheeks. He had never felt more connected to his family. He invited Sarah to join them, but she stood on the edge of the group.

They followed the hearse to the Iranian Christian church, where many of his father's business associates had arrived. Dana noticed Yazdan looking at him across the room, seeming to want to talk. But the priest asked everyone to sit down to celebrate the life of Caveh Armand. He gave a short eulogy drawn from the obituary Dana had written, adding his own words addressed to Dana's mother. "We feel your loss, Leila. You and Caveh have been leaders here in our church, and we pray for you in your mourning." He then led a service mainly in Persian, reading and chanting from the church's liturgy. Dana followed the script in the booklet in the church pew, feeling an intimacy with his Iranian Christian heritage that he had never felt before.

After the service, Dana and Sarah joined the procession of cars to the grave site. Dana brought Sarah with him to sit in the chairs provided for the family in front of the grave, although she protested quietly. The priest gave his blessings, and Frida stood with a bouquet of roses, offering one to each person to put on the casket. Dana's mother began crying again, and Dana grimaced with emotion. After all the roses were placed on the casket and the priest adjourned the grave service, Mehdi announced that everyone was invited to the Persian Grill for a buffet lunch.

On the way to their cars, people walked to the family members and expressed condolences. Sarah took Dana's arm, saying, "I've never seen such mourning at a funeral. So intense and from the heart." Dana nodded, as he watched his mother change from a grieving, sobbing woman to a warm and welcoming family leader, inviting everyone to attend their lunch. When the last person giving condolences left, she hugged Dana. "Your father loved you so much," she told him. He appreciated her gesture even though he still had doubts. She also hugged Sarah and thanked her for coming, and Sarah beamed with gratitude.

Dana turned toward his car and found Yazdan waiting for him with a tall, imposing man wearing an elegant gray herringbone suit. His silver-and-black-striped tie matched his silvery hair. Yazdan introduced him, saying, "This is Mr. Ghorbani, a longtime friend and business associate of your father." Dana was puzzled as he shook Ghorbani's hand because he had never heard of or seen this friend of his father.

Ghorbani stood upright next to the slumping Yazdan, looking confident and in command. His eyes, warm but distant, gazed directly at Dana's when they shook hands. "I'm sorry for the loss of your father, Dana. I look forward to meeting with you."

Dana nodded, although he didn't know what the meeting would be about. He said he also looked forward to it and then found Sarah talking to Frida—they were ready to drive to the Persian Grill. He first stared in wonder, though, at his mother. She approached Ghorbani and hugged him warmly, the top of her head reaching his shoulders. "I'm very sorry, Leila," he said.

Dana was curious. How did his father and mother know this impressive man? What role did Mr. Ghorbani play in his father and Yazdan's business partnership?

After they arrived at the Persian Grill, the waiter led them to a private room upstairs. The priest gave his blessing when people were seated, and Mehdi welcomed everyone. Mehdi's heartfelt words impressed Dana—he asked people to join together in this meal to honor his father's life. Waiters removed the covers from each dish, and a delicious aroma of meat, vegetables, and spices filled the air. The mood changed from grieving to celebrating. Dana was happy to see his mother going to each table, smiling and thanking everyone for coming. He was moved by how strong she was. The room became noisy with conversation.

That afternoon, Dana joined Frida, Mehdi, Tara, and their mother at her house to spend the evening with her. After supper, when they gathered in the living room to watch TV, Mehdi surprised them by pulling a rented video out of a sack. They spent the evening watching episodes from *The Danny Thomas Show*, also titled *Make Room for Daddy*—their father's favorite comedian and TV show. They remembered how he liked to remind them that Danny Thomas was the son of Middle Eastern immigrants with the birth name of Amos Muzyad Yaqoob Kairouz. Dana joined the others in laughing at the episodes, reminding him of a side of his father he had rarely seen.

6

When Dana had dropped Sarah off after the funeral, he studied her before she opened the car door. "Who were those men talking to you in the parking lot?" she asked.

"Just some of my father's business partners," he told her, ready to switch topics. "It's been almost a week since you wanted to talk to me. How are you feeling now?" he asked.

"I'm fine. I'm sorry we fought."

Her apology affected him. He felt his forehead smoothing, and his arm on the wheel relaxing its grip. "I think this break has been good for us," he said.

She nodded. "Let's have dinner on Thursday. We can plan our weekend."

A weight lifted off of him. Even though Sarah had been friendly and respectful to him during the funeral, he hadn't known how she felt since their quarrel.

"It's been hard not knowing your feelings," he said. "I'm so happy you aren't angry." He kissed her goodbye with a smile.

———❖———

At their Thursday dinner, Dana loved catching up with her, her eyes sparkling in the dim light as she talked. They were both on good behavior, as if they'd never quarreled. They enjoyed a bottle of wine, lingered over a seafood dinner, and ordered a piece of chocolate cake with ice cream, Sarah's favorite dessert.

She suggested they see the new exhibit at the Los Angeles County Museum of Art that weekend, and Dana agreed. Their relationship had weathered a storm. He knew they would eventually need to discuss his father's request, but he avoided talking about it for now. Maybe she avoided it as well.

She instead chose a familiar topic. "My boss is driving me crazy."

"How?" Dana asked, inwardly groaning—he would rather have continued talking about the art exhibit. He knew he would have to listen to Sarah vent about her boss.

"You know how much I admire the dean of Continuing Ed. She's so impressive."

Dana nodded.

"I was excited because she agreed to give a welcome to one of my events with a large number of registrants. Before the welcome, she complimented me on the great job I've been doing."

Dana nodded again, wondering what the problem was.

"When the dean was talking to me, James, my boss, joined us. She barely acknowledged him, just a quick nod and then turned back to me. It was weird."

"I've seen that happen," Dana said. "In my first year at BG Hill—"

She raised her hand to stop him. "You're interrupting me. Just listen."

She described how James had been distant to her since the event with the dean. He had reviewed their event plans in staff meetings and moved quickly through Sarah's without mentioning the dean's praise. She tried to be friendly to him, but he didn't respond to her, just nodding and going back to what he was working on. She was fed up with it.

"I'm making him look good, but he pouts because the dean was attentive to me, not him. I don't know how to deal with such immaturity," she said, looking at Dana like she expected him to say something.

Dana was uncertain whether she wanted advice. He finally said it wasn't unusual for managers to act that way when an executive recognizes the workers more than the managers. "Their jealousy can make them forget their role. A good manager would reinforce the praise from the dean and help you become even more successful," he said.

"James is an idiot. I don't think he could ever do that," she said.

Dana frowned. "If you see him as an idiot, that could influence how you behave around him, and he could become even more resentful."

"But he is an idiot!—also an overweight, balding slob trying to grow a mustache."

Dana looked over Sarah's shoulder at the table behind her, where two couples in their thirties were laughing and enjoying themselves.

"Maybe you should look for a new job," he said.

"No—I love my job. He's the one who needs a new job."

"Then you might have to learn how to deal with him," he said. "Treat him as one of the things you need to manage. Maybe praise him now and then since he seems sensitive."

"He makes more money than I do! I shouldn't have to manage him."

Dana was silent, looking again at the table with the two couples, who were clinking their wineglasses together for a toast. "I don't really want to talk about it anymore if you're not going to take my advice," he said.

"I don't need your advice. Can't you just listen to me?" she asked.

Dana looked down at his plate with a furrowed brow. He had five more years of work experience than Sarah, but she didn't seem to value what he had learned.

"I'm listening, but you might need to just accept reality," he said.

Sarah looked at him silently, pressing her lips together. She seemed to be as fed up with him as she was with James.

"I could do it—it wouldn't be hard," she said. "But how ridiculous!"

He nodded, trying to act understanding but mainly ready to change the topic. She got up to go to the restroom.

He wished she was at a point in her career similar to his. She was twenty-five and employed in a relaxed academic environment. Maybe they would have more stimulating discussions about work if their experiences were more equal.

In his junior year at Irvine, Dana had applied for a summer internship posted on the English department bulletin board by a local communications consultant, BG Hill. His experience that summer was eye-opening. He helped outline communication goals and tactics for clients and helped with the participation of neighborhood groups. After he graduated, BG Hill offered him a job and a salary that allowed him to move into his own apartment. His mother was proud of him, but his father became more distant than ever. His words, when he had learned Dana was going to college, still rang in Dana's memory: "So, what? You think you're better than me?"

Dana was now thirty. He had been promoted to project manager and was the principal staff person for facilitating large meetings of stakeholder audiences. He was proud of what he had accomplished and had a vision of someday leading his own communications company.

Sarah returned and Dana quietly watched her straighten her napkin. The chocolate cake and ice cream arrived at a good time, breaking the silence they had retreated to after the frustrating conversation about her job. His wishes for her to be closer to his age and maturity were swept away when she gazed into his eyes and laughed her infectious laugh. "You've been hoping this cake will put me in a better mood, haven't you?" she said.

"If that helps," he said.

She offered him a bite of her cake, and he laughed, glad she had stopped talking about her job. He dropped her off early since he was facilitating a neighborhood meeting the next day. He looked forward to spending time with her on the weekend to see the art museum and be together, confident they would enjoy two interests he knew they had in common—art and sex.

7

Two days after the funeral, their mother had asked Dana and his siblings to begin looking through their father's things. She had started putting aside what she wanted, planning to donate the remaining items after her children had made their selections. She seemed to be executing a plan she had been thinking about for more than a few days. She asked Dana and Mehdi to go through their father's things in the garage, which he had used as a shop and office.

Mehdi suggested that Dana start with their father's desk and files as soon as possible, particularly to look for important paperwork related to their company and current projects. Dana decided to start on Friday after work. Mehdi would follow up on the weekend.

When Dana sat down at the large antique desk, with its many slim drawers and brass handles, he felt apprehensive. This was his father's private space, a space he had never been invited to enter. He hesitated, not knowing where to start. The desk's surface overflowed with papers, many related to concrete work on construction projects. He put those aside to go over with Mehdi.

He began with the drawers. The first one he opened contained articles and newspapers from Iran, written in Farsi, of which Dana was a poor translator. He leafed through these papers, his heart racing. They were from a world his father had never talked to him about. Another drawer contained his father's Bible and photographs of boys in Iran at church and school. Dana recognized his father as a boy and thought about the story of his father being chased by the Muslim boys.

Dana sat back in the chair, feeling he was looking into a life he had never known. He blinked, paralyzed, not knowing what to look at next, beginning to sense a force that held him back from opening the next drawer. He worried about what he was supposed to do with the information he found. He wasn't the right person to decide on these private things.

He forced himself to open a third drawer. It included paperwork related to becoming an American citizen. He knew his father was proud of his citizenship. He imagined how difficult it must have been—the move from Iran, learning a new language, finding a job to support his family, and the citizenship process, which, if failed, would have left his father and family with an uncertain future.

This struggle had never been shared with him. He was left out, not born until after his family had left Iran. Maybe his father had thought he could never imagine what it had been like, so he never bothered to share those experiences—experiences that Dana now felt would have helped him better understand his father and better understand himself, growing up as an immigrant's son.

He again sat back in the chair, lacking the motivation to go further and despondent over the distance between him and his father. A weight pushed down on his shoulders. He opened the fourth and final drawer and found pictures of his mother, including a picture of their wedding party, which he had seen before. He also found a picture he had never seen—of his mother and father standing with Mehdi in an airport. He assumed this was taken right before their flight to America in 1964. In his best clothes, Mehdi held his mother's hand and looked up at her, smiling and excited. Tears came to Dana's eyes as he quietly said, "Oh . . ." He felt a tremendous distance from what this picture showed: a happy, united family about to go on the most exciting adventure of their lives.

He stopped and sat with his eyes closed. He finally overcame his physical immobility and moved to the file cabinet next to the desk. He opened the top drawer and saw several files related to Armand Concrete. The weight on his shoulders increased. He couldn't go any further—he didn't even open the second file drawer.

Sweating and nervous, he felt like he had as a boy when his father criticized his piano playing, his poems, and his interest in acting. But this was deeper. The stifling pressure in the room began to nauseate him. He was not wanted here. Overwhelmed, he left the garage and entered the house. In the kitchen, Frida looked up from preparing sandwiches for lunch.

"What's the matter?" she said. "You look like you've seen a ghost."

"That's a good way to describe it," he said. He quickly turned to his mother and initiated the conversation before she could remark on how he looked.

"Maman, I went through Papa's office, and there's nothing I want. Tell Mehdi that he should look at the papers piled on top of the desk—they're related to recent concrete projects he knows about. Tell him that I think we should keep all the papers in the file cabinets since they're related to the company. The other drawers have personal items you should look at to see if you want to keep them."

"Don't you want supper?" his mother asked.

"No, thanks. I have leftovers to eat."

He hugged his mother and Frida goodbye, then left. He could sense they were looking at each other, both curious about him. But he wanted to avoid any more words about his time in the garage. He drove home, glad to be alone.

He lay on his couch and gradually recovered from the feelings he had experienced in his father's office. He tried to step back and analyze them. What had happened? He had never been so paralyzed. He went into the office with a job to do, as requested by his mother, and he couldn't do it. A simple job, like cleaning up his room when he was a boy—something he didn't like to do, but something he could complete to satisfy his mother. He appeared to do what she had asked in his father's office, but he knew he hadn't. He hadn't even opened the last drawer, so anxious to leave and escape the heavy presence he felt pushing down—a sensation that compressed his chest and nauseated him.

It could only be one thing—the presence of his father. His father didn't want him in his office. He didn't want him going through his drawers, touching his personal items. And he didn't want him meddling with his company, pushing him out before he even opened the last drawer. But why did his father want him to join Mehdi as a partner? Why did he say those words of praise and love in the hospital as he neared death? Were they only to push him to accept the offer to partner with Mehdi? Were his father and Yazdan so worried about Mehdi's ability to keep the company going that his father had used those words as a bribe to get him to say yes? Were those words false? Was the truth what Dana had sensed his whole life—that his father didn't love him and never would?

He felt better as he defined the questions. If it was true that his father didn't love him, did that change Dana's mind about leaving BG Hill, leaving a job that he loved? If he didn't leave BG Hill, how would Mehdi feel? Were there other ways he could offer to help Mehdi?

Exhausted, he fell asleep. When he woke thirty minutes later, he went to his piano and played one of his favorite Beethoven pieces, "Für Elise." The opening sadness in the music gradually turning to joy calmed him.

After a long Saturday at the museum, Dana and Sarah had a glass of wine and a selection of appetizers in the museum café and then drove to Dana's apartment. Sarah put her hand on Dana's knee and smiled at him, and he anticipated the pleasure of being close to her. They wasted no time in undressing each other and getting into bed. All the insecurity Dana had felt—his fear that Sarah might leave him—disappeared. They were playful with each other, smiling and laughing, until their desire grew intense, with Sarah holding him tighter than she ever had. When they lay back and rested, he sensed a distance from her as she looked at the ceiling. He kissed her and felt tears on her cheek.

"What's the matter? Are you all right?"

"I'm fine. I'm just happy we're getting along."

"Are you sure?"

She nodded and smiled, turning toward him, but he still felt she was holding something back. He ignored it and brought her close to him, ready for them to sleep.

The following day at breakfast, he cautiously brought up his father's company, well prepared after the disaster of their last conversation on the topic. Sarah, too, seemed prepared and sensitive, concentrating on listening. He told her he had been thinking about his father's offer and had talked to one of his father's business partners. He didn't tell her he had accepted the offer at his father's deathbed. He didn't tell her about his experience in the garage, where it seemed his dead father was pushing him away. "I'm leaning against taking the offer," was all he told her. "I still have doubts about my father's intent."

Sarah smiled and looked at him tenderly. "That is so much the right decision," she said.

Dana was satisfied with that resolution for now, or at least relieved their conversation had not led to conflict. Sarah had plans with friends that afternoon, so Dana dropped her off at her apartment. He then drove to Frida's, eager to hear her reaction to his experience with his father's ghost.

8

Frida welcomed Dana into her apartment, still dressed in the skirt and blouse she had worn to church. His eyes were drawn to new flowers in the vase on the coffee table. Their colors and fragrances immediately relaxed him.

"I'm glad you stopped by," she said. "I've been thinking about you since you left the house looking like you'd seen a ghost."

"You don't know how fitting those words are," Dana said. "I think there was a ghost in the garage. The spirit of Papa."

"What do you mean?"

"I felt his presence. Like a weight on me that didn't allow me to move. I don't think he wanted me to be looking at his things."

Frida pushed her hair back and looked at Dana intently. "Maybe he's communicating to you through a Persian spirit. What do you think he wants?"

"I don't know, but I'm unsure about helping lead the company, given what I'm feeling from him."

"But he asked you. He loves you. Why would he be pushing you away from what he asked?"

"I have no idea, but I don't feel loved."

Frida looked at him with concern. "What are you thinking of doing next?"

"I'm not sure, but I'll need to talk to Yazdan. What would Maman and Mehdi think if I changed my mind?"

"You first need to decide what you want. I can help with Maman and Mehdi."

Dana left feeling much better. His thoughts turned to Yazdan and Ghorbani, and to Mehdi. What would these three men say about his doubts? Before asking them, he needed to talk to the one person who knew more about his father's business than anyone: his mother.

———••———

"Maman, you've cooked my favorite food!" Dana said, smelling mouthwatering spices in his serving of kebabs and vegetables with dolmeh. His mother always seemed happy when Dana was with her, although she probably wasn't expecting the questions he had for her at this dinner. He started by telling her his move to Armand Concrete was complicated.

"Yazdan wants to talk to me this week. I'd like to know more about how he and Papa developed their business relationship."

His mother looked at him silently and refilled his water glass before responding.

"Yazdan was one of the Iranian men who got together at the Persian Grill with Caveh," she said. "They were Christian immigrants who left Iran because they disagreed with the revolution and were at risk of persecution. They helped each other succeed in this country."

Dana could feel a reluctance in his mother to talk about those days. "When did they start doing business together?" he asked.

She took a deep breath. "Your father learned that Yazdan worked for a construction company, and he persuaded his bosses to let him bid on concrete work for Yazdan's projects. Your father increased his company's concrete work and gave Yazdan discounts, saving money for Yazdan's clients. They both looked good to their bosses, and their business together grew."

"Is that all there is to it? Did Papa trust Yazdan?"

A look of discomfort came over his mother's face. "Why are you asking me all these questions?"

"I want to know more about what I'm getting into. I'm curious about the bombing. Did that have something to do with Papa's and Yazdan's business?"

His mother closed her eyes for several seconds, then took another deep breath, seeming resigned to giving Dana answers about a subject she didn't want to talk about.

"No. Caveh and Yazdan played card games organized by Ali. They would drink for hours. Ali invited Christian and Muslim Iranian men—that distinction had lessened after years in this country. But your father got in over his head and owed money to two Muslim men, money he didn't have. They were furious and threatened Ali, Yazdan, and your father if they were not paid."

Dana hesitated, taking in information he had never known. "Is that who bombed our garage?"

"I never heard if they found out for sure."

"How did Papa pay back the money he owed?"

"After the bombing, Ali paid off the debt, and Caveh and Yazdan committed to building him a movie theater at a low cost."

"Did Papa owe Yazdan for anything else?"

His mother hesitated again. "When Yazdan was in Iran, he was a member of SAVAK, the Shah's secret police, until the Islamic Revolution—that was in 1979. They were known for torturing people who disagreed with the Shah."

"Wow," Dana said. "But that was in Iran."

His mother got up and took their dishes to the kitchen sink. She sat down again and looked at Dana with a seriousness he had rarely seen.

"Your father believed Yazdan led a network of former SAVAK agents in Los Angeles—maybe he still does. We didn't know what happened, but he hated the Islamists who overthrew the Shah. Those two Muslim men were never seen again at the Persian Grill."

"Really!" Dana's mouth hung open. "So, if Yazdan somehow made the Muslim men disappear, how did Papa repay him?"

"He connected Yazdan to the Ghorbani Group, a land development company. Your father grew up with Mr. Ghorbani, and Yazdan asked him to use his friendship to develop an agreement. Yazdan would do the construction work for Ghorbani's projects and Caveh would do the concrete work."

Dana's mind raced. So, this was the connection to Ghorbani. "I imagine Yazdan wants to make sure this continues after Papa is gone."

"I'm sure he does, but I want you to be careful. Yazdan is a dangerous man."

His mother got up and served rice pudding for dessert. He knew he had reached her limit on questions. As he ate, he couldn't stop thinking of Yazdan—a torturer of the Shah's Islamic and other dissidents in Iran thirty years ago—now slumping, overweight, and bald.

Dana had begun paying attention to Iranian politics when he was fourteen. He and his family watched TV reports on the Islamic Revolution in Iran led by Islamic clerics and students against the secular policies of the Shah. They created an Islamic republic, causing the Shah to depart to Egypt in exile. They also took fifty-two American diplomats and citizens hostage before they could escape.

He had listened to his father express frustration to his mother about how the Iran ayatollah was affecting Americans' views, causing U.S. citizens from the Middle East to be abused and attacked. Dana had not experienced racist actions like his father described. His light complexion, longish hair, and tall, slender build were not typical of Iranian men. Mehdi, however—with his beard, short hair, and dark complexion—was easily identified as Middle Eastern.

One evening after the hostage-taking, when their father was working late, Dana's mother suggested that the four of them go to the mall for dinner. The parking lot was full, and they parked a distance from the entrance. As they walked back to their car after dinner, a beat-up car full of white teenage boys pulled into a parking spot in front of them.

"Hey, look at the A-rab!" one boy shouted at Mehdi.

Dana's mother told Mehdi to ignore the boy and urged them all to keep walking.

A second boy joined the first and walked toward them. "What the hell are you doing in this country? Go back to the hole you came from!" Two more boys got out of the car and moved toward them.

Mehdi positioned himself between the boys and his family, telling his mother to keep walking.

One boy started yelling, "Allah Akbar! Allah Akbar!" He moved closer to Mehdi as he mocked him.

"Dana, get Maman and Frida to the car," Mehdi ordered, and then turned to face the boys.

"Look at this tough guy!" the first boy said, spitting on the ground in front of Mehdi.

Dana had walked quickly with his mother and Frida a short distance, and, once he saw the boys weren't following them, told his mother and sister to continue to the car. Then he returned to join Mehdi, who was in a standoff with the four boys.

"Hey, tough guy, who's this skinny rat with you?" the second boy said before moving in quickly to push Dana.

Mehdi stepped in front of Dana and yelled, "So you want to fight? Come on, assholes!"

None of the boys were as old as Mehdi, and none were built like him, a stocky former wrestler. They surrounded the two of them, their arms jabbing at Dana. One got too close, and Mehdi punched him in the face, knocking him to the ground.

"What the hell? Let's rush them—it's four against two," one boy said. But nobody moved.

A car suddenly appeared, barreling down their row, its horn blaring. Dana's mother was driving. Mehdi took advantage of the confusion and punched another boy. He yelled to Dana, "Get in the car!" As Dana jumped in, Mehdi stepped toward the other boys and they retreated. He turned back quickly to the car and leaped in.

"Drive, Maman! Faster!" Mehdi shouted. The group of boys jumped out of the way, yelling as Dana's mother drove past. Mehdi looked out the back window to see if they were being followed. "I think we're in the clear," he said.

They all started talking at once, relieving the tension each of them felt. Dana looked at his mother closely. He had never seen her so angry. Mehdi was breathing heavily, his eyes intense. Frida, only twelve, chattered. She had many questions: "Why did the boys attack us? Why did they think we're Muslims? Why did they call us Arabs?"

Dana calmed her. "Some people are bad, but Mehdi and I won't let them hurt you." Mehdi, who was starting to relax, turned and smiled at Dana, who sat in the back seat.

"I'm glad you came back, or I would have been in trouble," Mehdi said. "And, Maman, your timing was perfect!"

When they got home, their father's truck was in the driveway. Frida ran in first. "Papa, some boys tried to beat us up!" she said. Their father looked at their mother with raised eyebrows. She described the threats from the white boys and Mehdi's punches, and their father was silent, shaking his head. He told them this was also happening to other Iranians. "You should all be careful," he said.

He then turned to Mehdi and asked if he had seen these boys before or recognized the type of car they drove. Mehdi shook his head, and their father sat silently, reflecting. He finally said, "If we find them, we'll show them why they shouldn't attack Iranian families."

Dana finished his rice pudding dessert, thinking about his mother's stories about Yazdan, Ali, and his father. Sixteen years after the confrontation with the white boys at the mall, he still remembered his father's words: "If we find them, we'll show them why they shouldn't attack Iranian families." His father had been talking about the Iranian men who gathered at the Persian Grill.

———••———

After driving home from his mother's, Dana sat on his couch. The incident at the mall had shaken his assumptions about fitting in as an immigrant's son in America. Those four white boys saw him as different from them. They saw him and his family as intruders in their country and mocked their differences in looks, language, and religion. Dana understood why his father and friends gathered at the Persian Grill. He imagined that all of them were challenged with figuring out how to live in a new country. They came together over food and drink to learn from each other—their drinking and gambling was how they escaped the constant pressure.

Dana stood up to close the blinds. He watched a flock of birds move from one bush to another. In two days, he would meet with Yazdan again. How would Yazdan react to his doubts about accepting his father's offer? He remembered meeting Yazdan as a boy at family cookouts in the park. Yazdan had seemed to be an overweight, fun-loving man who liked talking about the old days in Iran. He knew now that he had tortured the Shah's enemies.

Dana also had met Ali, another of his father's friends, at the cookouts. He knew that Ali ran a newsstand and was a big gambler. When Dana grew older, he learned that Ali's newsstand had expanded into a pornography bookstore and then into pornographic movies, shown in the theater built by his father and Yazdan. Ali contributed large sums to the church, and the community was surprised when he was convicted of tax fraud and sentenced to ten years in prison.

Dana went to bed early and lay wondering what he might be getting into if he accepted his father's offer—a network of men who used threats, strong-arm tactics, lawbreaking, and potential violence? What if he didn't accept the offer?

He dozed, sleeping restlessly. He awoke with a start, dreaming about the bombing of their garage. It had happened late at night when he was eight years old, waking them all with a bang that he now knew had a more significant impact than the actual destruction itself. He remembered police cars arriving with bright flashing beacons and lights being turned on in their neighbors' houses.

Dana remained scared for weeks after the bombing. His whole family was scared, even their father, though it was plain to see that he covered up his feelings with anger and action. He installed a new garage door the very next day after the bombing, seeming to want the neighborhood and his family to quickly forget about this unfortunate incident.

Dana lay awake thinking. His mother had answered questions that he'd long thought about. He now knew more about his father's network of Iranian men and their use of power. But what he didn't know was how all of this might affect him. That was what made him so uneasy.

9

When Dana entered Yazdan's office, he had a new perspective on the pictures of Yazdan shaking hands with the Shah. Was the Shah thanking Yazdan for silencing his critics? How often had he and his police broken into the houses of politicians or Islamic leaders opposed to the Shah and dragged them to prison, where they were tortured until they confessed to crimes that kept them locked up indefinitely?

Yazdan greeted Dana with a smile, which put Dana on guard. "It's good to see you, Dana. You remind me of your father—I've missed him."

Dana nodded. But how he could remind anyone of his father was beyond him.

"I'm happy that I will have a chance to work with both of Caveh's sons," Yazdan said. "And I'm glad you and your father reconciled the differences that kept you from joining Armand Concrete."

As Dana listened, he thought of going through his father's things in the garage, where he felt as if he were an invader of his father's territory—an invader whom his father's spirit had successfully beaten off. There were no feelings of reconciliation in that garage and no indication that his father wanted him to join Armand Concrete.

"Do you have a date set when you'll start working with Mehdi and me?" Yazdan asked.

"I'll be honest. I'm struggling a bit with the decision to leave my job at BG Hill," Dana said.

"What do you mean? This is a great opportunity for you. You will make Leila proud. I know how much your reconciliation with Caveh means to her."

Dana hesitated. Yazdan had immediately played one of his strongest cards. He was aware of how close Dana was to his mother. And he was right—Dana worried about how his mother would feel if he changed his mind.

"I know my mother wants me to be happy."

"Then come work with Mehdi and me. You will be happy, and she will be happy." Yazdan continued to smile as he talked, but Dana could sense that he was becoming impatient.

Dana decided to be direct. "My dream has been to own my own consulting firm. I'm having trouble letting go of that."

"If Caveh was alive, he would join me in helping bring reality to your dream. He and I found how difficult it is to establish your own business. It takes years, decades. Here, you can lead your own business in a matter of weeks."

"I know, and I'm honored. But I'll need to think more about whether this change is right for me."

Yazdan stopped smiling. For a moment, his back stiffened, even though he slouched in his chair, reminding Dana of the picture of him shaking hands with the Shah, ramrod straight and confident. Yazdan looked out the window, and when he turned back, his eyes bored into Dana's, making him uncomfortable.

"There is more at stake here than your happiness. You remember Mr. Ghorbani. He is waiting to hear how our arrangement will work without Caveh. He was pleased to hear that you'll be joining Armand Concrete."

So Ghorbani was pleased. In other circumstances, Dana might feel flattered—Ghorbani was clearly an impressive leader. But Dana wondered what sort of leader he was.

"I don't understand why this business relationship can't continue working as it has for years," Dana said.

Yazdan kept staring at Dana, then, with a raised voice, said, "For one thing, your brother is an imbecile. Neither Caveh nor I have involved him with Ghorbani."

Dana narrowed his eyes. Mehdi didn't have the education Dana had, but he was no imbecile.

"I disagree about my brother. What role would I play?" he asked.

"Caveh and I thought you would be perfect as liaison to Ghorbani. You would meet with him, as Caveh did, to discuss property development projects he and his partners are pursuing. Then you would work with Mehdi and me to estimate the costs to build the development. It may require negotiating with Ghorbani, but once he accepts our bid, you would ensure he was satisfied with our work."

Dana grew curious as he listened to the role his father and Yazdan had designed for him. "Why weren't you the primary liaison for Ghorbani, since my father was your subcontractor?" he asked.

"Your father grew up with Ghorbani," Yazdan said. "I don't have that kind of relationship with him."

"Why would my relationship with Ghorbani be better than yours?"

Yazdan looked around his office, coming to rest on the pictures of the Shah. "Ghorbani's politics in Iran were very different from my own. Ghorbani worked in the Shah's ministries—he was an influential leader. But he left Iran because he disagreed with the Shah's direction for the country. I thought he was naive. Long story short, I let Caveh deal with Ghorbani because I didn't want our political differences to get in the way of business."

"Was Mr. Ghorbani seen as a threat to the Shah?" Dana asked.

"No, I believe he left on good terms. Some of his investment money may come from friends in Iran. That's another reason I stay separate—these friends of his might not like it if they knew their investments benefited me."

Dana imagined Ghorbani's friends might not like their investments benefitting a former SAVAK torturer. How close was the partnership between Ghorbani and Yazdan?

"I appreciate this information. It's a lot to think about," Dana said.

Yazdan shook his head with a look of irritation. He raised his voice again to say, "It's already been thought about! I want to tell Ghorbani when you will begin. What is your start date?"

"I'll let you know." Dana stood, tired of Yazdan's persistence and ready to leave.

"Sit down—I'm not done yet." Yazdan slowly got out of his chair and ambled to a file cabinet. He opened the top drawer and took out a piece of paper, placing it in front of Dana as he returned to his chair.

"What's this?" Dana asked.

"I have another factor besides your happiness for you to think about. This receipt shows that Caveh owed me money—four hundred thousand dollars. You and your family now owe me. If you're not joining Armand Concrete, I want it paid back immediately."

Dana, still standing, stared at Yazdan. "Why did my father owe you money?"

"Ghorbani offered Caveh the chance to join him in an investment that he said would return double or triple the amount invested. Caveh didn't have the cash, so he borrowed it from me. We agreed to split any net gain, and Caveh agreed to pay back the full four hundred thousand if the investment lost money."

Dana was silent, his heart beating rapidly. "Are there any other documents for this loan?" he asked.

"No, we shook hands, as we would have in Iran. This receipt shows the transfer of four hundred thousand from my bank account to Caveh's."

Dana looked at the receipt and shook his head. "My family and I don't have that kind of money for full payment."

"Then join Armand Concrete, and we won't settle until we see the return on Ghorbani's investment, as I would've done with Caveh," Yazdan said.

Dana's throat tightened. "That should happen regardless of whether I join the company."

Yazdan's dark eyes glared at Dana. "Don't get smart with me! Without Caveh or you working with Ghorbani, I'm at risk with that loan. I want it paid back in one week if you don't join Armand."

Yazdan stopped staring at Dana and stood. "You will pay, or my friends will persuade you to pay. We're done talking." He turned his back toward Dana and looked out the window, not moving as Dana left.

It was midafternoon, too late to return to BG Hill. Instead, Dana drove to Newport Beach, his hands trembling, even as they gripped the wheel, and his mind replaying what Yazdan said. Did Yazdan's threat mean his friends would beat him as the SAVAK had beaten people in Iran? Were Yazdan's flattering words about working together trying to increase his control over Dana, keeping him close—as if to imprison him—to make sure Yazdan got his money back?

Dana parked his car and sat on a bench facing the ocean, alone except for a few people out in the cool weather. A brisk breeze and the sound of breaking waves helped him focus. He faced the wind and closed his eyes.

Surely, his father knew on his deathbed that if Dana joined the company, he would soon learn about Yazdan's loan for the Ghorbani investment. How much had his father worried that his death would leave his family in a financial crisis? Armand Concrete was at risk, not only from losing $400,000 on one investment but also from losing future business because of a breakdown in the partnership with Ghorbani and Yazdan.

It was logical that Yazdan would pressure Dana to join the company. He needed Dana's help, given his political differences with Ghorbani. Maybe his father was asking Dana to join the company because he believed Dana's skills would help rescue this situation.

A dog barked, and Dana watched it prance through the quickly dissipating foam left on the sand by an incoming wave. He thought of Mehdi, Tara, and their unborn baby possibly losing everything if the company went bankrupt. His mother and sister could lose their shares of the company, and his mother might have to give up her house.

His father had lied about wanting to be closer to him. What his father was really trying to do was to get Dana in a position to help prevent the company's failure. It seemed to him that the rejection he had felt in the garage from his father's presence was the true indicator of his father's feelings for him. After thirty years of knowing his father, he should have known not to trust a last-minute statement about wanting to be closer.

So, what should he do next? Given what he knew now, he had no desire to help lead Armand Concrete. He had exciting opportunities at BG Hill, which he saw as stepping stones to establishing his own consulting company.

But he couldn't stand by and watch Mehdi and the family business get ruined. How could he help it avoid financial failure? He could think of two things. One was to convince Yazdan to allow him to repay the loan with the return on the investment at the end of the project, as Yazdan said he would if his father were alive. This was doubtful, given Yazdan's insistence on the one-week deadline. The second was to talk to Ghorbani without Yazdan's knowledge so that he could better understand Ghorbani's relationship with Yazdan and his father. He might learn, then, if Ghorbani had any influence over the loan repayment.

A gust of wind blew so hard that tiny particles of sand stung his face. He got up and walked to his car, realizing he should meet with Mehdi before going further with Yazdan and Ghorbani. He didn't want Mehdi to be blindsided by his change of mind—to feel alone in a situation created by their father, Yazdan, and Ghorbani.

———— ••• ————

Dana met with his brother at a coffee shop the following day. Mehdi came from a project site, wearing jeans covered with flecks of cement.

Other workmen dressed in coveralls and construction boots stood in line.

"I'm rethinking my decision to join you as a partner," Dana said. He braced himself, expecting that Mehdi would feel betrayed and angry.

Instead, Mehdi replied with a tone of resignation. "That doesn't surprise me. I told Papa that it was a stretch."

Dana felt relieved. "But I don't want to leave you all alone, especially in dealing with Yazdan."

Mehdi scowled. "I appreciate that because he is scum."

"You said he got so angry with you that he threatened to kill you."

"I know he's a former SAVAK agent. I know he helped protect Papa after the bombing. But I think Papa was drinking too much then and made a deal with the devil."

Dana was impressed with how much Mehdi knew. He motioned to the waiter to fill their coffee cups.

"Yazdan was always reminding Papa of how much he owed him," Mehdi said. "It was a lot of pressure. I think it made Papa too dependent on work from Yazdan and Ghorbani. Yazdan knew that I opposed this."

"But he threatened to kill you?"

"We had a huge argument about a bill he submitted to Ghorbani. Yazdan claimed expenses for things that never happened, and I called him out on it. He got so angry that he threatened me, saying losing an arm or leg from a chainsaw would teach me respect. If not, I would disappear forever. I told Papa, and he fixed things—he even got Yazdan to apologize. But since then, I only deal with his foreman at the jobsites." The men at a nearby table had lifted their heads when they heard Mehdi say "chainsaw."

Dana rubbed his chin and closed his eyes for a moment. Yazdan was turning out to be quite the bastard. He debated whether to tell Mehdi about the loan and decided he should reveal everything.

"Are you aware of a loan Yazdan made to Papa for a Ghorbani investment?"

"Just vaguely. Papa kept me out of dealings with Yazdan after Yazdan threatened me. How much is it?"

"Four hundred thousand." Dana hesitated. "He wants it paid back right away if I don't join the company and help him with Ghorbani."

"That asshole! He knows we can't come up with that amount of cash."

Dana was glad Mehdi saw the situation as he did. "I'm hoping Mr. Ghorbani can help if Yazdan's mind can't be changed," Dana said.

"I hope so. But I don't want you to do something you're uncomfortable with. I'll go to the other old men from Iran to get help if we need protection from Yazdan."

Dana thought again about the masculine power he had always sensed in his father's network of Iranian men. Mehdi was much closer to it than he was. Dana feared the consequences if Mehdi played that game, a game that could become violent. "Let me first see what I can find out from Ghorbani," Dana said. Mehdi nodded, acquiescing to his suggestion. He dropped his head into his hands—Dana had never seen him so beaten down. The few times their lives had intersected, Dana followed Mehdi's lead. But now it was different.

"Mehdi," Dana said gently. "Do you remember the time Papa threw us out of the house after we were yelling at each other before supper?"

Mehdi lifted his head. "Yeah. We found a place to eat, but when we came home, the front and back doors were locked. No one answered the doorbell, and we were cold, so we walked to Hassan's."

"The whole five miles," Dana added. "Do you remember how Hassan laughed when we told him what had happened? 'That Caveh!' he said. We slept on his couches, and he dropped us off at our parents' the next morning on his way to work."

"Just as Papa was leaving for work—I remember," Mehdi said. "But why are you telling me this story?"

Dana shrugged, but he knew why. As they passed their father on his way out that morning, he hadn't looked at them. Dana cherished that memory—for once, he and his brother had been equals.

After meeting with Mehdi, Dana spent Friday afternoon in his office, focusing on a new communications opportunity with UC Irvine. He tried to write notes for an upcoming meeting with university leaders, but his thoughts kept turning to Yazdan threatening Mehdi with a chainsaw.

10

Dana often picked Sarah up on Friday after work to begin the weekend with her. But this Friday, Sarah's college girlfriend from San Francisco was in town staying with her. He met them for dinner Saturday night and then spent most of the weekend alone. He read poems from a collection he had recently bought and played his piano for two hours on Sunday. He didn't know what would happen in the coming week, but poetry and music calmed his nerves.

He called Ghorbani's office Monday morning and found that the earliest he could meet was the following week. That was after Yazdan's deadline to pay him the $400,000, but he would have to take that risk. He spent the rest of the morning writing a final report for a developer who wanted BG Hill's help overcoming neighborhood opposition to the design of an apartment building. He summarized the findings of a neighborhood meeting he had facilitated with the architect and the developer—they'd been lucky to get a thumbs-up on an alternative design.

After finishing the report in midafternoon, he went for a walk in the bright sunlight beaming down on the streets and sidewalks. He was happy with his role in developing a solution for his client that pleased the neighborhood. When he returned to his office, he sat back in his chair and closed his eyes, dreaming of building his own company to serve this special role—dealing with conflict and working to reach a consensus.

His ringing phone jolted him out of his peaceful reflection. It was Yazdan. Dana cleared his throat after exchanging greetings, not knowing what to expect.

"When are you joining the company?" Yazdan asked.

Dana took a deep breath. "I've decided not to. I'm glad to be an advisor, but I'm not leaving BG Hill."

Yazdan was silent.

"I believe my father wanted my help to ensure the company wouldn't fail. I can do that without joining the company. I can perform that role as an advisor, and help you that way."

"I don't care one way or the other," Yazdan said calmly. "If you're not joining Armand, when will I get my four hundred thousand?"

"We can't come up with it immediately. But I'll work with Mehdi to make sure it's repaid once we know the results of the Ghorbani investment."

Yazdan didn't reply. Dana tried to wait out his silence but broke it with one more attempt. "I'm confident we can work this out for the sake of my family, given your and my father's long friendship."

The phone stayed silent until Dana heard the click of Yazdan hanging up.

Dana put his phone down, his shirt damp with sweat. He worried about what Yazdan would do next, remembering his warning that his friends would persuade Dana to pay and his chainsaw threat to Mehdi.

That evening, Dana tried to take his mind off his concerns and fears by playing his piano again. It only half worked.

On Tuesday, Dana turned his full attention to the UC Irvine project, immersing himself in his work. It was a new type of project for BG

Hill, with a new type of client—a university—and involving more than communications. UC wanted Dana's help in reaching out to the business community, which the National Science Foundation grant awarded to them required. His proposal to involve business leaders in helping govern the project and participate in strategic planning had been well received.

By the end of the day, he had roughed out a plan that recommended appointing business and UC leaders to a steering committee, and connecting UC researchers to business users with technical teams and seminars. He put his notes in his briefcase, planning to refine them at home that evening.

Deep in thought, he walked down the stairs to the underground garage. He started his car and drove to the exit ramp, moving slowly, his thoughts still focused on ideas for the UC meeting. Turning onto the street, he noticed a black sedan behind him. It followed him as he pulled onto the freeway, keeping the same distance from his car whether he sped up or slowed down.

When the car followed his exit off the freeway, he knew this was no coincidence. He decided not to go directly to his apartment building; instead, he made turns on city streets. The black car followed him for three turns, then accelerated and passed him. He could make out the driver through tinted windows, a man wearing a watch cap rolled above his ears. Dana drove to his apartment and finally felt safe after turning the deadbolt lock on his door.

He looked out his living room window, assuming Yazdan had sent him a signal. This was the part of his father's world that had always made him uncomfortable—where his father punched people who owed him money, Ali violated tax laws, and Yazdan most likely had people beaten or worse. These men lived by their own rules, united in overcoming barriers to succeed in America. That world now threatened Dana and his family. He went to bed worried, hoping nothing else would happen before he met with Ghorbani.

On Wednesday, he continued fleshing out the schedule and plans for the UC project, preparing for a meeting with UC leaders the following week. He called Sarah over the lunch hour, and they decided to wait for the weekend to see each other, given his need to work long hours and Sarah's catching up after her friend's visit. When he drove out of the parking garage that evening, he looked for a black car and breathed a heavy sigh of relief when he didn't see one.

He arrived at his apartment building and parked in his usual spot. As he walked into the building entryway, he was startled by a black car slowly passing by the building. The driver wore a watch cap and looked at him with a sneer. Dana hurried into the hallway, locked the door behind him, and walked up the stairs, breathing rapidly. He entered his apartment, closed the door, and turned the dead bolt lock. Standing still, he closed his eyes. They now knew where he lived. What would happen next?

Dana had blocked out time Thursday afternoon to work with his team to prepare presentations of their recommendations to the UC leaders. They filled their BG Hill conference room's whiteboards with ideas. The ideas excited him, and he forgot his worries about Yazdan. He worked alone late to draft the slides and handouts the team would create the next day for their presentations to UC.

He finished around seven o'clock and walked down the stairs to the parking garage. His mind was buzzing from the ideas his team was developing—they were creating new roles for BG Hill. The garage was empty except for a couple of cars. He stopped—one car looked like the black car that had followed him. No one was in it, and he nervously looked around, not seeing anyone. He quickly opened his car door, and a guttural voice behind him yelled, "Where's Yazdan's money?"

Dana's stomach dropped, and he turned and saw the man with the watch cap step out from behind a pillar. The man walked toward him with a rolling gait, arms and hands bowed out from his sides and swinging with each step. Dana knew that no one else was likely to enter the parking garage, and the man was too close for him to jump in the car and drive away. He looked at the man, his throat dry.

"We don't have the money yet," Dana said, his heart beating rapidly.

The man swiftly covered the remaining distance to Dana and grabbed him by the lapels of his sport coat, his jaw clenched. He bent Dana backward over the hood of his car, his face inches from Dana's. It was a hard face with grizzled whiskers and scarred cheekbones. Dana didn't move or cry out for help, his breathing constrained by the man's grip on his lapels and shirt. The man pushed him even farther backward.

With nostrils flared and eyes wide, the man growled, "If no pay next week, we do more than threaten you!" He pushed Dana again, released him, and strode to his car, speeding out of the parking garage with screeching tires. Dana's body shook from fright. The man could have stabbed him or shot him or broken his bones, with no one aware of it. He entered his car and sat behind the wheel for several minutes, but he couldn't get his racing heart to settle down.

He finally drove out of the parking garage, constantly checking to see if the black car was following him. He thought of Sarah. He was alone and wanted her to comfort him—he longed for her hugs and kisses. He drove to her apartment and rang her doorbell. Her roommate opened the door and called for Sarah, who came out of her bedroom, her surprise at seeing him turning to concern.

"You look upset. What is it?" Sarah said.

He smoothed his hair back and tried to compose himself before speaking. "Can you come with me, so that we can be alone?"

Looking puzzled, she got her jacket out of the closet, and they drove to his apartment. He could only say in the car, "Wait until we get to my place," in answer to her questions. When they finally got there, they sat down on the couch together.

"Tell me—what's wrong?" Sarah asked, her forehead beginning to furrow.

"My father owed money to his business partner, and he's threatening me if we don't pay." He scooted closer to her, wanting her to reach out and put her arms around him.

"Threatening how?"

He described the car following him and the demands for money. He didn't tell her about the parking garage altercation. "I didn't mean to worry you—I just need you to help me calm down."

"Help you calm down? Don't calm down, please. You're in danger! Me too, if the car followed you today. What are you going to do?"

He hadn't realized he might be endangering Sarah, but he needed her hugs before he thought more about what to do. "I'll figure it out, but I want you to hold me right now."

"I can hold you. But what are you going to do about these threats? Aren't you going to go to the police?"

"I don't know, Sarah. I just want to be with you right now." How many times did he need to ask her?

She leaned over and kissed him on the cheek but then pulled away. "I knew something like this would happen as soon as you started considering your father's request."

"I told them I'm not taking the offer." He turned away from her, closing his eyes. He couldn't believe she wasn't being sensitive to him.

"I'm not comfortable with this situation," she said. "I want you to forget about your father's company and be the Dana I used to know and love."

"I'll try to do that, but it would help if you held me and showed me your love."

She leaned over again and hugged him, but again without her usual tenderness. She pulled away quickly, folding her hands in her lap, a gesture he had never seen her make.

"Can you stay the night?" he asked, and she shook her head. He moved away from her, leaning into the back of the couch and putting his head against the wall above it.

She turned to him. "I don't want you involved in Iranian conflicts, especially if they might affect me."

"Okay. I'll take you home now." He felt empty and numb, not knowing what else to say to her.

They drove back to her apartment without either of them saying anything. She leaned over to kiss him quickly before she went inside. On his drive home, Dana swore loudly, angry and hurt. He had tried to communicate his need for comfort, but she hadn't listened. She was only concerned that he might become an Iranian businessman like his father.

He didn't know what was next for Sarah and him. The following day was Friday, and they hadn't even discussed whether they were getting together for the weekend. He needed to talk to someone who would understand his situation with Yazdan, someone to be a sounding board. When he got home, he called Frida to see if she was available for lunch the next day.

11

Frida suggested they meet Friday for a Middle Eastern lunch at Babani's. When they arrived, two of the waitresses waved to Frida, and she waved back with a smile. The crowd was larger than when Dana ate there with Mehdi—maybe because it was a Friday and people were getting an early start on the weekend. After they were seated at a table with aluminum chairs, Frida ordered stuffed cabbage leaves and Dana his usual falafel sandwich. Then Frida looked at him, ready to listen. But he didn't want to talk immediately about Yazdan, Sarah, or any other aspect of his life. He needed something to distract him—calm him—before he could get into any of that.

"Tell me how the nursing job is going," he said. "I know you love it, but you don't talk much about what you do there."

She smiled. "Well, there are some wonderful storytellers there who just want someone to pay attention to them." She described a woman in the beginning stages of dementia who, longing to go home, was skilled at quietly leaving the nursing home, using unlocked doors or attaching herself to groups of exiting people. "She's certainly creative. We've become good friends, but"—Frida laughed—"you'd be amazed at how manipulative she is."

Dana was glad to hear her talk so enthusiastically about her job. "They're lucky to have you," he told her. He knew she was responsive and intuitive in meeting their needs, just as she was in providing support to him when he needed it.

As he listened to her, he was reminded of his first piano recital when he was seven. He played well initially, and his confidence grew until he realized he had forgotten to repeat a section of the composition. He stared at his sheet music intently, not wanting to make another mistake. He could feel the melody becoming choppy, with little emotion. He ended and quickly walked to his seat, shocked at his mistake, while the audience applauded. His mother leaned over and told him he had played well, patting him on his hand, and then went back to listening to the next student. Frida, however, kept looking at him. She was five years old and had no interest in music. Her main curiosity, as Dana heard his mother describe to a friend, was about people—she was sensitive to the emotions of others. She had watched him struggle to hold back tears, and she began tearing up herself as she took his hand and smiled up at him.

"You know," Dana said, pulling himself out of the sweet memory, "you'd be a great nurse practitioner. Have you thought about going back to school?"

"I don't think so," she said quietly, sliding her plate away toward the edge of the table and placing her dirty napkin next to it—she was one of those people who always tidied up for the waitress. "I'm not like you. What I'm really hoping is that Babak and I will be married soon so we can have children and raise a family."

"It makes me happy to hear that you know what it is you want from life," he told her, but inwardly, he was envious and insecure. Mehdi and Frida were moving forward in creating families while he was moving backward.

"What about you and Sarah?" she asked.

"We have our ups and downs. Right now, she doesn't understand the situation I'm in."

Frida looked at him with sympathy. "You mean your situation with the company?"

Dana nodded. "I've decided not to take Papa's offer and told Yazdan. He said Papa borrowed four hundred thousand dollars from him. And that I need to pay it back next week if I don't join the company." He took a sip of his coffee.

"Next week! That seems impossible."

"Yeah, and I'm feeling threatened by Yazdan. Maman told me he was a SAVAK agent in Iran."

Frida's eyes widened. "I've never felt good about him."

"I'm going to see Mr. Ghorbani. He invested the money Papa borrowed from Yazdan."

"I hope he can help straighten things out."

That was all the conversation Dana needed. With just a few words, Frida had made him feel understood and not alone. He then asked her for help on one thing. "Maman could be upset when she learns I'm not joining Mehdi to lead the company," he said. "Could you talk to her?"

"Of course."

He returned to work after lunch with his step a little lighter—he was glad, as always, for Frida's understanding and caring.

Dana didn't know what to expect from Sarah after their awkward interaction the previous evening. Even though he was frustrated with her, he still wanted to be with her. Who else would he share fun banter with? He would miss so many things if they went their separate ways. The adorable way she pouted when she had the facts wrong about some painting or artist, although always conceding when he was right. And that dimple in her cheek when she grinned.

He called her Friday afternoon and got her voicemail, which he hoped he would, not ready to talk on the phone without knowing if she was angry with him. He left a message that he would pick her up unless he heard differently from her. "Maybe we could try this new deli near campus," he said, and ended the call.

He didn't hear from her, so he pulled into the drop-off circle at her building around five o'clock and waited for her.

Sarah walked to his car with a neutral look on her face, one that he couldn't read. When she sat down, he leaned over and kissed her, which she returned somewhat tentatively. She started talking about her day at work, particularly her frustrations with her supervisor. She filled the air with words, depriving him of the opportunity to apologize to her as he had planned. He tried to show an interest in what she was saying, listening carefully to her and providing sympathetic nods.

He finally found an opening and said he was sorry about how the previous night had ended. "I thought about it all day—about you—and I wanted to clear the air so that we can enjoy the weekend." He briefly turned his eyes from the road, smiled at her, and reached out to take her hand.

"I'm sorry, too," she said. "I don't know why our conversation was so awkward . . . so intense. I do want us to talk about it." Although she kept her hand in his, it lay loosely, and she stared forward, seeming to focus on the surrounding neighborhoods. He gave her hand an affectionate squeeze and smiled at her again.

He parked near the restaurant, and she abruptly turned to him before he opened the car door. "I'd like to talk here instead of in the restaurant," she said.

"Okay," Dana said. He looked at her and saw that her eyes were glistening. A worry started to grow in him as he waited for her words.

"I think we're more different than I thought," she said.

"But that's a strength." The words came out more quickly than he intended them to. "It's why we enjoy each other so much."

Sarah took a deep breath. "It wasn't a strength last night. I just can't come to terms with how you're letting yourself be drawn into your father's business and all its drama. I don't understand it, but I do know that it's ruining everything. We couldn't even talk about it without both of us becoming emotional wrecks."

He felt himself becoming defensive but realized this was more than their usual disagreement over Armand Concrete. "I think we can work it out," he said.

"I don't know."

A lump rose up in his throat as he feared what was coming next.

"I've been looking into graduate school, and NYU has accepted my application. It's a huge opportunity. I can study toward my goal of becoming an art museum curator."

"Have you decided to go there?" he asked, afraid of her answer. What he didn't vocalize was the fact that she had applied without even telling him. How many weeks ago?

"Yes," she said quietly, her lips trembling.

Dana felt he had been punched in the stomach. "What about us?" He sensed there was no chance, but he couldn't just let her go.

"I was planning to persuade you to come with me, but after last night, I realized it isn't a good idea. And you have obligations here."

His eyes filled with tears. "What are we going to do?"

"I start at NYU next semester. I think it's best if we ended things."

Dana slumped. He let his head drop down and rubbed the back of his neck. He tried not to cry.

She looked at him and bit her lip. "I know this is sudden," she said. "Are you going to be okay?"

"No, I'm not." He continued to rub his neck. "I'll take you home."

"I don't want to hurt you." She looked at him closely and began crying, wiping her eyes. "You've meant so much to me."

He remained silent and started the car. The ride to her apartment was painful—he could barely drive. When they neared her place, she touched his shoulder, saying, "I want you to be okay." He stopped the car without looking at her and concentrated on his breathing. She leaned over in tears, kissed him on the cheek, and then got out and closed the door.

He went home and lay down on his couch. He curled up on his side and closed his eyes.

He had not seen this coming. He had looked forward to a pleasurable weekend with Sarah—making up after their quarrel, picking out things to see and do, and sleeping together, their physical intimacy healing their wounds. Now, he felt lost and unloved. He rubbed his neck again. It was stiff as a board.

His whole life seemed to be falling apart. He was drifting alone, with sharks circling.

He tried to eat a sandwich but took only a few bites. He turned on his TV and watched a nature program about African predators and their prey. Eventually, he went to bed early and lay awake for hours, finally dozing but constantly moving from side to side, never finding a comfortable position.

He didn't leave his apartment all weekend, spending most of his time watching a series of movies on TV. On Sunday afternoon, he gave up any hope Sarah would call and felt motivated enough to play his piano and heat up some dolmeh from his mother. Before he went to bed that evening, his mind turned to his meeting the following day with Ghorbani. He didn't have any idea of what to expect.

12

Dana sat across the boardroom table from Mr. Ghorbani, his eyes drawn to the landscape paintings of Iran and Los Angeles.

"These paintings are beautiful," he said.

"All by local Iranian artists I've supported," Ghorbani explained. Dana was impressed, just as he had been when he arrived at Ghorbani's office building.

He had driven up the hills surrounding Los Angeles on winding roads through neighborhoods of expensive homes and modern office buildings, the scenery enhanced by the midafternoon sun and blue sky. When he turned on the street of the address for the Ghorbani Group, he came upon a three-story building constructed of travertine stone on the side of the hill. He entered the building and announced himself to the receptionist, a striking Middle Eastern woman with carefully styled brown hair swept back and down to her shoulders. She took him up the elevator to Ghorbani's office.

"How are you and your family?" Ghorbani asked. "Caveh died too young."

Dana ignored the abruptness in Ghorbani's greeting, noticing his expensive three-piece suit. He was glad he had worn a coat and tie.

"We're all coping, but my mother is taking it hard."

"Leila is a wonderful woman. I remember at their wedding thinking how fortunate Caveh was to have her as his wife."

Dana thought of the hug Ghorbani gave his mother at the cemetery. He asked Ghorbani how he and his parents knew each other in Iran, a question on his mind ever since the funeral.

"Well, Caveh and I grew up in the same neighborhood. We were always playing soccer with neighborhood boys. It was a special time." Ghorbani looked wistfully out the large floor-to-ceiling window. "We followed different paths, with me going further in schooling and taking a government job—Caveh stopped his studies to become an expert in concrete masonry. I met your mother when Caveh was already engaged to her—I was honored to be best man at their wedding."

"Why did you come to America?" Dana asked.

"I disagreed with Shah Pahlavi's use of power. At first, as a young man, about your age, I believed in his desire to improve the economy through market approaches, even though I didn't support the coup that overthrew the previous government." He stopped and asked Dana if he would like water or coffee. Dana declined.

"I worked hard in a government ministry to modernize the economy, but I was shocked by the arrests and torture of the Shah's rivals. I didn't fit in with those loyal to the Shah or those advocating an Islamic revolution."

Dana smiled. "So, instead, you came to America and built a company."

Ghorbani laughed. "It wasn't quite as easy as you make it sound. I started by working for a couple of brokerages in downtown L.A. and learned how to invest other people's money. Long hours. Grueling. But I was successful in real estate investments and eventually established the Ghorbani Group with my partners. We became a resource for Iranians still in Iran and those recently immigrated who wanted to move their savings to American investments."

"I could fill the afternoon with questions about you and my parents," Dana said. "But we should get to my reason for meeting. I'd like to learn more about your business arrangement with my father and Yazdan."

Ghorbani nodded. "Yes, I've been thinking about this. Your father told me he wanted you to join Mehdi in leading Armand Concrete when he was gone."

Dana couldn't tell whether or not Ghorbani thought that was a good idea. "I'm thinking about it," he said. "I understand you've used my father's and Yazdan's companies to construct your property development projects. One question is whether that will still be possible without my father."

"That depends. I will give you some more history and then ask you some questions."

Dana looked steadily at Mr. Ghorbani, fearing that his words or gestures would reveal his eagerness to hear this history. He moved back in his chair and tried to calm his emotions—the office brightened momentarily with sunlight coming through the large windows. Ghorbani's eyes narrowed as he began to speak.

"After the wedding, Caveh and I didn't see each other again until the celebration of Mehdi's birth. A couple of years later, when I decided to leave Iran for Los Angeles, Leila made a delicious dinner for my farewell gathering. Then we lost touch again until Leila called me from their apartment in Los Angeles. I wasn't aware they moved to America. We got together occasionally, most memorably, to celebrate the births of you and your sister."

Dana had never heard this part of his family's history before. He again thought of the hug Ghorbani gave his mother. She seemed closer to Ghorbani than his father. He waited silently, not wanting to interrupt the story.

"I had no more contact with Caveh until Leila called me. She asked me to keep Caveh in mind for concrete work needed for my projects."

Dana was surprised. Why would his mother have taken such an extraordinary step? "Was that after the bombing of our garage?" he asked.

"I didn't know about it at the time of her call, but I was aware of the reputation of the Persian Grill group. I made inquiries and then found out about Caveh's debts and the bombing. It helped me to understand why Leila had called me."

Dana recalled the night he was awakened by his mother yelling after his father came home drunk from the Persian Grill, telling him to sleep there if he was going to drink so much.

"A few months later," Ghorbani continued, "I asked Caveh to bid on a concrete project for one of my developments. Caveh won the bid and did excellent work. After several more projects, Caveh proposed that the Ghorbani Group contract with Yazdan's company to oversee the construction of their projects and take care of non-concrete work."

"And you agreed?" Dana asked.

"Caveh described it as a successful business development strategy he and Yazdan used for other clients, so I agreed to try it. But I required that Caveh be responsible for the quality of Yazdan's work. We had success with this arrangement, but I sensed that Caveh proposed it because he owed Yazdan, not because he wanted to pursue a business strategy."

Dana nodded, remembering his mother's words about Yazdan fixing his father's gambling debts after the bombing. His breathing quickened when Ghorbani said he had questions.

"What is Yazdan expecting of you?" Ghorbani asked.

"He wants to continue the partnership, with me replacing my father as your liaison." Dana hesitated and decided to be open. His mother seemed to trust this man—maybe he could too. "Yazdan doesn't know about this meeting."

"Do you and Mehdi want Yazdan to be involved in this partnership?"

Dana hesitated again. "Mehdi doesn't get along with Yazdan and is leaving it up to me. I'm uncertain about everything, including my role."

"You might not join Armand Concrete?"

"I'm having second thoughts." He described his current position at BG Hill and his dream of establishing his own consulting company that would focus on integrating organizational strategy with communications. He also said his relationship with his father was difficult.

"Caveh was tough. I think he could be a challenging father. Especially for a son so unlike him," Ghorbani said.

"Yes. Mehdi was his ideal son."

"Is Mehdi ready to take over the company?"

"Definitely," Dana said, "and I'm willing to advise and help Mehdi in the transition. But I'm concerned about Yazdan."

He stopped talking and waited to hear Ghorbani's reactions, uncomfortable about how much of himself he had revealed.

"Your father valued Mehdi," Ghorbani said. "But you have your mother's people skills and sensitivity." Ghorbani smiled, appearing to think of her, but he quickly recovered. "I understand the need for organizations to integrate strategy and communications. You have a vision, and I think you will reach your goal of building your own business."

Dana relaxed, feeling bathed by these warm words of support.

"I want Mehdi to continue doing my concrete work," Ghorbani said. "And I would value having you as an advisor in the transition." He stopped and looked directly at Dana. "Now, how can I help you in your situation with Yazdan?"

Dana felt a great sense of relief, his heart slowing. But he hesitated. He remembered Yazdan's words about his friends persuading Dana to pay.

"Yazdan became angry when I expressed doubts about joining Armand," Dana explained. "I think Yazdan wants my help as a liaison because of his political differences with you."

Ghorbani laughed. "Political differences is an understatement! When I learned—after agreeing to use Yazdan's company—that he was a former SAVAK commander involved in arresting and torturing the Shah's opponents . . . well, I was disgusted."

"My mother told me Yazdan's network of former SAVAK agents in Los Angeles probably helped my father after the bombing of our garage."

"I believe your mother. Yazdan is a dangerous man to cross."

Dana closed his eyes for a moment. "He is demanding I immediately repay a large loan if I don't join Armand, a loan he made to my father for an investment with your company." There, he had said it. Yazdan wouldn't be happy if he knew that he had revealed this to Ghorbani. But it was too late to worry about that now.

"That was Yazdan's money that Caveh gave me to invest?"

"Yes. They agreed to split the net return for the investment."

"I don't have a problem with that. But you have a problem paying him back immediately?"

Dana remembered the watch cap man violently bending him backward on the hood of his car. "I proposed settling the debt when we know the investment results. But Yazdan is using his demand for immediate repayment as leverage to get me to join the company," he said. "Yazdan fears that, without me, his company will lose its special arrangement with you. He feels so strongly about this that he sent one of his goons to threaten me last week. He pinned me to the hood of my car."

Ghorbani sat silently, turning his head to look at the paintings on the wall. His eyes lowered to look at the floor and then at Dana with a seriousness Dana had not seen before.

"Many Iranians, like Caveh, left the politics of Iran behind, focusing on their new lives in America," Ghorbani said. "But there are three factions of Iranians in Los Angeles still tied to Iran: former SAVAK agents and others sympathetic to the Shah, Muslims sympathetic to the ayatollah and the current Islamic regime, and prodemocratic advocates like me, who hope to influence a democratic movement in Iran. Each has connections to friends and relatives still in Iran and knows the history of bloodshed among these and other groups. They have tried to keep a truce in America, not wanting to disrupt their lives in a country where many have succeeded beyond what would be possible in Iran."

Ghorbani paused before saying, "Yazdan, whether he knows it or not, is violating that truce by threatening you. I will make sure that it is communicated to him. I'm confident that will end his threats."

Dana opened his mouth slightly, having heard words beyond his expectations. "Yazdan will know I talked to you. Are you sure my family won't be at risk?" he asked.

"We will tell him what he is doing is unacceptable."

"I'm grateful," Dana said. "But what about you? Will you continue to use his construction company?"

"No. This is convenient for me. My preference has been to only work with Armand Concrete. I was prepared to continue the current arrangement if you joined the company. But now it's clear: My business relationship with Yazdan is over."

Ghorbani looked satisfied, happy to have reached a resolution. Dana nodded—his relief and gratitude made it difficult for him to speak.

"I wouldn't repeat what we've discussed here," Ghorbani said. "All people need to know is that the arrangement has ended."

Dana nodded again, sensing Ghorbani's power.

"One more thing," Ghorbani said. "Please tell Mehdi I would like to have lunch with the two of you in a few weeks to discuss a new arrangement for working on our projects. Armand Concrete is the best concrete contractor in Los Angeles."

Dana's face warmed, basking again in Ghorbani's praise.

They shook hands, and Mr. Ghorbani walked him to the elevator. The doors opened, and an imposing man wearing a white shirt and tie exited, his shoulders thrown back like a soldier. Ghorbani introduced him to Dana as Darius, and he shook Dana's hand with a strong grip, his eyes concealed by dark sunglasses. Dana entered the elevator, wondering what role Darius played for Ghorbani.

Dana silently replayed his conversation with Ghorbani several times on his drive home. He was excited to tell Mehdi and Frida about the resolution of the Yazdan problem. He was also deeply affected by what he learned about his mother and father's lives in Iran and Los Angeles and the role Ghorbani had played. He had thirsted for information like that for years.

His excitement diminished, however, when he entered his apartment. He felt the absence—the loss—of Sarah. He would have loved for her to be the first to hear about his meeting with Ghorbani. She would have been overjoyed with the news, her eyes lighting up as they looked up at him, setting off her freckles. But that was over. The positive meeting with Ghorbani helped lessen the depression he felt over her, but it could not overcome his loneliness. He settled into an uneasy balance.

<hr>

Dana woke up the following day without sunlight streaming into his room. He looked out his window toward the horizon. The sky was a brown tint, a sign of smog, and he closed the window to keep from breathing the polluted air. He showered, forcing his thoughts away from the breakup with Sarah. As he dressed, a feeling of fear welled up. What if Ghorbani failed to persuade Yazdan to wait on the loan? What about the threat from the man in the watch cap? His deadline was in a few days. "Yazdan is a dangerous man to cross," Ghorbani had said.

For several days, Dana was cautious whenever he left his apartment. He watched cars behind him as he drove, often taking circuitous routes. He left work on time, joining others walking to the parking garage. As the days passed, he didn't hear from Yazdan or Ghorbani. He hoped the situation was resolved.

13

Dana entered Frida's apartment, immediately noticing the delicious aroma of Persian cooking. The pleasure provided by the bright flowers on her coffee table was secondary to the savor of Persian spices.

"I knew you wanted to hear about my meeting with Mr. Ghorbani, but I didn't know you were cooking for me," he said.

"Babak is on a business trip, so I thought I would test this recipe on you first. I know it won't compare to Maman's."

Dana smiled. His sister was preparing to be a model Iranian wife when she and Babak were married. She served Dana lamb kebab with rice mixed with nuts, fruit, and mouthwatering spices.

"It's every bit as delicious as Maman's," he told her when he had mopped his plate with pita bread.

"Good! Now, tell me all about your meeting with Mr. Ghorbani," she said.

"He supports my plan to start my own company—I've never received that kind of encouragement from Papa or his friends."

"That's great, but what about Yazdan?" she asked.

Dana gave Frida background information from Ghorbani about the three competing Iranian networks in Los Angeles. She surprised Dana by knowing about them already.

"You know much more than I do about Iranian immigrants," he

said. "I guess I lost connections to the Iranian community when I went off to college."

When he told her that Ghorbani would deal with Yazdan and wanted to meet with Mehdi and him to discuss a new partnership with Armand Concrete, she reached across the table to grasp his hand. Her eyes glistened. "I'm so happy to hear that news," she said.

He helped her clean the table and asked how their mother was doing.

"She's being strong. I think she feels more alone than heartbroken."

He promised to see her more often. "Now that things with Yazdan are settled, I have more time. And with Sarah . . ." He almost blurted it out. But now was not the time.

"What about Sarah?" Frida said, raising her dark brows at him.

"Oh, she's just been very busy. We haven't been seeing each other as much."

"I'm sorry, Dana," Frida said, turning to take the plates into the kitchen. "This probably has her a bit stressed out too."

"I should be going."

Frida nodded. She offered to walk him to his car. "This warm ocean breeze," she murmured when they left her apartment building. "I just love it here in the spring." The sun was setting, and the evening walkers had returned to their homes. Dana and Frida appeared to be the only ones outside in the quiet neighborhood.

He opened the gate and turned to say goodbye to Frida. He stopped, realizing the sedan parked across the street looked familiar— it was the black car. When he spoke, his voice cracked. "Frida . . ." He took her elbow to quickly lead her back through the gate, but he heard rapid footsteps behind them. The watch cap man moved between the gate and Dana and Frida so they couldn't close it. He pointed a pistol at them and told them to walk to Dana's car. Dana stood still, his heart racing, not sure what to do. Frida held Dana's arm so tightly that her fingernails dug into his bicep.

"Move it!" the man said, poking his gun into Dana's back.

Dana looked at him, trying not to appear afraid. He thought of Ghorbani's assurance that there would be no more threats. "There's no need for my sister to come," he said.

The man laughed, the scars on his face visible under the streetlight. "Armands don't pay debts—better to bank on two. You drive!" he said to Dana while motioning to Frida to sit in the front passenger seat.

Frida covered her mouth and looked at Dana with eyes full of panic. He wondered if she was thinking, as he was, about SAVAK torture, imagining their techniques of inflicting physical pain.

The man got into the back seat, his gun pointed toward the front. "Drive to the next light," he said.

Dana thought of the old men Mehdi knew. "Tell Yazdan I'll get the money to him in the next couple of days."

The man laughed again, seeming to relish what was to come. "You had your chance."

Dana felt a heavy pang in his chest. "Where are you taking us?"

"Where no one will see or hear you. Now shut up."

Frida stifled a cry of fear. Dana thought of what he might do before getting locked up in a place where they would be at the mercy of this man and perhaps others. He could open the door and jump out as the car moved, but he couldn't leave Frida. He thought of calling the man's bluff and driving to a police station, hoping the man wouldn't shoot. No—too risky.

He continued to drive, seeing the stoplight a distance away. His mind raced with what he might say to Yazdan. He wondered again what had happened to Ghorbani's pledge of being able to control him.

When they reached the light, the man told Dana to turn right. Dana grew alarmed as an oncoming car drifted across the center line. "Faster!" the watch cap man yelled. Before Dana could complete the turn, the oncoming car crossed into his lane and struck his car's left front fender and headlight. Metal screeched against metal, headlight glass exploded, and Frida screamed.

Two men stepped out of the car with guns drawn, one wearing a white shirt and tie. Dana's hopes soared when he recognized it was Darius. But his fear grew again when the watch cap man bellowed into his ear in panic, "Back up! Back up!" Dana winced, feeling as though his head had been struck.

Just then, another car hit the rear of Dana's car, pinning it between the two vehicles. Two more men got out of that car, also holding guns. Darius shouted to the watch cap man, "Drop your gun and get out!"

Dana wondered if the man might try to use Frida and him as hostages, but the man dropped his gun on the street and exited the car when Darius repeated his command in Farsi. Darius then turned to Dana. "Leave now," he said, "in case the police arrive." He told one of the men to move his car out of Dana's way.

Dana worried that the crashes might have pushed his fenders into his wheels, but his car rolled forward without obstruction, its path illuminated by only one headlight.

Lights flickered on in the houses in the neighborhood, and Dana drove away. Looking through his rearview mirror, he saw Darius and his men cuff the watch cap man with a zip tie, push him into one of their cars, and quickly drive off in the opposite direction.

Dana couldn't speak as he and Frida drove to his apartment, his stomach churning as he imagined where they would be if Darius hadn't arrived. He looked at Frida; her eyes were closed and her arms crossed. She sobbed quietly.

Why had this happened? He and Frida had been threatened over a business arrangement. Over a *loan*. He had been part of many business negotiations where tensions escalated, but no one was followed, threatened, or kidnapped at gunpoint. Dana wasn't only angry at

Yazdan. His father had gotten him into this situation, involving him and his sister in a world of strong-arm threats and violence.

Dana and Frida entered his apartment, and he locked the door behind them. She still appeared terrified, and he hugged her. "Are you okay?" he asked.

"You said everything with Yazdan was resolved!" she said, dabbing her eyes as her fear turned into anger.

"I thought it was."

"Did Ghorbani lie to you?" she yelled.

"No. I think we're safe now. Those were Ghorbani's men who rescued us."

"I hope so. I was scared for Mehdi and Maman when that man said the Armands don't pay their debts."

The phone rang. It was Ghorbani. "We have the SAVAK gunman under our control. You won't be attacked again," he said. "Send me the bill to repair your car."

Dana looked at Frida and nodded with relief. "We're glad your men showed up when they did. What about Yazdan? Will he threaten us with other SAVAKs?"

"No," Ghorbani said. "We've made it clear to Yazdan that taking you hostage was a major violation of our truce. He knows his life will be in danger if he misbehaves again. The ayatollah's spies in this country have little time for former SAVAK agents."

"How about the four hundred thousand?" Dana asked. "Can we handle it as he and my father would have?"

"I told Yazdan that I thought you would propose that. Is that true?"

"Yes, if you agree."

"I do."

Dana hung up and turned to Frida. He was exhausted, as she seemed to be. "I'm going to sleep on your couch, if that's okay," she said.

"Please, take the bed," he answered, gesturing toward his bedroom.

He wanted to be the one to stay near the front door, and he doubted there would be much sleep.

———◆◆◆———

The following morning, Dana told her he didn't plan on telling Mehdi or Maman about being kidnapped by Yazdan's men. "There's no point in worrying them. I'll just tell them the arrangement with Yazdan is over."

"I'll do the same," Frida said, "as long as we can trust that Ghorbani has him under control—he already said he did once. If something like this happens again, we have to tell them."

After driving Frida to her apartment that morning, he walked her through the gate. It was hard to believe what had happened there the previous night. Before she entered her apartment, he hugged her and looked at her.

"I'm going to ask Maman to pick a night for a family dinner," he said. "It's time to talk about the future of Armand Concrete and the Ghorbani Group."

———◆◆◆———

Dana threw himself into his work at BG Hill. He led a successful meeting with UC leaders, obtaining their approval for establishing a steering committee with business leaders. He and his staff began planning the invitations and agenda for the initial meeting. But when he returned home in the evening, he felt an emptiness and sadness. He thought of calling Sarah, telling her he had cut off all ties with Yazdan, but remembered how adamant she was about ending their relationship, and how motivated she was to start a new life at NYU. He realized he needed to tell his family that their relationship was over.

At the end of the week, he stopped by to see his mother after work and asked her how she was doing without Papa. "The house is quiet," she said, "and I sometimes get lonely, but I'm busy helping Tara. Baby is almost here." He envied his mother's joining with Mehdi and Tara to help plan for the addition to their family. Now was as good a time as any to tell her the news, he supposed.

"Sarah and I . . . we've broken up."

Dana's mother gave him a sympathetic look but remarked, "I wondered how long it would last. Like Frida said, she is so American."

This surprised and intrigued him. He had never thought of Sarah that way and was unaware that his mother or sister had.

Moving to his main reason for visiting, he asked his mother if she would host a family dinner where they could talk about the future of Armand Concrete.

"I would love to, but I'd also like to know what's happening. Before that dinner."

With some trepidation, he replied, "Well, I won't be joining Mehdi in running the company."

"But you told your father you accepted his offer."

"I'm sure Papa cared about me, but I think he cared more about the company's future."

His mother's face softened, gazing at him with love. "I don't blame you for not trusting your father," she said. "He was hard on you for many years. But tell me what you and Mehdi are planning. Will Yazdan still be a business partner?"

"No. That relationship is over," he replied.

His mother's eyes widened. "Dana, I'm sure you have good plans, but Yazdan is a powerful man."

"I know, but I've worked out a new relationship with Mr. Ghorbani, who helped end things with Yazdan."

His mother looked at him silently and began to smile.

"I have prayed for this for many years."

"For what?"

"I always thought your father was too loyal to Yazdan, that he should have worked directly with Mr. Ghorbani, his childhood friend. I imagine his loyalty to Yazdan had to do with the bombing of our garage—Caveh owed Yazdan for helping us get out of that mess. And I thought Mr. Ghorbani probably distanced himself from your father when he began drinking and gambling."

Dana nodded with understanding. "He wants to meet with Mehdi and me on future concrete work for his projects."

His mother smiled again, seemingly not surprised by his words. "Mr. Ghorbani is a great man. I met him in Iran through your father before we got married. We did things together as couples. But his wife was killed in a car accident. He left for America soon after."

Fascinated, he wanted to ask her questions. But he stayed quiet, watching his mother continue to react to this good news. She stared out the window and then turned back at him with a mischievous look that he loved but rarely saw.

"Let's invite Bijan to our dinner," she said.

"Who's Bijan?"

"Bijan Ghorbani!"

It was Dana's turn to look out the window as he considered this idea, an idea that he would never have suggested, an idea that would never have come to his mind. Laughing, he smiled back at her and nodded.

14

Dana called Mr. Ghorbani a week before the dinner to invite him on behalf of his mother. Ghorbani hesitated but then said, "I can't say no to an invitation from Leila. Please tell her I'll bring wine and dessert."

Dana also talked with Mehdi about the future business partnership with Ghorbani. He found Mehdi looking at blueprints in a trailer at a construction site. "Come in!" Mehdi said, greeting him warmly. "I bet you haven't been at one of our sites since your summer jobs in high school."

"No, and I don't plan to in the future. I've met with Ghorbani about the money we owe Yazdan," Dana said.

Mehdi's face dropped. "Am I going to have to talk to the old men?"

"No. Ghorbani solved everything. We'll pay back the money after we know the results of the investment, as Papa had planned. And we no longer will have a partnership with Yazdan."

"You're kidding!" Mehdi said. "I didn't expect this. Ghorbani is more powerful than I thought."

"He still wants us to do his concrete work. He liked my idea of you running the company, while I'll be an advisor to the two of you."

"That's great!" Mehdi said. "It will be an honor to have Mr. Ghorbani consider Armand Concrete for work on his projects." Dana sensed that Mehdi was also excited to be the company's sole leader.

Dana's mother prepared a meal of chelo kebab, with skewers

of spiced ground lamb and beef served on Persian rice. Mr. Ghorbani, wearing a casual but expensive sweater, brought several bottles
of wine and a large platter of sohan—a toffee with pistachios on
top—for dessert. After the meal and wine were served, his mother
sat down, taking off her apron and revealing a fashionable dress
Dana had never seen. Ghorbani offered a toast to the Ghorbani and
Armand partnership.

They clinked their glasses together, and Mehdi raised his glass
again. "Let's also toast our mother for preparing this delicious meal."

Dana noticed how closely Frida watched their mother as Ghorbani
touched their mother's glass of wine with his. Was Frida seeing possibilities he had not? He opened his mouth slightly as he thought of what
was happening between his mother and Ghorbani, who were now each
alone, after knowing and respecting each other for over thirty years.

Thinking about the evening on his ride home, he could not recall
when his family had eaten together so peacefully, genuinely enjoying
each other. Even Tara, who was usually cautious around her in-laws,
had them laughing as she joked about her pregnancy. "I'm hoping for
a girl," she said, "because I don't think I could handle another Mehdi
in the house. But whenever I say that, the baby kicks me."

Mehdi had grumbled good-naturedly, replying, "It's most likely
my *son*, telling you to watch what you're saying!" Dana watched his
mother, Tara, and Frida laugh, and Frida took a risk by saying, "God
forbid that the baby is another Caveh!" His mother and Ghorbani
smiled knowingly at each other, and Dana wondered about experiences in their former lives that he knew nothing about.

———————

The next day, Frida stopped by Dana's apartment with leftovers he
had forgotten to take home from the dinner.

"Do you think there's a potential relationship between Maman
and Mr. Ghorbani?" he asked her.

"There already is," Frida said. "I think they care for each other deeply and maybe always have."

"Do you think they'll start seeing each other?"

"I asked Maman and she said, 'Don't be silly—it's not even two months since your father died.' She needs to wait for a grieving period to end before seeing another man, or people will talk."

"I feel like an outsider when I hear what you know," Dana said.

Frida smiled at him and nodded. "You've been an outsider for years. In some ways, Papa put you there. But now, nothing can keep you from being more involved with our family but yourself. Your breakup with Sarah may help."

He grew serious. "Sarah never really understood the Iranian part of me. I have trouble understanding it myself. But I still miss her."

Frida looked at him sympathetically.

"What are your and Babak's plans?" he asked.

"We're going to announce our engagement soon. I can't wait to surprise Maman."

Dana smiled. "I know how happy Maman will be. But, I have to tell you . . . I'm envious—you and Mehdi are building families."

"You will too, one day. And you would be quite a catch for an Iranian girl!"

He laughed. "We'll see—life is unpredictable. I doubt if Papa and Maman knew they would move from Iran to a foreign country when they married. No matter what I think of Papa, I know that took courage."

"Papa never gave you the guidance and support he gave Mehdi and me. Tara talked about it after you and Mr. Ghorbani left."

"What did she say?"

"That you may have found someone who can support you as a father should, someone you respect and trust."

That night, Dana thought about Bijan Ghorbani, a man he looked up to, whose guidance he valued tremendously. He wondered, though, as a leader of the faction supporting democracy in Iran, how different

Ghorbani was from the leaders of the other factions. Although his cause was more admirable, he had sent Darius and three men with guns to rescue Frida and him. Maybe Ghorbani had to develop that power to survive and succeed as an immigrant, but Dana didn't see it as something to model himself after.

He also thought of Frida's words about Sarah—that their breakup might bring him closer to his family. He loved Sarah so much, and his heart ached when he pictured her sitting closely beside him, remembering all they had done together. Were his mother and sister correct when they implied that Sarah might be too American for him—that she was so comfortable in her own world that she could not understand the world he came from?

Sarah was drawn to what he escaped to—music, poetry, and art. She was repelled by what he escaped from—the Iranian network with complex dealings involving families and friends. In his escape from that world—encouraged by Sarah—he may have lost part of himself. For their relationship to work, she would have needed to understand and appreciate the Iranian side of him. He knew now that she could not do that.

When he prepared to go to bed, he looked at himself in the bathroom mirror; he could see the sadness that descended on him. He had accepted the loss of Sarah but still missed her. He decided to write her a note before she left for New York. He didn't want their last interaction to be his brooding silence in the car as she cried.

———••———

Dana and Mehdi discussed the transition to the new partnership on the way to their lunch with Ghorbani.

"I'll be glad to advise you and Ghorbani on Armand projects for Ghorbani's developments," Dana said. "But my UC Irvine project is my priority—I'm hoping to use it in forming my own company."

Mehdi nodded in agreement. "That sounds good. By the way, Maman told me you and Sarah broke up. I'm sorry to hear that."

"Thanks."

"I think Frida is already looking for women for you," Mehdi said. "It may take time, but you'll bounce back and find someone."

Dana appreciated Mehdi's brief words of sympathy and support, knowing there was no need for either of them to say anything more.

Darius greeted Dana and Mehdi at Ghorbani's private club in downtown Los Angeles. They followed him through the halls of dark wood paneling and mirrors until they reached the club's restaurant with its striking black-and-white-tiled floor. The hostess took them to what she called Mr. Ghorbani's corner, seating them at a table that looked out on the downtown skyline.

"Wow. This view," Mehdi commented. His eyes, however, were scanning the tables of well-dressed men near them. Dana understood their impact on Mehdi. This was a place of privilege, where power was defined by how much money a person had accumulated.

They watched Mr. Ghorbani make his way through the tables, nodding and smiling to men he knew. He sat down, welcomed Mehdi and Dana, and then beckoned to the waiter to take their orders. After their meal was served, Dana began the conversation about their business partnership, confident in taking the lead. Ghorbani acted somewhat surprised but deferred to Dana with a slight smile. Mehdi was silent, intently observing the two men.

"We've appreciated the relationship that has led to Armand Concrete working on Ghorbani projects," Dana said. "We hope it can continue."

"Yes," Ghorbani said. "I'm prepared to commit to a set of contracts for the upcoming year to be awarded to Armand Concrete. I suggest we do this every year."

Dana paused. He had been concerned that Ghorbani might make it too easy and Armand would become dependent on Ghorbani.

Dana didn't want Ghorbani to take the Armand family under his wing and provide for them after the death of their leader. Ghorbani's courtship of Dana's mother might have added to his motivation to do that.

"That's good," Dana said. "But I believe we should compete by preparing bids for your major projects."

"I don't think Mr. Ghorbani is asking us to do that," Mehdi said.

"We have competitors who we must keep up with," Dana said. "Bidding will keep us competitive."

"I'm fine with that," Ghorbani said.

Dana nodded, the tension in his forehead lessening. "I also would like to have a goal that at least half of our projects be for Ghorbani clients who are not Iranians."

"Why?" Mehdi asked.

"We don't want to be perceived as only working within the Iranian community and network. We want to be positioned to work for any client."

This was important to Dana. He felt it was time to move beyond immigrant relationships like his father's and Yazdan's, no matter how valuable they were in helping their families succeed in a new country. He wanted to move Armand toward practices he used with BG Hill clients, which he would use in establishing his own company.

Ghorbani nodded and smiled. Dana wasn't sure he was in agreement.

"One more thing: my role," Dana said. "I suggest we meet here monthly to discuss our progress. I don't need to be part of day-to-day decisions—Mehdi is running the company. But I'd like to be an active advisor."

"We have a deal," Ghorbani said, smiling broadly. "Are you okay with it, Mehdi?"

Mehdi looked at both of them and laughed. "I guess so!"

"Great. One more thing for both of you," Ghorbani said. "From now on, please call me Bijan."

When Dana got home that evening, he put a record of Beethoven's sonatas on his stereo. He sat back and listened to the music, thinking about the meeting with Ghorbani. He was satisfied with his facilitating role and with the new partnership between Armand Concrete and the Ghorbani Group. He knew that he and Mehdi might still find themselves in business dealings influenced more by Iranian alliances than by qualifications and performance, potentially led by the man he admired so much. But Dana was prepared to resist those approaches. He valued the wisdom and support of his elders, but he wanted to make sure their business dealings were professional.

He closed his eyes and listened to the sonatas. His mind swirled with images of what had happened since his father's death almost two months ago. He again thought of his mother's dinner. Why had he never experienced a dinner with his family like that? It had to be because of the presence of his father—his outspokenness, demands, and criticism. Had the others experienced the same impacts as he did? Probably not. They each saw a side of their father that was good, and they were able to manage and ignore the side that wasn't. But he could neither see the good side nor manage the bad, and the result was his intense need to escape. He escaped in music, poetry, and drama, and those things led him to make friends outside the Iranian community. Going to college made him even more of an outsider.

What if he hadn't felt the need to escape? He still might have pursued his interests, but he might not have felt so apart from Iranian life. It was easy to blame his father, but perhaps he should have worked harder to appreciate his good side. If he hadn't made such a dramatic break from his family, he may have appreciated Iranian traditions more, as he did at his mother's dinner—the loyalty to family, the delicious food that brought people together, the loud conversation and laughter, the joking and good-natured teasing, and the genuine care and love for each other that overcame inevitable conflicts and tensions.

The sonatas ended, and Dana selected a new album, Beethoven's Fifth Symphony. He sat back and listened to the orchestra, feeling the emotions of the music—threats of danger and despair, efforts to escape, momentary peace interrupted with new threats, calm observation and hesitation, only to be challenged again, engaging and climbing, reaching triumph and celebration. A feeling of acceptance passed through him, warm and enveloping. He was part of something bigger.

Acknowledgments

I'm grateful for my editor, Ava Justine Coibion. She saw the promise in these three novels and recommended revisions that transformed them into vibrant stories of characters struggling with their lives. Whether it was characterization, plot, dialogue, setting, language, or restructuring, her revisions improved my stories and educated me. She was a joy to work with.

I'd like to thank The Loft Literary Center in Minneapolis for its leadership in making the Twin Cities a welcoming place for writers. Its programs help writers of all types advance their craft and celebrate their accomplishments. I'm forever grateful to my Loft instructors, Patricia Hoolihan and Maya Hlavacek. They create a safe place in their classrooms for students to write, read our work, and receive supportive feedback.

I am part of a writing group of Loft students facilitated by Maya that has been active for close to five years. I'd like to thank Judy Anderson, Kolina Cicero, Dan Satorius, and Maya for their knowledge, skills, encouragement, and patience in helping me improve my writing. They have read sections from each of these three novels and provided valuable feedback multiple times. I've also benefited from reading their wonderful stories.

I'm grateful to the outstanding team of Greenleaf professionals: Justin Branch, Morgan Robinson, Adrianna Hernandez, Laurie MacQueen, Madelyn Meyers, and Tiffany Barrientos. In addition to my gratitude for Ava Justine Coibion's developmental editing,

I'm thankful for Jeffrey Curry's superb copyediting and to Anna Jordan for creating a compelling design.

Finally, I'm thankful for the support of my family. My relatives are faithful and encouraging readers of my stories, which I'm able to write with the love and support of my wife, our daughter, and our daughter's family: Linda, Anna, Adam, Charlie, and Sophie.

About the Author

Robert Johns is an author of fiction in St. Paul, Minnesota. After receiving a master of arts in English in 1976 from the University of Iowa, he dreamed of writing stories about personal choices in the face of cultural forces and conflict. Forty years later, following an academic and public sector career in transportation research, he began writing fiction with guidance from The Loft Literary Center in Minneapolis. His debut novel, *O'Brien's Broken Play*, was published in October 2023.